THE
MURDSTONE
TRILOGY

MAL PEET

David Fickling Books

31 Beaumont Street
Oxford OX1 2NP, UK

The Murdstone Trilogy
is a
DAVID FICKLING BOOK

First published in Great Britain in 2014 by
David Fickling Books,
31 Beaumont Street,
Oxford, OX1 2NP

Text © Mal Peet, 2014

978-1-910200-15-5

1 3 5 7 9 10 8 6 4 2

David Fickling Books supports the Forest Stewardship Council (FSC), the
leading international forest certification organization. All our titles that are
printed on Greenpeace-approved FSC-certified paper carry the FSC logo.

Mixed Sources
Product group from well-managed
forests and other controlled sources
www.fsc.org Cert no. TT-COC-2139
© 1996 Forest Stewardship Council
FSC

DAVID FICKLING BOOKS Reg. No. 8340307

A CIP catalogue record for this book is available from the British Library.

Typeset in 12/16 pt Sabon by Falcon Oast Graphic Art Ltd.
Printed and bound in Great Britain by Clays Ltd, St Ives plc.

For Elspeth, as in all things

Book One

Dark Entropy

1

The sun sinks, leaving tatty furbelows of crimson cloud in the Dartmoor sky. From somewhere in the bracken, tough invisible ponies huff and snicker. Final calls: rooks croaking homeward, a robin hoping for a last territorial dispute before bedtime. Voles scuttle to holes, their backs abristle with fear of Owl. It is early spring. Lambs plead for mothers. Below ground, badgers, ripe and rank with oestrus, prepare themselves for the night's business. A fox flames its ears and clears its throat.

Darkness takes possession of the earth, then the sky. Now the only light is small and square. It comes from the window of an isolated cottage. To be exact, it comes from a Habitat anglepoise lamp hunched upon a small folding table inside and below the window. The lamp shares the table with a plate upon which tomato sauce has congealed, a bunch of keys and a somewhat out-of-date London A to Z.

These things, and the cottage, belong to Philip Murdstone, who sits, still wearing his overcoat, gazing into the illusory heat of his coal-effect electric fire. He is holding, and sometimes remembers to drink from, a pint glass containing cloudy cider from the two-gallon plastic container on the floor next to his chair. The false fire sits on the hearth of a gaping fireplace formed from large, irregular blocks of granite.

On the mantelpiece a small number of trophies gleam faintly. One is a slab of glass, or more probably Perspex, the accolade buried within it only readable from an oblique angle. Another is a rather kitsch statuette of a child sitting cross-legged intent upon a book. There are three others, and all five are in need of dusting.

For some time now, since well before sunset, Philip Murdstone has been reciting a brutal phrase as if it were a mantra that might console him.

It is: *I'm fucked*.

It has failed to console him.

Usually, in his life as well as his fiction, Philip tends to leave the weightier questions unanswered; now, in self-lacerating mode, he addresses them. Or, rather, it. His bitter self-interrogation has resolved itself into a single query: why has he agreed to sell his soul?

Answer: because he is broke. Skint. *Poor*. He is a poor man. Famous – OK, well-known – but a pauper. This ugly truth frequently visits him in the dark marches of the night. He tries to deflect it by turning on his bedside radio and losing himself in BBC World Service programmes about leech farming in Cambodia or the latest dance craze in Saudi Arabia, but it doesn't always work.

4

His penury had not always dismayed him; there was after all, an honourable tradition of writers living in poverty. Russian ones, especially. Dying in poverty, however, had less appeal. Dying *of* poverty had none at all.

Philip knows why the sales of his books are in drastic decline. It has nothing at all to do with their quality. He buys the *Guardian* every Saturday, Brian at the corner shop handing it, in its plastic sheath, over the counter as if it were a pornographic version of the Dead Sea Scrolls. He also subscribes to *The Author*. So he knows what's going on. Oh yes. Writers no longer work in solitude, crafting meaningful and elegant prose. No. They have to spend most of their time selling themselves on the fucking internet. *Blogging* and *tweeting* and *updating* their bloody Facebook pages and their wretched narcissistic *websites*.

Minerva has mentioned his failure to do likewise on several occasions.

'But it has nothing to do with real *work*, Minerva. Surely you can see that.'

'I do see that, Philip. I'm not actually a fool, you know, even though I am your agent. But it has a very great deal to do with *money*. Gone are the days when you simply write a jolly good book and wait for the queues to form. Readers need to be *friended*, darling. They need to be *subscribers*. They need to be *followers*. You can't just sit in splendid isolation. Not that your isolation is particularly splendid, is it?'

But he'd refused to do any of it. Not that he was a

Luddite, by any means. Not at all. He regularly caught the monthly bus to Tavistock with his handwritten list of Things To Find Out About and spent a good hour, sometimes more, at one of the library's computers. He considered himself a bit of a dab hand at Googling. That was work. That was useful. The rest of it, though, the incessant, vacuous web-witter . . . No. *No!*

He'd regarded himself as a dignified – all right, *stubborn* – refusenik. Until now. Now – what a day of ugly truths it was turning out to be! – he was forced to admit that he had deluded himself. Led himself up his own tiny garden path. The absolute bloody fact of the matter was that he had allowed himself to be left behind. He was like some ancient artificer – a clockmaker, perhaps – who looks up from his bench to discover the world has gone digital and that his days are numbered. Or a loyal and expert employee who goes to work one day to find that he has been replaced by a bit of software devised by a teenager in Bangalore.

He, Philip Murdstone, had become – the very word had a murderous thud in it – *redundant.*

He gulps scrumpy, because even that isn't the worst of it.

Oh no.

Because, swelling and looming over the horizon of his own small tragedy, cometh the Ultimate Cataclysm. The ascendancy of the darkly glittering Californian Overlords of Cyberspace, those latter-day Genghis Khans sweeping civilization aside, burning libraries, impaling editors in long rows, razing ancient honey-coloured colleges and glass towers alike in a venal and rapacious lust to control language, turn authors into drones servicing its throbbing Amazonian hive and children into passive dabbers at electronic tablets freeloading downloads. And soon, their philistine conquest achieved, the Overlords will stand there in their ironically democratic jeans and T-shirts, surveying the wasteland with their hands on their hips, at the head of vast phalanxes of slobbering intellectual property lawyers, sneering at the last writers still able to crawl and say, 'You got a problem, you backward-looking ink-addicted Neanderthals? What was that? Who said "copyright"? Drag that fuckin' nostalgia junkie up here, boys, and break his goddamn fingers.'

As Minerva had rather chirpily reminded him.

'It's all going to go pear-shaped when Apple rules the world, darling. So if you're a writer the only sensible thing to do is make a ton of money before it happens. And you're a little late off the starting block, if you don't mind me saying so.'

There was worse yet. He is in love with her. Hopelessly – and that is the *mot* both *juste* and *triste* – in love with Minerva Cinch. And, although the gooey cliché makes him atrabilious, it had been love at first sight. On his part.

Their first meeting had been in the foyer of a Marriott hotel. He had just scooped the Blyton Prize and a Costa for *Last Past the Post*, and she'd walked in and scooped him. He'd had no idea what a literary agent might look like. Intense and bespectacled, perhaps. Middle-aged, at least. And then this astonishing creature had swanned in, turning all heads, and exclaimed, 'Philip Murdstone! I feel like I've known you for *years*! Let's have a glass of bubbly and talk about fame.'

He had almost swooned like a callow girl in a bodice-ripper. And ever since, after their increasingly infrequent meetings, he would fantastically eroticize their brief and businesslike kisses.

He does so now, groaning into his scrumpy. Like most solitary men, he has a wide repertoire of groans.

He'd just once asked her out on a date. It had taken him a month to crank himself up to it. She'd turned him down, fairly gently, giving him to believe that it was her unnegotiable principle that professional and emotional relationships should not overlap. Actually, 'cross-contaminate' was the word she'd used.

He is also afraid of her. He'd been all right with this at first. Fear and attraction share chambers in the human heart, after all. But after a while fear had commandeered most of the space and furniture in that cramped accommodation. He was afraid of her not only because she was (he bitterly assumed) more experienced in the bedroom department than he was. No, it was more that she lived confidently in a world that he both despised and depended upon. She knew about the publishing business, whereas he only knew about writing.

In so far as he deigned to think of it at all, Philip pictured publishing as a vast river fed and polluted by unmapped and unpredictable tributaries. He had no idea how its flow worked. Where its snags and shallows, its navigable channels, were. Minerva did, though. By God, she did. She stood gorgeous, masterful and unshaggable at the helm of the SS *Teen Lit*, steering it through perilous currents and gaping alligators while he, the award-winning Philip Murdstone, clutched white-knuckled at the rail.

Part of it, of course, was that *he* always went to *her*. Apart from one aborted occasion. She would send for him, and he would go. Eagerly and hopelessly, as he'd gone today. To that bloody hell hole, that stew, that *sump*, London.

2

'Table for two,' she'd said, breezing in. 'Name of Cinch. Thanks.'

Philip had ordered the Mexican Platter and been given an enormous square plate upon which, apparently, a cat had been sick in neat heaps around a folded pancake. The heaps were necklaced together by what looked like thin red jam. One of the things the cat had eaten was green.

Minerva used an opaline fingernail to remove a pomegranate seed from her teeth. She dabbed it onto the tablecloth. In its tiny smear of red flesh it resembled something left over from the dissection of a small mammal.

She said, 'I think the problem is, darling, that you've lost your appetite.'

'No,' he said robustly. 'This is delicious, honestly. You can't get this sort of thing in Devon.'

Minerva held her hand up. 'I'm not talking about the food, Philip. I'm talking about your *work*. And not just your work, OK, but about your *motive*.'

'Ah,' Philip said. He poured more Moldovan Pinot

Grigio into his glass, pretending to be thoughtful. 'What do you mean, exactly?'

She sighed like a teacher. 'This isn't easy for me, OK? But let's get down to basics. Philip, why do you write novels for kids, sorry, young adults?'

'Well, God, what a question. I mean. You're my agent.'

'Yes, for my sins. So. You write for kids because you have a unique insight into the pain of childhood. No one, and I mean *no one*, has ever written so sensitively, so poetically, about a child with learning difficulties as you did in *First Past the Post*. A wonderful, wonderful book. It deserved all those prizes. It broke new ground. It made Asperger's cool.'

'*Last*,' Philip said.

'Pardon?'

'It's *Last Past the Post*. You said *First*.'

'Sorry. Anyway, you've made that whole area, you know, boys who're inadequate, your own. Which may be why no one is writing that kind of thing any more. In your five lovely sensitive novels you've said all there is to say.'

'Well, gosh, I don't know about that. I mean, in the new book I think I've gone into a whole new, er, dimension.'

'You mean football?'

'Well, not just the football . . .'

'The football is cool,' Minerva said. 'Definitely a selling point right now.'

'Yeah, but it's not really *about* football, obviously.'

11

'Right, OK, and that's Problem One. Have you ever actually played football, darling?'

'Well, no, not really, but—'

'I didn't think so. But that doesn't matter, you were about to say, because *Sent Off* isn't really about football. It's about a sensitive adopted boy of mixed race with learning difficulties who's good at football and believes his real father might be a Premiership footballer and so he sets out to make contact with him and gets rejected and then realizes that he doesn't need a paternal role model because he has his own inner strengths. Basically.'

'Well, yes, and—'

'And I can't sell it,' Minerva said.

'What do you mean?'

'I mean that I've walked the length and breadth of this city on my knees and begged and wept and no one wants to publish another book about sensitive retarded boys. Even with football in it.'

'Ah,' Philip said. He gulped wine.

Minerva studied him. He was still good-looking, in a crumply vicar sort of way. He was still recognizably the seriously smiling young man whose photograph appeared on the jackets of his books. The hair was untouched by grey, and it was rather sweet that even at his age he still didn't know where to get a decent cut. The skin tone was starting to go, though; his face had the texture of an apple that had been left just a teeny bit too long in the fruit bowl. She wondered, briefly and more or less professionally, whether he'd had any sex recently. Since

Tony Blair was Prime Minister, say. She dabbed the edges of her lipstick with the paper napkin, sighed, and put the boot in.

'And, darling, I've just seen the sales figures for *Waldo Chicken*.'

Bravely, he looked at her.

'Three hundred and thirteen,' she said.

'Christ. No. But – but it got great reviews, Minerva!'

'*One* great review. In *Merry-go-Round*. By Toby Chervil. Who owes me a favour. About whom I know a thing or two. To be fair, there's also been a couple of so-so blogs, but you won't have seen those, of course.'

Philip had the stricken, disbelieving face of a man who returns home to find a dead cow in his living room.

After several attempts to say something angry or dignified he blurted 'What are we going to *do*?'

Minerva reached across and laid a gentle hand on his wrist. 'Move on,' she said. 'Surprise everybody. Get hungry again.' She removed the hand and wiggled it at the waiter who had been leaning on the bar, ogling her. He came over to the table as though it were only one of several entertaining options available to him.

'Some sing else?' he said.

'*Fantasy?*' Philip repeated the word in a whisper, as if it were something shockingly filthy that might have been overheard at the neighbouring tables.

'Or, to be more precise,' Minerva said, '*High* Fantasy. Sometimes spelled *Phantasy*, with a pee-aitch.'

'And what is that when it's at home in its pyjamas?'

'Tolkien with knobs on,' Minerva said. 'Necromancers. Dark Forces. Quests. For Mystical Objects that have got lost, usually. Goblins, gnomes, faeries, often also spelled with a pee-aitch. Dwarves. Beards. Time and dimension shifts. Books with a deep serious message that no one understands. You know.'

'Oh, God. Minerva, you can't be serious. You know I can't write that stuff! I *hate* Tolkien. I mean. Bloody pretentious escapist nonsense, isn't it? And you know, come on, it's not my *genre*.'

'Philip, darling. You are actually in no position to get all mimsy about your genre. Your genre, which you more or less invented, OK, the Sensitive Dippy Boy genre, lovely as it is, isn't *selling*. Fantasy, on the other hand, is flying off the shelves. It's selling by bucketloads, containerloads, downloads. You know why? Because it's what kids want to read. Especially sensitive dippy boys.'

Philip managed a reasonably good impersonation of a British POW ignoring a serious flesh wound. 'You can be harsh, Minerva. Did you know that? This pudding is disgusting, by the way.'

'I told you not to order it. Now listen, OK? I'm going to tell you something. Three months ago, a manuscript landed on my desk. A huge great wodge of paper, typed. Years since I'd seen such a thing. I nearly put my back out trying to lift it. It was called *The Talisman of Sooth*.'

Philip groaned.

'The author is a Baptist minister and part-time masseur

from Huddersfield. He wrote it, he said, in a three-month phrenzy of inspiration. I skimmed the first couple of chapters, then gave it to Evelyn to read.'

'Evelyn?'

'Evelyn Dent, my PA. She likes that sort of thing. She came in late the next day, all hollow-eyed, and said it was triff. So I gritted my loins and had another go at it. It had no structure, no character development, just one mad thing after another at breakneck pace. Dead religious, of course. The White Necromancer turns out to be a thinly disguised Jesus in a pointy hat.'

'Well, of course,' Philip said, 'they usually—'

Minerva raised a shapely hand to silence him. 'Three weeks later – just *three*, darling, OK? – I sold *The Talisman of Sooth* to Pegasus Books for an advance of . . . well, let's just say not far short of a bent banker's bonus. Plus, there are so many American publishers climbing all over each other to get it that I'm going to have to hold an auction. And last week I agreed a fee of a half of a mill for the computer game rights. I'm flying out to LA on Tuesday to close the deal.'

Philip shook his head slowly. 'The world's gone mad,' he said, as if he were alone.

'The dogs bark but the caravan goes by,' Minerva said.

He squinted at her suspiciously. 'What does that mean?'

'It means, darling, that you've got to decide whether you are a tethered dog barking in the night or part of the caravan. Or the bandwagon, if you prefer. Do you know the last thing Wayne Dimbleby at Pegasus said to me, after we'd shaken hands on the *Talisman* deal? He said, "Minerva, dear heart, you don't happen to have any more where this came from, do you?" He was practically *begging*. "I might have," says I.' She leaned back in her chair and fixed her client with a firedrake eye.

'Minerva, I told you. I can't write that dreadful hobbity stuff. I just simply . . . *can't*.'

'Of course you can,' Minerva said quite sharply. 'You're a professional, Philip. You could turn your hand to anything, if you put your mind to it.'

Philip clasped his hands together until the knuckles whitened. 'Minerva, please. Listen to me. I—'

'No, darling. You listen to me for just another tiny minute. Your total income for last year, from all five books, OK, was twelve grand and some change. My share of that was a measly eighteen hundred quid plus VAT. Now, you may be perfectly content in your badgery little cottage living on poached mice and hedge fruit, but my tastes run a little richer. Eighteen hundred hardly pays for lunch for a week. Unless you eat here, of course. People are starting to wonder why I keep you on. And to be frank, darling, in my stronger moments so am I.'

'You can't mean that,' Philip cried, aghast. 'Don't say that. I mean, good lord, it's true that I'm having a bit of a dip at the moment, but—'

'It's not a dip, Philip. It's a ditch. It's a rather deep

trench. One might almost say a canyon filled with darkest night.'

'Well, I think that's—'

'Write me a phantasy, Philip. Let's make lots of money. Then if you don't like being rich you can go back to writing about loopy boys. That's fair, isn't it?'

'But Minerva, *Minerva*,' he wailed. 'I don't know how to do it!' He seized her hand in both of his.

'Oh, come on, Philip. It's not quantum physics. There's a *formula*.'

'Is there?'

'Of course. I'll show you. Would you like a brandy first?'

'Oh God, yes please.'

Minerva spoke rapidly, simultaneously scrawling key words and sentences on the back of a sheet of scrap paper taken from her bag. She wrote in purple-ink felt-tip. The scrap paper was the tragic final page of Philip Murdstone's manuscript of *Sent Off*.

'So. The world – "Realm" is the proper term – of High Fantasy is sort of medieval. Well, pre-industrial, anyway. Something like Devon, I imagine. Vaguely socialist, in an idyllic, farmerish – is that a word? – sort of a way. But the Realm has fallen under the power of a Dark Lord who wants to change everything. He was probably a decent sort of a guy originally, but went mental when he got a sniff of power or got snubbed or something. You know. Anyway, the Dark Lord is served by minions. That's a word you *must* use, OK? The top minions are the Dark Sorcerers. Some of them conspire against the Dark Lord, but he is much cleverer than they are and always finds out what they are up to and does terrible things to them. Below the Dark Sorcerers there are hordes of brutish warriors. They're usually something like warthogs wearing leather armour and are called Dorcs. The oppressed subjects of the Realm are of three sorts. There are dwarves, who live under the ground in old mines, burrows, that sort of thing. Then there are elves. They live in, up, or under trees. Finally, there are sort of humans. Some of them live in walled cities, some live in funny little hamlets a bit like whatsitsname, the one you live in. All three types can do magic, but it's pretty feeble stuff compared to the heavy magic the Sorcerers can do.'

She underlined 'feeble magic' and 'heavy magic'.

'I could murder a cigarette,' Philip said.

'In a minute. The young hero lives in a remote village in the furthest Shire – that's another must, *Shire*, OK – of the Realm. He thinks he's an orphan, but he's a prince, of course. He's being brought up by nice doddery old sort of humans. They probably get slaughtered by Dorcs and he has to flee. Somehow or other he becomes the apprentice of a Greybeard who is a Good Sorcerer, the last of the Twelve High Magi or somesuch. He knows the true parentage of the hero, but doesn't tell him. He does instruct the hero in the rules and uses of Magick – that's magic with a *kay* – but otherwise keeps him in the dark about what the hell is going on. The hero passes various tests and ordeals, sort of like Mystical GCSEs, then he gets a magick sword. The sword has to have a name. That's important, OK?'

Minerva underlined *sword has name* three times.

'What sort of a name?' Philip asked, dazed.

'Something a bit Welsh-sounding is usually OK. Something you can't pronounce if you've got a normal set of teeth, you know? Oh, and on the subject of names generally, it's a good idea to stick an apostrophe in where you wouldn't normally expect one. So. Where was I? Ah yes. Then the Greybeard disappears, or dies. Towards the end of the story the hero acquires an even more powerful and more mysterious mentor. He'll be a Whitebeard, not a Greybeard. But before that the hero has to go on a Quest. This is terribly important, Philip, OK? You've simply got to have a Quest.'

She wrote QUEST in purple capitals.

'Really?' Philip tried to sound arch. 'Surprising as it may seem, I am *dimly* aware of the importance of the quest in children's fiction. All great children's books are quest narratives. I think it's fair to say that my own novels might be seen as contemporary versions of—'

'Yes, darling, of course. But in the kind of quest I'm talking about, the hero has to overcome *real* dragons, not gropey games masters or embittered ladies from Social Services.'

When Philip had recovered from this stabbing he said, rather meekly, 'Dragons are compulsory, are they?'

Minerva considered this for a moment. 'Well, not

necessarily, I suppose. Some other monstery thing might do. Probably best to stick with dragons, though, to be on the safe side. Anyway. The idea of the Quest is to find the Thing. The Thing has mystical powers, of course. It'll probably be called The Amulet of Somethingorother.' Minerva paused. 'I'm not exactly sure what an amulet is, actually. It's a sort of bracelet, isn't it?'

'Um, no, that's an armlet. I think an amulet is a sort of totemic object, rather like—'

'Whatever. Anyway, the important thing, OK, is that this Thing gives the hero the power to overcome the Dark Lord. Which he does, at the end, in a huge battle between his lot and the Dorcs. In fact, he nearly loses the battle, but then the Whitebeard shows up and shows him a trick or two so that he ends up victorious. The Realm is saved. The End. Actually, not the end. Just end of Part One.'

'What?'

'These things come in trilogies, as a rule.'

'Oh, dear God, no.'

'Don't worry your pretty head about that, darling. We'll burn that bridge when we come to it. There you go.' She slid the sheet of purple graphics over to Philip, who stared at it.

'I'm amazed,' he said at last. 'You've certainly done your homework. How many of these dreadful epics did you have to read to work out this, er, analysis?'

'None. I pinched it out of the *Telegraph*. From a review of *The Dragoneer Chronicles*, actually.'

'And what might they be?'

'Oh, come on, Philip! Even you must have heard of *The Dragoneer Chronicles*.'

'Nope.'

'My God, darling, have you been living in a cave or something? Well, yes, I suppose you have, more or less. *The Dragoneer Chronicles* is the biggest thing since Harry Potter. You have heard of Harry Potter, I take it? You have? Good. Well, *The Dragoneer Chronicles* is a six-hundred-page fantasy blockbuster written by a seventeen-year-old anorak called Virgil Peroni. American, obviously. Actually, his mother wrote it for him, but that's not the point. He got half a mill upfront from Armitage Hanks. A full mill for the movie rights. Enough to keep him in Clearasil for eternity. Which just goes to show, darling. If a beardless youth and his mum can do this stuff, a writer of your calibre should find it a doddle.'

Philip said, 'Would you excuse me for a minute? I need to go to the toilet.'

When he came back Minerva was putting her iPad away. She glanced up at his face. 'Philip, have you been crying?'

'No.'

'OK. Now then. *Style.* The style for High Fantasy is sort of mock-Shakespearian without the rhyming bits. What you might call half-timbered prose. Characters "hasten unto" to places; they don't just piss off at a rate of knots. You have to say "dark was the hour", not "at night". Bags of capital letters. You know the sort of thing?'

Philip tipped the brandy glass until it wept its last burning tear into his mouth. 'Yeah. I know the sort of thing.'

'Good. Now then, what I suggest is this, OK? Take my notes away with you. Do a spot of research. Immerse yourself in the genre. Or take a quick dip in it, if that's all you can manage. Then go on one of those lovely long walks of yours across the boggy fells or whatever they are and dream me up a quick outline and a couple of chapters. I'll give you a bell when I get back from LA and see how you're getting on. Actually, come to think of it, darling, you're ideally situated, aren't you? It's all very misty and legendy down your way, isn't it?'

'Oh yes, very. Can hardly move for legends, some days.'

'There you are then.'

Minerva described a dying man's electrocardiograph on the empty air and the waiter hastened unto her with the bill. She slipped into her silk and flax-mix jacket, and hefted her bag onto the table. 'Now, darling, I really must dash, OK? I'm already seven minutes late for lunch with a Dark Sorcerer called Perry Whipple.'

'But you've just *had* lunch,' Philip pointed out.

'I know. It's a *nightmare*. You've no idea.'

She stood up, so he started to. Then she sat down again. He was left half up and half down, bent in the middle like a man with stomachache. Which, in fact, he was.

'I nearly forgot,' Minerva said. 'You have to have a map.'

'A map?'

'Yes. For the endpapers. You know, a map of the Realm with the funny names on. Showing where the Mountains of Shand'r Ga and the Mire of Fetor and so on are. Oh, and don't forget to leave a bit of the map mysteriously empty. *Terra Incognita* sort of thing. OK?'

'I used to enjoy drawing imaginary maps at school,' Philip admitted.

Minerva beamed at him. 'There you are,' she said. 'I knew you'd be ideal for the job. I said so to Evelyn. You'll do it marvellously, darling. I just know it.'

It was dark in the room now, but he could not bring himself to turn on the lights. He drained his glass, groped for the plastic flagon.

Redundant.

Obsolete.

Fucked.

Sold out.

He tried not to cry. He was assisted in the effort by his father, the late Captain Morgan Murdstone, who said from beyond the grave, 'Steady, the Buffs.' Philip had never understood the meaning of the phrase, but in his childhood it had halted the advance of pain, forced loss to retreat, driven tears back into their dugouts.

He snuffled up snot and sat to attention.

He would reach deep into himself. Yes, he would do that. He would draw from that quiet well of obstinate courage that had sustained him before. He had been forced to lower his spiritual bucket into it, so to speak, in order to endure the dreadful writer's block that had beset him halfway through *Waldo Chicken*. And again when the new septic tank had backed up. Those had been hard times, God knows. And this now was not much worse. He would get through it. He would boldly go into Hobbitland and bring back the goods. After all, he had a map, of sorts. It wasn't quantum physics. He'd amaze them all. He'd amaze – sweet thought, this – Minerva.

So tomorrow – yes, tomorrow, why not – he would visit the Weird Sisters and carry off whatever Phantastickal, Magickal and Phantasmagorickal crap they had in stock and work his way through every last page. Although, given the choice, he would rather endure an operation for piles.

As if the thought had conjured it, an appalling spasm forked through Philip's innards. Even as he doubled up and fell to his knees on the hearth rug he knew its cause. The farmhouse scrumpy had made alchemical contact with the Mexican Platter and, perhaps catalysed by the rhubarb and chocolate *torte* with Pernod cream followed by brandy, had triggered a seismic eruption. Just behind his navel, something huge and grotesque hatched from its egg. A brutal fist hammered at the door of his bowels. He climbed, whimpering, upstairs to the lavatory.

When he emerged, some forty-five minutes later, his face was white and waxen as a graveyard lily. He felt his way to his unmade bed, fell onto it and lost consciousness almost at once.

3

In the morning, delicately, Philip made himself a cup of tea and rolled a cigarette. He carried both out his front door and across the lane to where a warped and rusted gate was set into an ancient wall of stone. He sat his mug on the gatepost and lit his thin smoke.

The view from here was lovely, constant, and never the same. Somehow, it was always sympathetic to his mood. Today, it was a composition in weak watercolour lit by a pallid sun. Sheep Nose Tor was a couple of beige brushstrokes at the foot of a colourless sky. The clandestine outlines of the lost village St Pessary, halfway down Goat's Elbow Hill, were thinking about becoming indigo. Beyond Beige Willie the elusive meander of Parson's Cleft was a sepia vein running down the soft loin of Honeybag Common into the dark thicket of Great Nodden Slough. But, for once, this beauty did not comfort. Something slumped inside him. Could he possibly bring himself to leave this splendour to wander exiled in some ludicrous version of Middle Earth?

He stomped on his roll-up and turned towards home.

He had loved the cottage at first sight, ten years ago. Then, he had been flush with the optimism and the money that the success of *Last Past the Post* had brought him. He had treated himself to a long weekend break at a grand and expensive hotel near Moretonhampstead, secretly hoping to meet attractive young women who would melt into the arms of a rising star of children's literature. As it turned out, Blyte Manor specialized in golfing holidays. His fellow guests were all garishly dressed men who, in the evenings, talked about golf until they were too drunk to do so.

To console himself he took to walking on the moor. He found it surprisingly enjoyable. In the middle of an effulgent summer's day he found himself in Flemworthy, a small and nondescript town that had no apparent reason to be where it was. He took a liking to it, despite its drabness; perhaps it was because the inhabitants looked as dislocated as himself.

So he'd had a couple of pints in the Gelder's Rest, the stark pub at the corner of the Square, then found the lane that led towards Goat's Elbow, his target for the day. Beyond the low stone wall on his left, the ground tumbled into a leafy vale through which a stream murmured, then rose again into a landscape of interfolding, crag-capped hills that seemed to change shape as cloud-shadows stole across them. Sheep grazed, larks filled the sky with light jazz, etc.

If Philip had been less happy, less hungry-eyed, he might not have noticed the cottage. It was built of grey stone with a monkish hood of shaggy thatch. It was snugly hunkered into a kink in the hill like a wily old animal expecting a change in the weather. Its small windows squinted as though unused to so much sunlight. The faded *For Sale* sign leaned wearily against the rusting ironwork fence that separated the tangled garden from the lane.

Philip had knocked at the door, even though it was obvious the place had not been lived in for some time. Shading his eyes, he peered into one of the two downstairs windows. Heavy black ceiling beams, a green-painted door that led to some further room, a stone fireplace that occupied almost the whole of the gable wall. He'd had a sudden and irresistible vision of himself comfily ensconced in that room in front of the fireplace, his peaceful solitude illuminated by a great log fire. Of himself contentedly surveying the changing seasons as they worked their magic on that splendid view. It was the kind of place that Writers lived in.

He'd jotted down the name of the estate agent and, after checking out of Blyte Manor on Monday morning, presented himself at the offices of Chouse, Gammon & Fleece in Moretonhampstead. When he explained the reason for his visit, Mr Gammon was both incredulous and exceedingly helpful.

The independent surveyor (another Mr Gammon, as it happened) reported that the cottage needed 'a spot of updating', so Philip offered, as an opening gambit, a mere three-quarters of the asking price. To his surprise and delight it was immediately accepted. The paperwork, the legal stuff, was all completed at astonishing speed; Philip reflected that these Devon folk did not deserve their reputation for living at a slow and contemplative pace. Less than six weeks later, in a solemn little ceremony at the cottage door, he took possession of the keys to Downside Cottage and waved goodbye to Mr Gammon's speedily vanishing Range Rover.

Five years later the spot of updating (new roof timbers and thatch; new drainage; elimination of dry rot, wet rot, woodworm and deathwatch beetle; the installation of indoor toilet/bathroom; new kitchen; the underpinning of the subsiding rear wall; new electrics and plumbing; replacement of the crumbling window frames; damp-proofing and replastering; two new ceilings; new staircase and upstairs flooring) was complete. None of it, to Philip's ineffable pleasure, had done anything to damage the cottage's air of divine discontent and ancient stubbornness. Nor had it made even the slightest difference to the unique and timeless smell of the place, the smell that now greeted him as he pushed open the door and stooped under the low lintel. He had tried many times to analyse this subtle odour, to identify its many components. Damp boots, congealed sausage fat, stale tobacco, ripening cheese, mildew, the dung of tiny rodents; all these were part of the rich mix. But there was something else, something elusive, that made it so welcoming; he had never been able to put his finger on it. It was almost as if he had created the aroma himself, rather than inheriting it.

He inhaled, searching for a word.

'Badgery', that was it. Her word.

She'd visited him once and only once, three years ago. In a state of thrilled anxiety and troublesome tumescence he'd made preparations for her stay, feminizing the bathroom with the best unguents that Flemworthy could provide, ensuring that the spare bedroom was comfortable, but less enticing than his own. Her visit had lasted less than two hours and she hadn't taken as much as her coat off.

The memory unmanned him. Eventually he gathered himself and set off, brisk and resolute, for the village.

As usual, a small number of Flemworthy's more superfluous inhabitants had gathered in the Square to enjoy the spectacle of people parking their cars. Later, perhaps, they would venture into Kwik Mart to admire the more nerve-racking arts of the astigmatic girl who sliced salami at the cooked meats counter.

In 1898, the Elders of Flemworthy had decided that the latent sanitary and cultural needs of the town would best be served by the building of public conveniences and a library. Needless to say, there had been considerable opposition from those who believed that these wilful extravagances would pose a threat to order and tradition. But, by a stroke of luck, Queen Victoria died in 1901 and the objectors were persuaded to accept the construction of both buildings in her memory.

The Elders cast far and wide for a suitable architect, finally settling on a slightly avant-garde young man from Barnstaple. His thing was Harmony. He argued that because the two new buildings would dominate the Square, they should be built of the same local materials and to a similar design. Unused to such aesthetic considerations, and impressed by them, the Elders agreed. They failed to notice that the young architect had, in the interests of Harmony, designed buildings of the same size. Thus it was that Flemworthy came to have the largest thatched toilet and the smallest thatched library in the county; it was unsurprising that the locals occasionally used one when they meant to use the other. It was unto the less popular of these two buildings that Philip now made haste.

The Weird Sisters saw him coming. They abandoned their pastime of inventing suggestive catalogue entries and fluttered, like happy harpies, along the shelves in preparation for his entrance. In common with all the women of Flemworthy, they had pencil moustaches and a reluctance to assume a completely upright posture. They had names – Francine and Merilee – which Philip, in accordance with local custom, used interchangeably.

'Good morning, Merilee. Good morning Francine.'

'Mornen, Mr Murdsten. Us's glad to see you safe back from Lunnen.'

'Oh, tas awful you has to go up there. I cudden bear it, I swear to God. All that goin everywhere in tunnels an people speaken in langwidges. Make my flesh crawl just thinken about it.'

'Yes, well, it can be a bit—'

Francine sighed sympathetically. 'You has to go, acourse. You writers has to have your nights of wine an willen women on a reglar basis. Everyone know that.'

Merilee nodded agreement. 'Tas all part of it.'

'Well, um, I—'

The sisters leaned at him expectantly. Not for the first time, Philip felt strangely weakened by their skewed yet mesmeric gaze. It took a physical effort, a deliberate shudder, to free himself.

'Actually, I was wondering if you have anything on the shelves by way of what I believe is called, ah, High Fantasy.'

They gargoyled at him.

'For research purposes,' he added hurriedly.

'Ah,' Francine murmured.

'*Research*,' Merilee breathed. Her hands moved as if to cup her breasts, but Francine halted their movement with a subtle slap. She slid from behind the counter and with a conspiratorial gesture summoned Philip to follow her. After a short and distorted walk they arrived at an empty shelf.

'Bugger,' Francine said. 'All out agen. Tas always thus. Tas poplar, see? Us'll not order no more.'

'My God,' Philip said. 'People round here like that sort of thing, do they?'

'Can't get enough on'm.'

'Really? I'm amazed.'

'Reality's too good for'm, swot it is.'

'So,' Philip said helplessly, 'not even a copy of, um, *Lord of the Rings*?'

'Ah. Not as such. But us does have the filums. On cassette *and* VD.'

'Right. Unfortunately, I don't have the necessary equipment.'

Merilee stifled a snort.

Francine glimmered up at him.

''Tas not what I'd call a problem,' she said, 'seen as how us do. You'd be moron welcome to come rown an watch it at our place. Be lovely.'

'Well, that's very kind, I'm sure . . .'

'Ternight?'

Before Philip could respond Francine turned to the counter and barked, 'Book'n out!'

'Actually,' Philip said, suppressing panic, 'I'm not sure about tonight.'

'Tomorrer? Wensdy?'

'I'll check my diary.'

'You do. The special effecks is fantastic.'

'Ah. Right then. I'll get back to you.' He sidled slightly to his right, scanning the shelves. 'Looks like all my books are out again,' he observed.

'As ever,' Francine said. 'Can't keep'm in less we nail'm down.'

It was an ongoing puzzlement to him, this mystery of his local fan club. Somewhere hereabouts there must be a coterie of avid admirers who borrowed his books on a rotational basis. Yet he had never been buttonholed by a single enthusiast as he went about his daily business. Odd. A clandestine literary cell, unwilling to declare itself.

He was still pondering this enigma as he made the short journey to the Memorial Conveniences.

The Weird Sisters watched him go. When he was out of sight Merilee took the pristine copies of his works from beneath the counter and restored them to their rightful place on the shelf next to the undisturbed novels of Iris Murdoch.

Philip returned to Downside and, at the fourth attempt, persuaded his knackered and knock-kneed Ford to start. An hour later, he arrived at Tavistock library, where he was a familiar face. In addition to his net-surfing visits, he had given a good number of readings there; the last, at which he'd raised the possibility of being paid, had been almost a year earlier.

In answer to his query, Tania (her name was on a badge which rested on the gentle declension of her left breast) said, 'Well, gosh, it depends what you mean by "Fantasy". I mean, it's a broad-spectrum genre, as I'm sure you know. There's Post-Tolkien Traditionalist fantasy, obviously. That's your goblins and wizards and so forth. Reliable. Then there's Post-Tolkien Experimental, which has glam-rock angels and drugs and that sort of thing. Not to be confused, of course, with Mormon Vampire Fantasy, which is an entirely different thing. As is Steampunk.'

'Steampunk?'

'You know. Victorian time warp. Like *Blade Runner* directed by Isambard Kingdom Brunel.'

'Ah, yes.' Philip's brain scrambled for coordinates like a drowning spider clutching at the radials of a plughole.

'Then, of course, there's Portal Fantasy, in which the central characters find their way through some gap or tunnel in the cosmic fabric and find themselves in a different dimension of the spacio-temporal continuum, although, in my opinion' – here Tania sniffed disdainfully – 'these are often just sexed-up historical novels. Very popular with children of single parents, though. I have *absolutely* no idea why. Let's see. Right: Post-Apocalypse Fantasy. That's boys' stuff. Basically Post-Tolkien Experimental with continuous violence. Think computer games for the semi-literate. Tricky to tell the difference between that and Splatter SF, as often as not. It's provoked some lively discussions as to cataloguing, I can tell you. Baguettes have been thrown in the staff room more than once. Dystopian Fantasy is more or less the same thing, but with a girl as the main character because teenage girls are more miserable than teenage boys. What else? Philip Pullman. He's another problem. The Dewey System just wasn't designed with him in mind. Religious Fantasy, you might say, but that's the same as Theology, isn't it? Irene over there at the desk would call it Pretentious Fantasy, but then she only likes books about the SAS. There's Terry Pratchett, of course, but he's pretty *sui generis*.'

'Indeed,' Philip said knowledgeably.

'And needless to say there's Harry Potter, but you'll know those. No point you looking for them anyway. They're all out and reserved for the next two years. In fact, the books that J. K. says she's not going to write are reserved for the next two years.' She looked at her watch. 'Probably best just to have a browse. You've got about twenty minutes before the next lot of kids from the Community College come in for their Library Project. If you need help I'll be in the Security Room checking the pepper sprays and the dogs. Use the wall phone to the right of the door. The code is One Nine Eight Four.'

She turned away and then turned back.

'The ones with blue jackets tend to be better than the others,' she said.

An hour later Philip was nursing the Ford back up unto the Moor. On the passenger seat were: Volumes I and III of *The Alchemist's Daughter*; Part One of *Dragon Summoner*; *The Sword of Nemesis IV*; Parts Seven and Nine of *The Firedrake's Pestle* and *Dark Origin: The Prequel*. Perched on top of the gaudily coloured heap was a copy of Slothrop's *A Short History of Dartmoor Funerals*, which he had taken out on the grounds that he would need some light relief.

Back in the safety of Downside, he piled the meaty volumes onto the table below the window. He then carried a stepladder and a torch upstairs and climbed into the low attic. He brushed thick dust and dried droppings from cardboard boxes that had lain undisturbed for almost a decade. Towards the bottom of the third one, under a stratum of his A-Level essays, he found a copy of *The Hobbit*. The edges of its pages were as brown as the rind on smoked bacon. He carried it downstairs and added it to the heap along with a new A4 notepad, Minerva's scrawlings and two pencils. To fortify himself, he prepared and ate three rounds of Marmite on toast. He stood at the window, drinking a large mug of tea and smoking a roll-up. Then he turned away from the springtide glory of the moor, lowered himself onto his chair, and began to read.

Two days later he had acquired the hollow-eyed and unravelled appearance of a man who has stumbled away from the horrors of a medieval battlefield.

4

*T*enebrus *uttered a long, loud cry in an unknown language. At the summons, a legion of Gashluk reverse-melted from the dank flagstones, their dead eyes glittering at the intruders.*

The air inside the chamber grew suddenly rank with their stench.

Asrafel smiled grimly and drew Rethimnon from its scabbard.

Rethimnon? Philip was fairly sure that it was a holiday resort in Greece. Or Turkey. Xanthos, was it? Crete? Definitely not Welsh, though.

The weapon leaped in his hand like a rampant salmon.

Oh, God.

'Magus,' he roared. 'Before you enter this, your final battle, consider whether these foul minions of thine know

the identity of those they dare confront. I offer you, in the name of Pancreus, one final choice: surrender and return in peace to thy Foul Kingdom, or be consigned to the Eternal Ice by he who is the True Elect!'

Tenebrus' scornful laugh echoed hauntingly round the chamber. The Gashluk bared their slimy teeth in mirth also.

'Fool!' the Magus hissed. 'You think your pathetic weapon can prevail against this?'

Tenebrus reached inside his foul cloak and produced The Amulet of Bhang and with his hooked fingers caressed its

'Bollocks,' Philip cried, and dropped *Dark Origin: The Prequel* onto the heap of broke-backed books that lay at his feet. He buried his face in his hands and allowed himself a sob. After a minute or so he delved once more into his deepest resources and took up Volume I of *The Dread Palimpsest*. It was as thick as a tombstone and almost as heavy. The map on the frontispiece looked suspiciously like the Isle of Wight.

Fifteen minutes later he was drooped on one of the stools – cunningly wrought from ancient tractor seats – at the bar of the Gelder's Rest.

'Pint of the usual, please, Denis.'

Denis was new and young and from Birmingham; his speech consisted almost exclusively of interrogatives.

'Got a new guest beer in? Fiston's Dark Entropy? Bit like Newcastle Brown, but with a nice taste? Hoppy, hint of burnt toffee? Put some lead in your pencil?'

'Ah, no thanks, Denis. Just the usual. Feel a bit frail

today, to be honest. I probably ought to have something to eat.'

'We've got the liver and kumquats on special?' Denis asked.

Something in Philip's ascending colon murmured a gnomic warning. 'Sounds lovely, Denis. But I think I need simple fare today? The Ploughman's Lunch, maybe?'

Denis's intonation was infectious.

'The Crispy Chinese Pancake Ploughman's? The Spicy Thai Crabcake Ploughman's?'

'Um. Can I just have a cheese one? Oh, and Denis? Hold the pickled onion?'

Denis took himself off to the kitchen, looking peevish, while Philip took an exploratory sip of his beer and glanced cautiously over each shoulder to see if any dangerous conversationalists were lurking.

The two Ancients, Leon and Edgar, were sitting in their usual place below the dartboard. The curdled crowns of their pints of Guinness were aligned exactly halfway down their glasses as if they used a spirit level to coordinate the progress of their drinking. Their communication was entirely telepathic, but just occasionally one of them would say 'Yep', and then the other would shake his head in reluctant agreement. At this late lunchtime hour, the only other people in the bar were two women wearing cropped grey hair and complex walking boots; their heads were close together over a map. Philip relaxed. The Worm of Desperation eased its grip.

After his third pint, Denis persuaded him to switch to the Dark Entropy.

When Philip left the Gelder's Rest at ten minutes to four he was as drunk as a boiled owl. He made his way homeward, tacking skilfully between obstacles that only he, in his magickal condition, could see. Now and again he startled passers-by with sudden loud exclamations such as 'Yes!' and 'Hah!'. On Dag Lane, he was enchanted by the hawthorn blossom and paused to watch it tilt and shift in the still afternoon air like the lace on a bride's bum. Despite some gaps in his consciousness, he found himself, eventually, approaching his cottage. The green and ochre swathes of moorland opened up ahead and to the left of him. At the gateway in the stone wall he stood and conducted the landscape as if it were swelling and rapturous music.

But when he reached his own gate, at the very instant he put his hand on it, his good spirits fled. Something dark passed over his heart like a hideous shadow on an ocean floor. He could not bring himself to go into his house. His sanctuary had been possessed by necromancers and warlocks and shadowfaxers and alchemists and bloody dorcs and writers who were allergic to full bloody stops; he couldn't face them. He hiccupped, and it brought up a sour gas. The Dark Entropy was repeating on him.

So he turned away and trudged unsteadily towards the moor. He survived the perils of the cattle-grid, then took the path to his right because it led up to level walking, and he didn't like the feel of his legs. There was May blossom up here too, spread like a snowy quilt on its long bed of thorns; but he had lost interest in it. High above him, a dogfight was taking place between a buzzard and a squadron of rooks, but he did not lift his head. A cuckoo called; it sounded like derision.

He steadied himself and belched, then propelled himself into the blurred overlaps of the landscape.

As stone circles go, the Wringers are not especially thrilling. That hasn't stopped them being draped in legend; on Dartmoor, you pile three rocks in a heap and there'll be a legend doing the rounds in less than a fortnight. They say, for example, that the Wringers can never be counted; that no matter how many times you try you end up with a different number. There are fourteen altogether, although one of them has fallen in towards the centre. According to local lore, this, the dawn-facing Altar Stone, is where dreadful things used to be done to virgins, should any be available. In fact, it was toppled in 1763 by a local farmer trying to steal it for a barn lintel.

The stones are all about a metre wide. They vary in height from just over two metres down to a stumpy 120 centimetres or so, although it is hard to keep track of them because they change places on certain nights.

The Wringers are sometimes called The Devil's Clock, Old Nick's Bedpan or Old Horny's Freezer. It is said that fresh meat will never go off if it is exposed to the new moon from inside the circle, which might account for the pork-pie gastroenteritis epidemic that racked Flemworthy's population in 1913. The Wringers have the power to cure rickets, ringworm, scrofula, gout, nail fungus, stammering, baldness in women, heresy and wind. And also impotence, which perhaps explains why there is always a condom or two lying about.

A strange thing about the Wringers is that although you'd swear they were in the middle of a great stretch of level ground, you never see them until you're almost up to them. And on this spring afternoon they took Philip by surprise again, although he was glad to see them. He needed something to lean on.

He felt bad now. He had suddenly put on lots of weight, and there was that numbness at the top of his skull that would later turn into a lobster-shaped headache. The air had thickened, and he was sweating. He relieved himself against Long Betty, the fourth or perhaps fifth monolith clockwise from the Altar Stone. Then he subsided onto the grass with his back against Growly's Thumb. Very slowly he rolled a cigarette. When he told his hand to lift it to his lips nothing happened because he was unconscious.

It falls to me, Orberry Volenap, fourth and last of the Five High Scholars, to set this down. Dark and dire though the record be, I must make haste in the telling, for I have now lived two hundred and four Circuits, and already in my dreams I glimpse my ancestors behind the Glass waiting to greet me. When this my last task is completed, when the end of history is written and the Great Ledger is forever sealed, I shall willingly join them. Perhaps then I shall see again. Not that I am ungrateful to the Powers that took my sight. The great comfort of my blindness is that it hides from me the greater and more terrible darkness cast over the Realm by the foul Antarch Morl Morlbrand and his ever-spawning minions.

The voice spoke and the hand wrote at exactly the same pace, but Philip knew that they did not belong to the same person. The voice was ancient, and cracked all the way to the heart. The hand that guided the racing pen was not old. It showed no wrinkles, veins, scars or hair. The skin was light with a texture like coarse soap. The fingers were longish, narrow, with pale blue nails. The writing was in a language he didn't know, but understood perfectly. It consisted mainly of flowing diagonal strokes alternating with patterns of dots – never more than five – inside either circles or rhomboids. The ink continued to form itself into characters after the pen had moved on.

But blind I am, and needs must I dictate this to my only surviving Clerk, Pocket. He is a Greme, from the clan of Matriarch Wellfair, and, though stubborn like all his kind, has learned the Books and has fair mastery of Inkage. We shall begin, as the Law demands, with the Incantatory Preface in the Old Language. Venx Bilhatta, Venx lux Bilhatta, carpen hos . . .

A pig's arse to the Incantatory Preface.
This second voice cut in so brusquely that Philip was almost pitched headfirst out of dreamland. It was both light and hoarse, like the voice of a child suffering from mild laryngitis. At the same moment, the penmanship

changed: the flowing diagonals became fast slashes, the elaborate circles and rhomboids were reduced to quick wedges, dashes and curls. The ink writhed on the paper, trying to keep up.

The poor old darkler will never know what I'm writing anyturn. Long as he hears nibscratch he'll just keep droning on. All Doom and Gloom it'll be. Which is square enough, the fluking state we're in. The fluking state he's in. Beard-ends full of bits from the floor, and a clump of bleddy moss growing under his lip. His hatstrings dangle in his posset when I can get him to feed, and when I tell him so he just sighs and shakes his head like a fly-naggled goat. He arsebleats like there's no tomorrow, never mind my sensitive Greme nosehole. Sometimes he'll sleep two days or more at a stretch, only waking to use his foulpot (which I have to empty, and me a Full Clerk). When he's awake, it's gripe and bleddy groan about being stuck here in what he calls 'Subterranean Exile' living like a tunnel-fumbler. Comes natural to me, of course. And when I urge him on to cheerfulness, he gets the growls on and tells me I have to learn the Higher Resignation and accept that the Powers have changed their allegiance. And when I say a pig's arse to all that he'll put an Ache on me, which I hate, and call me a stubborn Greme like all Gremes. Well, maybe I am and maybe we are.

The pen raced on; behind it the inkage jostled itself into position.

Maybe that's why there's still some of us left. He blames hisself, is what it is. Broods on Ifs like they were eggs. If he had expunged Morl from the College when he whiffed what he was up to. If he had entrusted Cadrel with the Four Devices of the Amulet. If he'd twigged the shapeshifter Mellwax. Iffing hisself round in a circle till he meets hisself coming back. Does no bleddy good. Ifs is thorns, as my old Dame used to say.

So if I let him tell it we'll never get to the end. He'll be all Digressions Major and Digressions Minor and Reversed buggering Rhetoric and Footnotes and Pendicles like in the Ledgers and we'll never get at the meat of the matter. And it's maybe we don't have time enough. Morl's Swelts are everywhere, even here in Farrin. I've clocked them overhead, and I can't be sure the Library Seal will hold, not if they call in bleddy occulators. Listen to him. Still mumbling away in the Old Language. That Preface goes on for seventeen bleddy sheets. Why bother, I asked him, once. I got an Ache for my pains.

The pen paused and the ink caught up, but the voice continued; and in the depths of his coma Philip understood that it was addressing *him*.

Now then. What you need is a Layout. Can't know what happens less you know where you is, as the old Greme saying goes. We'll project.

Had Philip been awake, he'd have screamed. He seemed to rise, as if in a rocket-propelled transparent elevator, through rock strata and thick veins of earth, past the mouths of labyrinthine tunnels and burrows, past boulder-grasping roots of mighty trees. Pocket's voice came with him.

This is a Greme trick. Even Pellus can't do this. It naggles him, though he's too hoity to admit it. Right, here we be.

Philip experienced a silent bursting forth, and then he passed through a band of glow and came to rest hovering above a vast, impossibly beautiful landscape. It was lit by gently shifting beams of multi-coloured light, as though the sun shone through slowly-rotating filters. For a dreadful moment, he thought he might be having a religious experience.

The Realm, Pocket said matter-of-factly. *Or, as we are supposed to call it nowadays, the bleddy Thraldom of Morl.*

It began to scroll towards Philip and pass slowly and silently beneath him. Farrin was a high plateau of conical hummocks and copses of trees that cast orange shadows. It was webbed with tracks, although there was no obvious sign of dwelling places, merely scatterings of jumbled stone. The walls of the plateau dropped away, shrinking into long ridges of rock like the spinal plates of buried reptiles. These stretched into a harsh desert where blue-shadowed dunes were continuously transformed by winds that Philip could not feel.

A range of mountains came into view, rearing up almost vertically from the sands and sweeping in a great arc towards a dark sea far off to Philip's right. These crags were grey, but where their surfaces had been broken by collapse or quarrying they showed interiors of buttery yellow. The higher peaks were lightly dusted with what looked like snow, although it was white for only brief periods of time. Among the far foothills, light danced on the surface of a lake; close to its far shore a black castellated island cast a green shadow on the water.

The clerk's voice spoke, and his hand wrote, the names of all that rolled below them. Philip knew, with a dreamer's certainty, that every word was being inscribed indelibly on his memory, hard-wired to his brain. He felt consumed by an insatiable happiness.

His eyes tracked the course of a river; silver, then milky blue, then turquoise. It enfolded three walled cities before it vanished, beyond a mighty cataract, into what seemed a limitless forest. But this too passed, and a rich undulating plain appeared, patchworked with fields and meadows, woodlands and thatched hamlets and greens where children might have played but did not.

Some immeasurable time later, a darkness appeared in the approaching distance, spanning the horizon. At first, Philip thought that the clerk's Greme magic had rolled the world into nightfall; then as it drew nearer, he realized that he was looking at a vast, black, flat-bellied cloud. It cast onto the land below it a shadow that was an utter absence of light.

The Thule of Morl, Pocket's voice announced. *This is as far as we go. We don't know the Layout beyond here any more.*

The slow unfurling of the world stopped.

Peering ahead, Philip now saw that a mesh of perfectly straight roads spread from the darkness out onto the plain. Along it and across it columns of what looked, from his height, like termites moved steadily and unceasingly.

There were many fires, but the termites passed heedless through them.

Swelts, the Greme's voice said, and the word lowered the temperature of the dream.

The Realm now reversed its scrolling, and the Thule receded. Philip had not been aware of any loss of altitude, but they were closer to the surface now. He saw details that he had not seen earlier. On the plain, there were smudges where whole villages had been extinguished as if by a gigantic and filthy thumb. The forest was scarred by furrows of toppled trees. Of the three walled cities, two were derelict, their towers topless, their ramparts broached. Where the mountains plunged into the sea, he saw in isolated coves the blackened ribs and spines of burned boats. The jumbled stones on the surface of Farrin were wrecked townships, perhaps razed by some spasm that had rocked the plateau.

Someone spoke from the far distance, and Philip recognized the voice as his own.

'What happened?'

Instantly he turned liquid and was syphoned downwards. When he was himself again the world had gone. He somehow knew that he was back in a subterranean chamber. The old cracked voice was still mumbling gibberish. Pocket was talking eighteen to the dozen and the pen was flying across the paper and the ink was again desperately chasing the words. The story that they recounted Philip saw unfold.

He saw the fierce grim ritual in which the bewitched

Bradnor Lux rejected and cast out his infant son, Cadrel. He saw the casket containing the Amulet of Eneydos withdrawn from the Throne Room, carried aloft between two ranks of a thousand black candles.

He witnessed Cadrel's exiled childhood among the moth farmers of the Furthest Hills.

He watched the shapeshifter, Trover Mellwax, in the form of a giant mucilaginous toad, steal the Amulet from the Guardians who lay stunned by his narcotic breath.

He saw the blond youth Morl Morlbrand arrive at the College of Thaumaturgy and stand gazing at the inscriptions above the ancient doors.

He watched a caravan of tall, long-necked animals, their heads hooded against the whirling sand, cross the Shand'r Ga Desert under a mantle of stars. Glowing tent-like structures swayed on their backs. Somewhere in the night, dogs barked.

He watched, helplessly, the brutish slaughter in the Furthest Hills.

He saw young Cadrel's wanderings, watched him cross the sun-freckled floor of the mapless forest. He saw the youth's slow awakening under the tutelage of Orberry Volenap, his winning of the Lost Sword of Cwydd Harel.

He watched Bradnor Lux carried aboard the black-draped barge and depart on his last journey accompanied by keening Shades.

He saw Morl again, no longer young, clad in the green and silver necromantick cloak. Turning towards him, his eyes remote as a fish's, set deep in a bone-hard face. The mouth moving out of phase with the words: *Give it to me! Give it to me!*

Philip's mortal body groaned aloud in its sleep when the Megrum uncoiled its endless length from its spiral cave, eeling towards him and spilling toxic drool from its multiple banks of teeth.

He saw star-crossed love take root and ripen; he watched Cadrel take beautiful Mesmira, half-sister to Morl, in his arms.

He watched a rising blood-red sun slowly illuminate the impatient host of Morl's battle-hungry Swelts, their war-axes and serrated javelins raised to greet the dawn. He saw Cadrel and GarBellon the Sage survey the enemy from a vertiginous jut of rock, GarBellon's white beard restless in the morn-breeze.

He saw a screen of blank and perfect blue.

He watched it for several long moments, perhaps hoping that it was some kind of intermission or commercial break. He noticed that little dark specks swam in the blue; then, in a rush of comprehension, realized that they were birds and that he was staring at his own world's sky. He felt his weight return and knew that he sat on grass with his back against a stone, awake.

He suffered a momentary though unbearable sense of loss, as if he had died while fully conscious. Apart from that, he felt fine. There was a roll-up between his fingers, which, eventually, he lit.

5

Occasionally, in his writing, Philip Murdstone made use of dreams as a narrative device, or to suggest that rather dim characters led richly articulate lives when they were unconscious.

The fact was, though, that Philip himself did not dream; or if he did – and he had been assured that everybody did – his dreams never survived, could never be recalled. He awoke every day a blank page or perhaps palimpsest. He was secretly ashamed of this, thinking it a sort of disability.

Once, when he was still teaching English as a Foreign Language in Hove, a dating agency had matched him with a woman whose name was (or perhaps wasn't) Sonya. He had taken her to dinner at a Chinese restaurant, where she'd proved adept with chopsticks. Sonya had spent the better part of the evening vividly recounting her dreams, which were long, elaborate, and drenched in suppressed eroticism. He'd had trouble keeping his end up, and had resorted to inventing the kind of thing he thought she might like to hear. He had not done very well; he simply wasn't much good at imagining the poetic non-sequiturs that dreams, it seemed, consisted of. Which is probably why his editors were always trying to trim them from his stories, and why he never saw Sonya again. (A year later, he learned that she had abandoned social work and gone off to be a pole-dancer in Lapland. Or was it a lap-dancer in Poland? He couldn't remember which, nor – despite eating a deal of grilled cheese at bedtime – had he been able to dream of her in either role.)

So he was peculiarly ill-equipped for understanding what had happened to him up on the moor. Back in his dusky parlour, he fumbled at the experience like an ape looking for the edible parts of a digital camera.

For one thing, he couldn't have reached the Wringers much before four thirty. He'd then dreamed, experienced, whatever, an incredibly detailed epic spanning something like twenty years. When he'd woken up and looked at his watch it had told him that it was four thirty-five. Then there was the fact that, despite Denis's evil ale, he'd felt as fresh as a daisy. Still did, actually. Sort of spring-cleaned.

But what kept him immobile in his armchair was that the dream was still there. And not in his ordinary memory, either. The slightest shift in his concentration – nothing more than turning his eyeballs to the side, really – brought it up in perfect sequence and bright detail. The voice, the pictures, the alien but comprehensible writing, all seemed to have taken up residence in a district of his mind that he had never visited before. A district he hadn't known was there. He remembered understanding, in the dream, that this was happening, but that awareness was itself part of the dream, so, therefore . . . This line of thought petered out.

He looked at the dream again. It was as easy as clicking on a mouse. There was the speeding hand and coursing inkage of Pocket Wellfair. His light husky voice. *Click.* Gone. *Click.* Back again.

Christ.

Was it possible, Philip wondered, to become fully schizophrenic in less than five minutes while taking an innocent nap on a May afternoon? If so, it seemed deeply unfair. Surely there should be some warning, a bit of a build-up: the odd voice from inside the bathroom cabinet, a brief glimpse of an archangel in Tesco, that sort of thing.

Yet he didn't feel mad. Far from it. He knew who and where he was, although, come to think of it, he couldn't remember how he'd got from the Wringers back to his house. But he knew, for example, that the things at the ends of his legs were his feet, and that if he chose to waggle them they would waggle. There they went. He knew that if he wanted to he could go to the kitchen and make a cup of tea and not get lost. So he did.

Then the thought struck him that Pocket and Morl and the rest of them might not be in his head if he were absorbed in something else, so he took his cup across the lane, stood it on one of the gateposts, rolled a cigarette and tried to lose himself in the familiar but ever-changing vista.

Sheep Nose Tor was still edged with gold, but Beige Willie was aubergine now. From the dell a sheep began to bleat, then changed its mind. Tardy rooks drifted across the evening sky that was now a nameless blue hung with gauzy swags of amber cloud. Philip sipped tea, inhaled sweet smoke; then, cautiously, let his mind slip sideways. *Click*.

Oh shit, *Swelts*! Hell's teeth, what ugly bastards! *Click*. Come on, *click*, *click*!

Gone. God!

His forehead seeped dew. His fear was as physical as the need to pee. He went back to the cottage.

Halfway through emptying his bladder he understood.

He conjured up Minerva's purple paradigm of the fantasy novel and laid it, like a transparency, over his unsought-for vision.

The two matched. Up to a point. The point at which the dream, call it that, had simply stopped, incomplete. It was all there, though: the exiled prince, the quest, the amulet, the greybeards; all the old hokum that featured in those dire tomes downstairs. Except that Pocket Wellfair's tale had a sort of, well, *authenticity*. The word was both absurd and absolutely appropriate.

He zipped up and flushed, stood immobile listening to the cistern reluctantly refilling itself. Then, not really wanting to, feeling in fact an eerie absence of self-will, he went to his study, the mean little room that Mr Gammon had called the Guest Bedroom.

He sat down on his B&Q orthopaedic office chair. The enormousness – and, for that matter, the enormity – of what he was about to do paralysed him. Eventually, however, he turned on the desk lamp and his PC. He settled the wayward cursor onto the Word icon. When the terrifying white page came up he hesitated briefly, then pressed Ctrl B and Ctrl I and typed:

Dark Entropy
By Philip Murdstone

He wrote without pause for nine hours, then fell asleep where he sat. When he awoke he went downstairs and drank a glass of water. He smoked a cigarette. It did not strike him as odd that he felt no hunger. He returned to his computer and stabbed the space-bar to relight it. (His first PC had had an animated screensaver thing: increasingly complex, multi-coloured pipework, like psychedelic plumbing. He'd watched it for long periods of time. It was peaceful, in a rather hectic way. He missed it. Why had it gone?)

When the text reappeared he carried on and did not cease writing for a further six and a half hours.

It was more or less a simple process of transcription. Pocket Wellfair's script swarmed up from the bottom of the screen and Philip's flying fingers turned it into English, line by line. A lifelong peer-and-peck typist, he was at first profoundly surprised that he could touch-type using all eight fingers and both thumbs. When Pocket's upscrolling words left him uncertain, he merely clicked his brain-mouse and described the images that unreeled for him. He did not pause or tut when clichés appeared on the screen. He did not stumble over the outlandish names or pointless apostrophes. It seemed to him that when his fingers faltered the text ran ahead and led them on. There was none of the finicky editing that was a large part of his normal writing process. Not that he was aware of any of this, or anything else. He had forgotten who he was.

Standing on the rocky promontory that overlooked The Sour Plain, watching the blood-red dawn reveal the host of Swelts, Cadrel unsheathed Cwydd Harel. It slid from the scabbard with a sound like unto a serpent's dying sigh. He smiled when the Sage materialized beside him.

GarBellon's long beard shifted in the dawn's breath. He turned to Cadrel and said

Nothing. The words ran out. The screen filled with a pure and simple blue in which a few black pixels floated. Philip had known it would, but he stabbed the Page Down key nevertheless. Nothing happened. He switched to the new part of his brain, but it wasn't there. He'd known it wouldn't be, but he grieved for it anyway. He grieved for it bitterly, like a miser watching his money burn.

6

Denis served up a pint and a pitying look.

'No offence, Phil? But you look like shite?'

'Thanks, Denis.'

'No worries.'

'What?'

'No worries?'

'Oh, right.'

For two nights and three days he'd laboured, but he was no nearer finding an end to Pocket Wellfair's tale than he had been when the monitor turned blue. Minerva's purple blueprint, which he now studied with rabbinical intensity, suggested what should come next but offered no navigational aids as to how to get there.

It was obvious that, despite the intervention of the Sage, Cadrel must have lost the battle with Morl's hideous minions. Murdstone had, after all, seen Morl's dark Thule with his own eyes. Sort of.

But how had the battle been lost? How had Morl prevailed against the power of GarBellon's sorcery? And had Cadrel survived? Was he once again a fugitive, or was he perhaps held captive in one of Morl's non-dimensions? Had Morl at last gained possession of the Amulet of Eneydos? Probably not, because . . . Well, just because, somehow. So where the bloody hell was it?

These whirling and intertangled riddles had brought him to the suburbs of madness; but what threatened him with a one-way trip to its centre was the fact that he was asking himself such questions in the first place.

He watched the bar fill up and become almost festive. It was, he realized, Friday. People from as far away as Bishop's Writhing and Tormenton had come to sample Denis's avant-garde menu. The waitresses, Zoë and Bernice, scuttled back and forth, hunched, beads of perspiration on their young moustaches. He noted, with a slurred objectivity, that the waistband of Bernice's thong was seven or eight centimetres above the rear of her jeans which, apparently, contained three buttocks. With each drink his vision became more telescopic. In terrible close-up he saw varnished nails pull heads from prawns braised in tequila, watched greasy tongues tease ostrich fibres from false teeth.

Late in the evening, through a gap in the throng, he spied the Ancients sitting against the wall with their twin brothers. By closing one eye he made the twins disappear. He made the hazardous journey across the room and sat down.

After five minutes or so Edgar said, 'Orright, then?'

'Fine.'

'Several few in tonight,' Leon said.

Without turning his head towards Philip, Edgar said, 'You looks rough as a badger's arse, maister, don't mind I sane so.'

'Jus' bit tired. Work. You know.'

Leon said, 'Us had the red snapper. Tez like a big bleddy goldfish. Orright, though. Fair bit a meat on un.'

'Right,' Philip said.

After a noisy pause Edgar said, 'Writer's block agen, izzut?'

'Well, not zactly. Jus', well, you know. Smatter of fact, yes.' He drank, burped, set his glass down carefully on the distressed oak and cast-iron table.

The Ancients drank, simultaneously, three centimetres of Guinness.

'I was wunring,' Philip said.

'Ah?'

'Was up at the Wringers, other day. Jus' walking about, you know? And I, er, well. I've read the legends, nachrally. In books and so forth. Lot'v nonsense, I dare say. But I was wunring if there were other stories. Local knowledge sort of thing. You know.'

'Ah.'

When a full minute had passed Philip said, 'An I thaw to myself, I thaw, if anyone's sure to know, id be you two gennelmen.'

Edgar's gaze settled on something beyond Philip's left shoulder, Leon's on something beyond Philip's right.

'About the Wringers.'

The Ancients drank, wiped foam from their upper lips with the heels of their thumbs.

'Ah,' Edgar said. 'Well now. You'm right as far as that goes. Leon here's yer man. He could tell you things about they Wringers. Cudden you, Leon?'

'Gaw bogger,' Leon said, 'I could an all.'

Then he lapsed into an impregnable silence.

A bright and gibbous moon illuminated the moor as Philip made his unsteady way towards the Stones. Where the path levelled he paused to get the lumps out of his breathing and heard voices.

The approaching figures appeared to be a girl holding hands with a penguin. They paused when they saw Philip, then came on cautiously. The girl had long bare legs and tee-tered on them like a spavined colt. The penguin was a boy wearing a peaked cap low over his face and gigantic black jeans and trainers; his crotch dangled just below his knees.

'Gevening.'

The boy gargled a reply, a sound on the verge of human speech. He had a cider can in his spare hand. The girl sniggered. Moonlight glanced from the ring through her nose. When their laughter faded away behind him Philip soldiered on.

At first he supposed that the small figure sitting on the Altar Stone was a dwarfish hiker. The long and hooded garment might have been a cagoule, the footwear walking boots. On closer inspection, the coat appeared to be made not of Gore-tex, but of some oiled and blue-green fabric a little like suede. It was fastened at the front by loops pulled over buttons made of bone. The walking boots were actually stout sandals with hobnailed soles. The face was small and wide and pale and child-like, except for the eyes, which were ancient. The creature's hands lay slackly on its knees; they were almost white and the fingers were long. The nails were blue. When he spoke, the voice was as familiar to Philip as his own.

'Terrible spotty arse that boy's got,' it said.

'Are you . . . ?'

'Pocket Wellfair? Naturally.' The old eyes studied Philip. 'You look maggoty, pardon begged. Even worse than last time. You're a bugger for the brew, I'd say.'

'Please.'

'Please?' That frail, slightly harsh voice.

Philip's tongue had thickened in his mouth. 'Cadrel,' he managed to say. 'The baddle. I want. I must. Know what happens. How it ends. Morl.'

'Ah,' Pocket said. 'Ends. Well, no, not as such. Unfinished business, as you might say. The battle, yes. And some after. I can do you that. Common wottage, that. Like nests in bare trees. Down in the ledgers, in my hand. No problem there. The problem lies in a different parish altogether.'

'Please. I need . . . my agent, she'll . . .'

The Greme raised his left hand. Its palm was feature-less. 'Ah,' he said. 'Now we come to the quick of it. I know what you need. I know what *you* need. Ho yes. But what's the question needs asking?'

Philip knew, somehow. 'What d'*you* need?'

'Excellent! Excellent, indeed! The right man for the job, as we thought. So, we'll make a deal, shall we? A bit sharpish? Time's got its cap on and is heading for the door.'

'What deal? Whachew mean?'

'Straight arsy-varsy. I send you the rest, you get me the Amulet of Eneydos.'

'*The* Amulet of Eneydos?'

'No, any one of them. Of course, *the* Amulet of Eneydos, you stoolfungus. How many of the buggers do you think there are?'

'But. It's not. I don't understan. How do I?'

Pocket Wellfair sighed. 'It's in *your realm*. That's where Trover Mellwax hid it. Now he's dead, if that's what his bleddy trick is, we can't get to it. Morl might be able to, but we don't know. He's working on it, though, you can bet your wife on that. But you, Marlstone, *you* could get it. Ho yes.'

'Murd. Not marl.'

'Whatsay?'

'Nemmind. Doesn' matter. Look, I, I don' even know what the Amulet looks like. I didn' see it. I dunno know what it *is*.'

The clerk sighed. 'It's about this big,' he said, shaping his fingers, 'and it's got . . . Oh, in a pig's *arse*! You'll know it when you've got it. Now, do we have this deal or not?'

Philip felt his balance going. He put out a hand to lean

on a stone but it moved past. He leaned on the next one that came by.

'If I say yes, you tell me the rest of the story?'

'Every last curl and splot of it. As far as it goes.'

'OK then.'

'Sure?' The clerk's eyes were owl-bright, dark-adapted.

'Yes, abslutely. Abslutely sure.'

'Bleddy serious this is, Marlstone.'

Philip nodded vigorously. 'Yes. Very serious. Very, very serious. I unnerstand that.'

Pocket studied Philip's face unhappily. He sighed. 'Right, then. I fluking hope you do. So what do your lot do to seal a deal? What's your Oathmaking?'

Philip struggled towards translation, clarity. Blinked, worrying that it might all be gone. Found refuge in formality, as drunks do. 'Well, in the absence of a written contract, a handshake is usually considered adequate.'

Pocket pulled a face. 'Don't reckon I fancy that,' he said. 'We'll have to tether it the Greme way.' He got to his feet. 'Do this.'

The clerk put the thumb of his left hand on the lid of his left eye and the second finger on the lid of his right eye. Philip used the wrong hand, then got it right. Pocket waited impatiently. Then he parted his legs and grasped his crotch with his right hand.

'Now do this.'

'Do I have to?'

'Yes you bleddy do.'

Philip gingerly handled himself between the legs.

'Right,' Pocket said sternly. 'You got your fingers on your seeders?'

'My what?'

'Your seeders. Your cluster. Your eggs. Bollix.'

'Er, yes, yes, I think so.'

'Right. Now say after me. Word for word. Square, mind. Your brew-foggled brain upright enough for that?'

'Yes. Yes, I think so,' Philip said, and hiccupped.

Pocket sighed again and began:

'By the Four Vital Orbs, I, Philip Marlstone . . .'

'By the Four Vital Orbs, I, Philip Marlstone . . .'

'Do make this deal with Pocket Wellfair.'

'Do make this deal with Pocket Wellfair.'

'Which I shall honour lest all four shrivel.'

'Which I shall honour lest all four shrivel.'

The Greme then held his hands away from his body and shook them lightly, as though they were hot, or wet. He gazed at Philip with dire solemnity. 'We're square-set, then. I bleddy well hope you know what that means.'

'Yes. I think I do.'

Pocket turned away, muttering. Philip could not make out the words. Something about a pig's arse and making do. He waited.

'Right then, Marlstone. Let's get the bugger done. And when you get ahold of the Amulet, you bring it back here, and no pawky malarkey. I'll know when the times line up. Now, where was you sitting grogstruck last time? Over there, wasn't it?'

Murdstone found himself on the moonlit grass in the lee of Growly's Thumb. When he looked up, all he could see was Pocket Wellfair's eyes, huge, like the last thing a shrew might see before its death.

Then he was asleep.

A sword hissed from its scabbard.

Ink wriggled across a page. Battle-horns sounded.

A vermilion dawn revealed horrors.

The Sage turned to Cadrel and spoke words that Philip Murdstone could not have imagined.

On Monday morning, pinkly shaved and light-footed, Philip entered Flemworthy post office. His obvious cheerfulness caused his fellow customers to edge cautiously away from him. When he reached the counter he purchased a padded envelope, slid a CD into it, and addressed it, Special Delivery, to Minerva Cinch. This unusual transaction attracted a good deal of suspicious attention. He also bought a plastic wallet of coloured pencils.

When he recrossed the Square a niggardly drizzle was falling; but it seemed to the Weird Sisters, watching his progress from the lead-paned library window, that he was illuminated by a rogue sunbeam. They observed the casual gaiety of his stride, the new straightness of his shoulders, the privacy of his smile. Silently, they slid their thumbs into their mouths.

7

Wales is a net exporter of rain. Indeed, according to *Llyfr y Meirw*, the Welsh Book of the Dead, rain was actually invented in Wales when King Sagwynd appealed to the Gods for something to cool the sexual excesses of the dwellers in the Lower Valleys. Which it failed to do, as we know. But the myth remains popular and the rain persists.

The parts of England unfortunate enough to be closest to Wales are regularly drenched, so it's strange, really, that one of England's major literary festivals is held at Hay-on-Wye, bang on the border. Torrential rain does not suit books, but there are millions of them in Hay, a great many of them displayed out of doors. Consequently, the festival cowers beneath a vast higgledy-piggledy arrangement of canvas, tarpaulins and plastic sheeting, tents and marquees. Long lines of bedraggled people wind among these temporary shelters, queuing for food and drink, for toilets, for book-signings, for celebrity readings. Looking down from an aircraft flying below the cloud-ceiling, you might think you were witnessing a mind-numbing humanitarian crisis in Bangladesh or one of the more tormented parts of Africa.

Philip Murdstone, peering through the streaming window of the Mercedes, was deeply worried about the effect the weather might have upon his suit, not to mention his expensively tousled new hair job. He need not have been concerned. Just before the car squelched to a halt, the rain relented and a watery sun made a miraculous appearance. He and Minerva were able to walk the duckboards to the Gorgon marquee without even soiling their shoes. By the time the air-kissing and handshaking were over, the walls of the tent were bright and gently billowing like the sails of a Spanish galleon borne softly towards the coast of Hispaniola.

When Philip and his fellow guests were miked-up and sound-checked (the show was being recorded for Radio 3) the audience surged in. Once the rustle and whisper of rainwear and plastic book-bags had subsided, Val Sneed, Managing Director of Gorgon Books, publishers of *Dark Entropy*, welcomed everyone to the Gorgon Fantasy Forum, sponsored by Gorgon Books, and said how thrilled and honoured she and Gorgon Books were to have three such glittering stars of Fantasy here this afternoon. At this point the PA system squealed feedback like a pig being gelded. A thin skinhead technician scuttled across the stage, fiddled with a cable connection close to Val Sneed's feet, snuck a peek up her skirt, and scuttled off again. There was a light scattering of applause. Then, on behalf of Gorgon Books, Val handed over to the Forum Chair, Gloria Rowsel, presenter of the BBC's *Book Show*, who would introduce the guests.

Philip surveyed the audience. The marquee was full to capacity and then some. Disappointingly, most of the wet pilgrims were male. It was unfortunate that Gorgon's Fantasy Forum coincided with Germaine Greer's readings from *Painting the Pudenda* in the Virago tent. There was, though, a decent scattering of damp girls. They were here, he supposed, to relish the immensely long and intense youth folded into a seat to Philip's left, who was biting small pieces from his fingers and washing them down with gulps of water. This was Virgil Peroni.

'Who astonished the world,' Gloria claimed, 'with *The Dragoneer Chronicles*, written when he was sixteen years of age, which went on to be a bestseller on both sides of the Atlantic and inspired the movie of the same name which is currently breaking box-office records around the globe. Now, at the grand old age of eighteen, he has authored his second novel, *The Dragon Agenda*, published in England this very week. Welcome to the Gorgon Fantasy Forum, Virgil.'

The prodigy swallowed, nodded vigorously and said something like 'Glarr'.

Applause.

The second member of the panel was a middle-aged woman wearing a kaftan patterned with hieroglyphs above jeans and sandals. She was from Hebden Bridge and appeared to be asleep. Philip had forgotten her name as soon as Gloria had uttered it, but she was, apparently, the author of something called *The Hemlock Chalice*.

'A debut novel,' Gloria informed the audience, 'which attracted a deal of controversy on account of its several episodes of inter-species sex and its unflinching depiction of violence.'

A modicum of applause. The sleeping woman nodded without opening her eyes.

'Our third guest this afternoon is Philip Murdstone. What can I say? This is a man whose first novel, *First Past the Post*, won tributes too numerous to mention. He then went on to write a sequence of deeply sensitive, boy-centred novels that utterly revised the way we think about disability. Then, earlier this year, he made a massive transition into the realm of Fantasy which took everybody by surprise. He is, of course, the author of *Dark Entropy*, published by Gorgon Books.'

Huge applause.

'Philip, if I may come to you first. Not merely because *Dark Entropy* is currently the number one bestseller for the twentieth week running.'

Laughter, some applause. Philip smiled in a modest, even rueful, manner.

'The critics were united in hailing your book as an astonishingly original take on the classic Tolkienesque, um, template, as it were, for Fantasy writing.' Here Gloria paused and placed two thoughtful fingers on her cheek. 'I have to admit,' she said, 'that having read your earlier books, I found myself asking where on earth this came from.'

Philip leaned his chin on his fist and waited three seconds before responding, as Minerva had advised. Then, frowning thoughtfully but somehow smiling at the same time, he said, 'Well, I've always loved Tolkien, of course. He is the Everest we all aspire to climb. But I did not think that I was a mountaineer. So I explored the lower slopes, so to speak. The foothills of social realism. Of course, I always knew that one day I would have to tackle those peaks, let my imagination fly. But' – and here Philip directed a benign smile at Virgil Peroni – 'I suppose the fact is that until recently I felt too young to be truly original.'

A murmur of amusement swelled as the slower members of the audience caught on to this charming and self-deprecating paradox.

Gloria waited, then said, 'I suppose the most striking aspect of *Dark Entropy* is the narrative voice. The voice of Pocket Wellfair. Who not only relates the story but interrupts the flow with earthy comments, explanations, asides to the audience and so on. One critic described him as Bilbo Baggins re-imagined by D.H. Lawrence with a bit of help from Chaucer. Where did *he* come from?'

Philip shook his head wonderingly. 'I wish I knew. I can only say that it's as if I'd dreamt him. Which is to say, I suppose, that he must have always been there, somewhere in my unconscious, a voice that I'd previously refused to listen to. But when I made the conscious decision to write a fantasy, he just sort of *came through*. It's rather scary for me to admit this, but it might be that

Pocket is my real voice, the voice that I've spent years developing without being aware of it.'

'Amazing,' Gloria said. 'I have to admit that while I was reading *Dark Entropy* I felt, very powerfully, that I was being spoken to by Pocket Wellfair, rather than reading something written by Philip Murdstone. I hope you don't mind my saying that.'

'Not at all,' Philip said generously. 'That was precisely the effect I was trying to achieve.'

'And in which you triumphantly succeeded.'

'Thank you very much, Gloria.' He leaned back in his chair and met Minerva's warm gaze. She winked. Something south of his abdomen twinkled in response.

Later, at the lectern, Philip said, 'Um . . . I thought I might do a request. Rather than just read a bit I'd chosen. So if there's anyone who . . . ?'

Several hands shot up. Philip recoiled, as if alarmed by such enthusiasm. The uplifted faces were bathed in the mellow light that the sunlit canvas threw upon them. He picked the wrongly hinged boy in the wheelchair whom Minerva had pointed out.

'Well, let's see . . . how about you, sir? The young man in the . . . er.'

A BBC girl poked a furry boom mike towards the invalid.

'Yeff, err. I like when the Gremes, you know, err, when ve're like tunnelling, and vey break frew into . . .'

Philip leaned to the microphone. 'I think I know

the passage you mean.' He produced his copy of *Dark Entropy*, which he had held behind his back. A single yellow post-it protruded from the pages. 'By the strangest coincidence, I have only one passage marked, which happens to be that very sequence. When the Gremes accidentally break through into the Megrum's cave. Now, how weird is that?'

There was amusement, then someone called out good-naturedly, 'Fix!'

More laughter, more calls of 'Fix! Fix!'

The boy in the wheelchair twisted his head towards the voices, appalled. Viscid filaments stretched between his lips.

Smiling, Philip raised a hand. 'I am deeply shocked by these cynical allegations,' he said. He looked over at the disabled boy. 'Help me out here, would you? We didn't set this up, did we? Have you and I ever met before?'

'No! No!' The boy's eyes swivelled and his buckled fingers clawed the air. There was a panicky dismay in his voice. 'We never, I didn't . . .'

The man with him, whose only obvious disability was a grey ponytail, reached across and laid a restraining hand on the boy's arm.

'Thank you,' Philip said, and the audience applauded again, perhaps to muffle the last of the boy's cries. 'There you are, you see. I did not collude with my young friend here. No. The only reason I marked this particular passage is that it's the one I always get asked to read. I can't imagine why.'

Appreciative chuckles.

Philip opened the book. A silence like a warm snowfall filled the marquee. He began to recite, using a voice that was slightly lifted, slightly coarse, and overlaid with a vaguely West Country accent; the voice, it was assumed, of Pocket the clerk.

8

'Cheers, darling.'

Minerva sipped champagne, then sent her tongue questing among her teeth. Philip watched, fascinated.

'I love those king prawns in samphire,' she said, 'but the bits do *lurk*, don't they? Anyway. Shall we run through the schedule now? You feel up to it?'

'Absolutely.'

'Right, OK. We land at JFK at two, local time. There'll be a car to take us to the Fox studios. You get an hour to wind down, then . . . Bugger. Here comes that mislabelled blonde again. Bet you a quid she's after you.'

The stewardess with *Virgin* written on her breast came smiling through the Club Class cabin and rested her hand lightly on the rim of Philip's pod.

'I am *so* sorry to interrupt,' she said. 'I could come back later, if you like.'

'It's fine,' Minerva said. Her smile might have been acid-etched on a statue of the Madonna. 'Be my guest.'

'It's just that I happened to mention to the captain that

you were on board and – can you believe it? – he was literally reading *Dark Entropy* and he asked me to ask you if you wouldn't mind signing his copy. He loves it.' She proffered a copy of the novel.

'I'd be delighted,' Philip said, fumbling for his Montblanc fountain pen. 'And what is our gallant captain's name?'

'Kenneth.'

'Of course.'

Philip tried to think of an inscription appropriate to a man who was flying two hundred and fifty people across the Atlantic while absorbed in a book about gnomes and necromancy, but his imagination failed him. So he wrote 'For Ken, Best Wishes, Philip Murdstone', using his new signature, the capital *P* looking slightly Greek, the *S* like a rearing snake.

'So,' Minerva said, when she had recaptured his attention, 'you've got the second spot on Hope's show. The second spot is good, the second spot is cool. I pulled strings, no, I pulled bloody *hawsers* to get it. That's because the first spot is the freak spot. Hope has someone on that the audience will laugh *at*, OK? The third spot, the last spot, is someone the audience will laugh *with*, right? The second spot, the middle spot, your spot, is the serious spot. Hope's people have got this thing going where pretty serious people watch the middle of his show because they've—'

'Sorry, did you say *his* show? Hope is a man?'

'Only very rarely. But in this case, yes.'

'Right. Funny with names, aren't they, Americans? So, er, who's on first?'

'Misty Turbo. Porn star and Born Again Christian who's made a religious dirty movie called, um, *Nail Me Again*.'

'Right. And the third slot?'

'A gangsta rapper called No-Tag who's way up in the ratings for a TV show in which he plays a single dad whose estranged wife has been killed in a hit-and-run and he moves back in with their two kids and finds that his teenage daughter wants to be a nun and his teenage son is a tranny.'

Philip frowned. 'A radio?'

'No, darling. A transvestite.'

'Ah. That's the one they laugh at?'

'No, *with*. They laugh *at* the religious porno chick.'

'Right, fine. It's not live, is it?'

'God, no. What do you take me for? Now then, Tuesday. I've booked a separate suite at the Marriott for interviews. There are only three because we don't want people thinking you're easy to get. The first is with *Sword and Sorcery Monthly*, the second is with the *New York Review of Books*, then it's, um, something called *Dead Breast*.' She frowned at her iPad. 'No, that can't be right. God, my eyes are going. *Dread Beast*, that's it.'

'We're making the *New York Review* wait for second place? That's a bit cheeky, isn't it?'

'Yep, but *Sword and Sorcery* and Dread Thing are

both paying for exclusives. OK? So I don't want them meeting in the lobby. Besides, it means we can give the *NYRB* lunch, and they like lunch interviews because it's an excuse to eat lunch, which is normally considered to be uncool. You're supposed to use the break to take a bottle of Evian water for a jog. Anyway, that'll all be over by four, at the latest. We can have a nice little lie down before heading off to WNYM for the radio show.'

'Right. Remind me about that.'

'Tip Reason. Lovely man. It's a minority show, OK, but *terribly* influential. Everybody in the trade listens to it. Tip has the best radio voice in New York. There are people, unkind people, who say that he also has the best radio *face* in New York. And to be fair he does look like a boiled scrotum, but that's by the by. He's as gay as bunting, and if he cops a feel of your bum I want you to promise me you won't make a fuss, OK? It won't come to anything.'

'Gosh.'

Minerva glittered happily. 'Good,' she said, 'very *good*. When he feels you up, say "Gosh" just like you did then, OK? It'll suggest that you are flattered and charmed but, unfortunately, utterly straight despite being British. Tip'll be OK with that.'

'All right.'

'Promise?'

'Sure.'

Philip sipped from his flute. Minerva studied him, sidelong. Her client's rapid transformation from hopeless troglodyte to man of the world was surprising, to say the least. It ought to have reassured her. But it hadn't, quite. Yet.

'Where were we? Right, Wednesday. Up at seven for a workout in the gym. Only joking. Nothing for you in the morning. You might fancy getting pampered in Love Yourself, on the fourteenth floor. Jacuzzi, Turkish massage, aromatherapy, you know the sort of thing. They have this service where a shapely Jewish mother-figure gives you an oily workover while telling you that nothing's your fault and you are right to neglect her in order to live your life. Hugely popular. No? Don't fancy it? Never mind. Have the nine-course breakfast instead. Book signing at Barnes & Noble at midday, OK, catch the office lunchtime jog trade. Gorgon are organizing coverage. I'll get there at ten to check things out. Afternoon, toddle along to Megalo Studios to record your bits for *Weirdie Go.*'

'That's the game show?'

'It's a Virtual Contest show, darling. I sent you a DVD, remember?'

'Ah, yes.'

'Which you didn't bloody watch.'

'Well, I meant to, but . . .'

'But you've been a busy little celebrity, I know. OK, superstar, lissen up. Four contestants togged up as fantasy heroes compete to win this quest thing. They all wear these helmets with like visors over their eyes, OK, and what they see is computer-generated images of, you know, dragons and foresty bits and so forth. The audience sees what they see, if you see what I mean. Actually, it's all done in a studio in front of these blue screens but you'd never know it. It's terribly clever. Anyway, each week the contest is based on a different fantasy novel. Philip, sweetie, you're drifting, I can tell. Do pay attention, because, listen, *three* episodes of *Weirdie Go* are being based on *Dark Entropy*, which is pretty bloody amazing, OK? Unprecedented, actually.'

The champagne had filled Philip's head with a soft and manageable form of happiness. The view from his window, a flawless arc of morning-glory blue above undulating cloud-blossom, would have served as a metaphor for the state of his brain, had there been need of such a thing. He laid a sentimental hand on Minerva's silky arm.

'It's *absolutely* bloody amazing. It is. You mustn't think I don't appreciate all this. You're wonderful, Minerva. I mean it.'

'Lordy, Mr Murdstone, the things you writers do say. Where was I? Right. So each week the author plays a sort of God-like intelligence, popping up to issue warnings or give clues, that sort of thing.'

Philip focused an eye on her. 'You mean I have to act in this show?'

'No, no, darling. All you have to do is dress up as thingy, the Sage, and have loads of digital cameras take pictures of you. Then you get computerized into this moving hologram-type thing, OK? What you have to say is all pre-recorded and dubbed on when the computer nerds make your mouth go up and down.'

'What do I have to say?'

'Oh, you know, "The Swelts are seven leagues from the Chancery." "Remember Pellus's Third Rule." "Just open the door on your right, you fuckwit." Stuff like that. You just have to read them off a sheet of paper. You don't even have to worry too much about expression, because the computers will tricksy about with your voice. A piece of cake, darling. We should be able to knock the whole thing off in a couple of hours. Two hundred and fifty grand sterling, ba-boom.'

'Really?'

'Really. And when your hard day's toil has ended, ye shall gather your reward. I'm going to take you to a fabulous little Sudanese restaurant in Greenwich Village that I happen to know about.'

Philip gazed hazily at her. 'Shall we have some more champagne?' he said.

'What the hell,' Minerva said. 'We might as well start as we mean to go on.'

She reached for the attendant button, but the *Virgin* stewardess had already materialized at her side.

9

Philip stood waiting between two walls, one of which was real. His face had been painted Soft Californian Tangerine. He was holding hands with a bearded young man wearing a radio headset. Both of them were looking up at a TV monitor, which hung from the narrow ceiling. It showed happy cartoon chickens taking a bath in Stoller's BarBQ Marinade. The cartoon chickens were replaced by a sort of coloured explosion followed by the words *The Hope Withers Show Part Two*.

The young man touched his headset with his free hand and said, 'OK.' There was a huge eruption of applause from behind the false wall. A man who looked like a Presidential candidate appeared on the monitor. He was seated behind a desk, absorbed in a book. He seemed unaware that he was on television. After approximately three seconds the audience started to laugh and he looked up peevishly.

He said to Camera One, 'Gedowda here, willya? Cancha see I'm *reading*?'

Wild laughter became applause.

Hope threw his hands up in despair and closed the book with a show of deep reluctance. 'You guys showed up just when I got to the bit where Morl creates the proto-type Swelt. Wow. *Awesome*. But I guess if anyone's gonna interrupt your reading of *Dark Entropy*, who better than its author. Ladies and gentlemen, let's give it up for the incredible *PHILIP MURDSTONE!*'

On the monitor, multi-coloured studio lights played over a rapturous audience.

Philip's minder gave him a gentle shove between the shoulder blades. 'Go, baby, you'll love it. Stand four seconds at the head of the stairs, remember.'

Philip stepped through a gap in the false wall and found himself at the top of a short flight of immensely wide curved steps, blind, in a blaze and roar of adulation. He clasped his hands in front of his body and bowed, counting *one and two and*. He straightened and raised his hands in a gesture of reluctant acceptance. *Three and four and*. Then he set off down the steps. Each one lit up electric lilac when his foot touched it. A vast invisible orchestra played a few bars from the overture to Gounod's *Faust*.

In the Marriott, Philip reclined upon one sofa. Dyana Kornbester of the *New York Review of Books* perched, predatory, upon the other. On the low table between them was spread a goblin's banquet of rich and strange canapés, along with Dyana's voice-recorder and assorted bottles and glasses.

'Well,' Philip said, 'you'll probably find this a terribly English, good-sporty thing to say, but as a rule I don't like to criticize my fellow writers.'

'Go on, feller. Spoil yourself.'

'Well, let's just say that personally I find Zubranski's deployment of Dantean symbolism just a little bit . . .'

'Hokey? Ponderous? Apolaustic? Thrasonical?'

'Hmm. I guess it's just that I think the Fantasy novel should create, above and beyond all, an alternative world that is unique and perfect in itself. That has its own *dynamic*. So there's a problem if you start to introduce ideas that . . . Well, if you use the form as allegory. As *message*. That's always been the problem, it seems to me. That writers of Fantasy are actually tethered to reality. It's no coincidence that most Fantasy writers are either ex-teachers or ex-preachers. That they drag the reader back into human socio-political issues or traditional modes of thought.'

He glanced at the watchful Minerva. Her widened eyes said: *Thank you. Brilliant. I love you. Where* do *you get this shit from?*

'So,' the pursuant Ms Kornbester said, '*Dark Entropy* is devoid of extraneous reference, huh?'

'Well . . .'

'Let me tell you something,' Dyana said, swallowing a caviar tartlet. 'Last week I was at a reception with no less a person than the President's Deputy Spokesman on Homeland Protection, and he told me that the view in the White House is that *Dark Entropy* is, and I quote more or less accurately, "a dark but timely premonition of the imminent religious, ideological and military struggle between the forces of Freedom and the powers of Darkness and Terror, and a warning about what will happen if we do not prevail".'

'Praise the Lord,' Minerva murmured, 'a puff from the President. It's not every day you get one of those.'

'Amen,' said Dyana. 'I hope you don't mind me eating all your canapés, by the way. They're fantastic. Celestial. Preternatural. These little crunchy fishy things are to die for.'

She leaned forward to take another. The photographer was standing on a chair behind her in order to get a high angle. As Dyana moved in on the canapés he took the photograph that became the most memorable of the many portraits of Philip Murdstone. In it, his collar and tie are loosened and the unbuttoned cuff of his shirtsleeve hangs Byronically. His elbow rests on the arm of the sofa, and his chin rests on the fingers of his right hand. The fingers of his left hand are pressed against his chest. He looks slightly younger than he really is. His hair is gently disordered, as if by the uplift of intense thought. His legs sprawl apart; the body language suggests that he is either defenceless or immune. The expression on his face is equally enigmatic: it might convey benign surprise, sudden amusement, even slight alarm. In the foreground, slightly out of focus, is the back of the head and upper torso of Dyana Kornbester. The feared critic of the *NYR* is reaching forward to stab at Philip's monkfish goujons with a cocktail stick.

In the cab en route to WNYM Minerva said, 'You OK, Mister Murdstone?'

'Never perkier.'

'You're sure you're not too pissed? In the English sense of the word?'

'Whatever makes you think that?'

'The fact that you've been glugging champers since breakfast.'

He turned his head to look at her. Her profile was backlit by changing shades of neon. 'I was all right in the interviews, wasn't I? They went OK?'

'Oh, more than OK. Beautifully. You were *magisterial*, darling. You even managed to be charming when you were being snotty. You had that hard-nosed bitch Kornbester eating out of your hand.'

'I thought she was sweet.'

'*Sweet?* You know what they call her, behind her back? Dyana Thesaurus Rex. She eats writers' heads for lunch, broiled, on a bed of thistles.'

'She certainly has a hearty appetite.'

The cab driver reached up and adjusted his mirror. The back of his head was shaved into runic patterns like crop circles in a burnt wheat-field.

'Hey, 'scuse me,' he said. 'I catch the name Murdstone? You the same Murdstone, the *Dark Entry* guy?'

'Er, yes, I—'

'Hey, *respeck*. That is some good shit, man. I loved it. *Loved* it. I wanna tell you sumpun. There's a buncha kids in my hood, mean little motherfuckahs? Used to call 'emselves The Fire Crew, sumpun like that? Now they call themselves The Swelts. You unnerstan what I'm saying? You *made* it, man. You *street*. You mind signin' my copy? I got it up here with me.'

'I'd be delighted to.'

The driver held the book up. The covers were buckled. 'You wanna make it out to Legion? My name is Legion.'

Minerva gazed out at the flowing lights, the eddying souls on the sidewalk. 'Hell's teeth,' she said very quietly.

'But I suppose, Tip, the real answer to your question is that until recently I was too young to be truly original.'

Tip Reason leaned closer to his microphone and chuckled. It was the sound of honey trickling from the rock. 'I know the feeling.' He sighed. 'Philip, it's been a true pleasure. I could talk to you all night. But we're out of time, and it feels like a personal tragedy.'

He glanced across at the window into the control room. The young Korean man wearing a headset raised a single finger.

Tip said, 'You have been listening intently to *The Tip Reason Show*, which nourishes the mind, brought to you by the makers of True To Life Dietary Supplements, which nourish the body. Our guest tonight was Philip Murdstone, author of the astonishing mega-seller *Dark Entropy*, published by Gorgon. If you just missed it, *weep*. And tune in at the right time next week, when my guest will be an old favourite on *The Tip Reason Show*, Tom Pynchon. He and I will be discussing the latest volume of his autobiography. Until then, you'll just have to try to cope without us. Goodnight.'

The red light on the studio wall changed to green.

Philip said, 'I do hope that was all right.'

Tip smiled. The bright regular teeth were a surprise in the dark pudgy face. He said into the mike, 'Kim? Philip wants to know if that was all right.'

A click, then the sound engineer's voice emerged from a speaker that Philip could not see. 'Not orright. *Boodifuh.* Mr Murdstone is a radio naturah, I think. The accent is so nice.'

'There you go, sweetheart,' Tip said. 'If Kim says you were beautiful, you were beautiful. He knows about these things.'

Back out in the reception room, Tip put a hand on the small of Philip's back, then slid it downwards and curled the fingers inwards and upwards. Philip felt his trouser cuffs lift a few centimetres further from the floor.

'Gosh,' he said; he sounded almost rueful.

He looked across at Minerva, who rolled her eyes, smiling.

10

He sat at a long black table. Its feet and his own feet and those of the chair he sat on and of the people in the queue were lost in a low cloud of dry ice. Behind him, his vast photographic portrait hung from the ceiling on almost invisible wires. At either end of the table, Gorgon security men with wires coming out of their ears kept careful watch. The queue was apparently endless; he was vaguely aware of disturbances on the sidewalk outside the bookstore. His aching right hand dedicated copy after copy of *Dark Entropy.*

'*Thank you. I'm so happy that you enjoyed it.*'

'*Thank you for coming. I hope you enjoy it.*'

One book he took to sign was significantly heavier than the others. It looked just like the others but felt about a hundred pages longer. He felt a chill in his lower body which he recognized as fear.

He wanted to know what was in the extra pages but did not dare to look.

He didn't want to look up at the customer but had to.

Child-sized, but not a child. Clad in a greenish coat with a hood that shadowed the upper part of the smooth white face. Two small green lights where the eyes should be.

Philip let out a fearful cry.

The Gorgon man on his right leaped over the table and seized the hooded creature, grappling him to the floor. When he stood up he was gripping an empty coat and the creature had vanished. The Gorgon man turned to Philip, grunting frustration. He had the face of a Swelt.

Philip sat up while the room was still full of his cry. The two green eyes watched him from a distance. Eventually he understood that they were the small lights on the air-conditioning unit. His brain flickered with nonsensical memory like a rebooted laptop, then steadied, showing a darkened hotel room.

The bedsheet was wet. Piss?

No, sweat. Christ.

Red digits winked at him from the bedside: 3.24 A.M. In a series of panicky robotic movements he found the light switch, crossed the room, opened a door, saw a row of twitching coat hangers, tried another door. The harsh bathroom light came on automatically. He washed his face, drank water from his cupped hand, dried himself with an impossibly soft towel.

'I have had a dream,' he said aloud.

'I do not have dreams.'

'This does not happen to me.'

The man in the mirror who looked more or less like him said, 'None of this happens to you.'

Philip, in GarBellon costume and beard, having been comprehensively photographed by both fixed and hand-held cameras, was escorted into Digital Realization Studio 3. A glass wall separated an array of technology from the performance floor, a space twice the size of a squash court in which a maze of blue partitions had been devised. Minerva, trembling slightly from nicotine deprivation, was not very deep in conversation with Jerzy Karmakemelian, the show's director.

'Philip,' Jerzy cried, spotting him. 'Welcome to the Warlock's Workshop. Seems to me like you're the only one properly dressed.'

'Ah yes, thank you,' Philip said, fingering beard-frond out of his mouth. 'Was I all right? Did the pictures come out OK?'

Jerzy looked puzzled for a second. 'Come out? Oh, yeah. We had a coupla gremlins locked them up right at the beginning, but we fixed it. Come over to the desk and we'll check it out.'

He led Philip and Minerva to where two men and a woman sat in swivel chairs churning images through a bank of monitor screens.

'Hal? Have we imported Philip yet?'

Hal was a bald person who looked approximately thirteen. He said, 'Twenty-seven seconds.'

'Cool. So then how about we give him a taste of what we're gonna do to him?'

'Sure,' Hal said, still watching his screen. Three dialogue boxes popped up, which he rapidly mouse-clicked into oblivion. The screen turned purest blue. Hal patted the seat of the chair next to his own. 'Sit, maestro.'

Philip hoisted up the skirts of his shamanistic robes and sat.

'OK,' Hal said. 'Let's bring you in on what we call a bloop. We're still working on the *Dark Entropy* mats, so we'll bring you in through a generic. That OK?'

'Absolutely.'

Hal clicked his mouse and the screen filled with icons. 'Right, er . . . yeah. This'll do.'

He clicked again and a sky appeared. A brooding greenish sky above a circle of stone monoliths. Hal parked his cursor towards the top right of the scene.

'The dialogue comes through a different matrix and it ain't ready yet, so I can't make you speak. But I can patch in an entry dub for now. Here we go.'

Where Hal's cursor had been there now occurred a sort of writhing in the sky. A tiny, pinkish-white, three-dimensional nodule materialized. Simultaneously, there came from somewhere a faint noise that swelled alarmingly into the sound of an angry rattlesnake being thrashed against a cymbal. As it did so, the nodule enlarged and unfurled like a hirsute haemorrhoid extruded from a vent in the spacio-temporal continuum. It ripened into the head of Murdstone-GarBellon. Its mouth moved silently.

It scowled. Then, to the reverse of the first sound, it was sucked back into the louring nothingness from which it had emerged.

'That's your basic bloop,' Hal said. 'We can bring you in on a bolt of lightning, and other stuff. There's a really cool one we're working on where you're like ripples in a chalice of blood.'

'Brilliant,' Minerva said, and snuck a look at her watch.

Philip sat gazing like a stunned carp at the point of his vanishing.

The restaurant was lit only by guttering candles within lanterns cunningly wrought from recovered materials. On the ceiling, dots of luminous paint replicated a desert starscape. The music was a slow thrilling lament for lost erotic opportunities. On other divans other diners conducted their business in murmurs. The food was soft, delectable, unidentifiable. Minerva and Philip ate it reclining on embroidered cushions that smelled vaguely of beautiful animals in oestrus.

She reached over and laid a hand lightly on his wrist. 'OK? Nice place?'

'Hmmm?'

'Did I do well? You like it here?'

He swallowed something that might have been marinaded suckling kid, then focused on her liquescent eyes. He tried on a smile that had once belonged to Cary Grant.

'Well, it's a long way from Flemworthy.'

'I can think of no higher commendation. More wine?' She poured from a smoked glass carafe with an antique silver stopper. 'Darling,' she said, 'you've done fantastically well this last couple of days. I'm quite awed, actually. You have been a revelation. An absolute bloody *revelation*.'

'Thank you, Minerva.'

'Oh piss off, Murdstone,' she said tenderly. 'The thanks travel in the other direction. I can admit this now, OK? I was ever so slightly dreading it. No, I was, really. I've brought clients to New York before, and some of them have screwed up most awfully.'

'Really? Who?'

'When they're all dead, you can read my memoirs. No, what I was going to say was that you've handled it, all of it, like a true pro. Taken to fame and fortune like a duck to Chablis. And I know why. And so do you, don't you?'

'Do I?'

'It's because you bloody *love* it, Phil. Simple as that.'

'Well, I . . . It has its moments, I must say.'

Minerva studied his face, nodding seriously as though at some slow-dawning mystery. Then she lowered her eyes to her glass, unable to meet his gaze any longer. 'It does. And I think this might be the moment for me to make a certain . . . confession. Something I've been wanting to say to you for some time. But we haven't had many *private* moments, have we?'

She glanced at him; she might have blushed, although the dim lighting made it uncertain. But he was stirred by the discrepancy between her demure expression and the languorous dispersal of her limbs upon the divan.

He tried to say 'No', but a sudden tightness in his throat reduced the syllable to a dry ejaculation. He swallowed wine from his trembling glass.

'When I, that first time, finished reading the manuscript of *Dark Entropy*,' Minerva began hesitantly, 'I was, well, as I've told you, amazed. Astounded. I heard birdsong.' She smiled. 'Well, it was five o'clock in the morning. But you know what I mean. And what I thought, OK, was *I don't know this man at all*. You know what I'm saying?'

'Yes, I think so.'

'Because I knew straight away that you'd produced something *huge*. And do you know what? It *frightened* me.'

'God. Did it?'

'Yes. Because I knew that all this' – her small gesture suggested that her client's global success and this intimate moment were the same thing – 'was inevitable. And I seriously doubted that you were up to it. I thought about your *seriousness*. Your self-imposed rustic exile. Your privacy. Your *integrity*. I imagined you crushed and wilting under the weight of the world's attentions. But I was wrong. Dead wrong. So here I am thinking, again, *I don't know this man at all*. You're a series of unfolding bloody enigmas, Philip Murdstone. And I don't know what I'm going to do about you.'

He was deeply moved by this confession of inadequacy. He put out a hand in the general direction of her shoulder, but she shrank away from it.

'No,' she said. 'Don't touch me. Not yet. There's something else I need to say. In a previous life' – and here she frowned with the effort of recalling the memory – 'I said to you something like, "Write me a book that'll make loads of money, then you can go back to writing about inadequate boys". Remember that?'

'Erm, yes, I think so. I had the Mexican Platter. It—'

'So, OK, here we are. We have made boodles of money, like I said we would. And now the moment has arrived, OK, when I release you from your bond. Like whassisname, Prospero and Ariel. We can call it a day, now. I dare say you've been spending the time between celebrity engagements developing a new novel about a boy with OCD or something. Tell me about it.' She leaned toward him attentively. The movement deepened her cleavage; the single pearl on her pendant was softly enfolded.

Philip managed to disguise a sob of desire as a thoughtful clearing of the throat. 'Well,' he said. 'Not really. I mean. I hadn't thought. No.'

'I don't believe you.'

'Believe me.'

'I could probably sell it to somebody now.'

'It's not that. There isn't anything.'

'We could sleep on it. You could tell me in the morning. You might feel differently then.'

'I'm sure I would. But not about this.'

Minerva plunged a hand into her tumbling hair and lifted it. She consulted the astrological ceiling of the restaurant. 'OK,' she said at last. 'Thank you. I realize what it must have cost you to say that. I respect you for it.' She pressed her teeth into her moist lower lip. 'So,' she said.

'So,' he said. It came out higher-pitched than he'd intended.

'Part two of the trilogy, then. What d'you reckon? Three months? Four, tops? You go like a fucking train, Phil, once you've got started. You obviously know where we're going. Even a non-fantasist like me can tell that.'

He nodded and drained his glass. As before, the wine filled his mouth with dark satin fruit. Its long complex finish contained notes of aloe, wormwood and gall.

Book Two

Warlocks Pale

1

Philip Murdstone sat considering the phrase 'depths of despair'. Its plural implied that there were, even now, levels of it he had yet to experience. He found himself thinking of a TV documentary he'd once watched, in which an unmanned submarine descended into the unplumbed darkness of some oceanic chasm. Its lamps had lit horrors: vast sightless worms; fish that were no more than X-rays with sets of fangs; forms of living slime.

He poured himself another shot from the duty-free bottle of Glenmorangie.

He was at the gate-leg table in his living room. Three days previously he had abandoned the study and the sleek new laptop with its bright blank screen, and had reverted, in a desperate act of superstition, to pens and paper. He had filled one and a half ruled notepads with scrawl, most of it crossed out, and doodles – several of them inept pornographic sketches of Minerva. Then he'd recalled reading somewhere that certain authors mapped out their plots on big sheets of paper. So he'd driven the

Lexus to Tavistock and bought two thick pads of A3. Now sheets of it – some fastened to others with Sellotape – covered the table top. They were diagrams of madness, maps of nothingness. From boxed and circled names and phrases, arrows in multi-coloured felt-tip headed out on purposeful expeditions that ended nowhere. In blank space. In question marks. In ghost-circles left by tea mugs or whisky glasses.

Just once, he'd thought he might have hit upon something. He'd listed the name of every single character in *Dark Entropy* and, using two colours of highlighter, separated the living from the dead. Then it had occurred to him that Morl was a necromancer and, therefore, could resuscitate deceased characters at will. This seemed to offer rich possibilities. But, in a horrible lurching moment, he realized that rich possibilities were the opposite of what he needed; they were merely extensions of the labyrinth of mirrors in which he was hopelessly lost.

He could not write volume two of what Minerva had taken to calling 'The Murdstone Trilogy'. He hadn't written volume one. Pocket Wellfair had. And of the Greme there had been no further sign. No message of any sort from the little bugger. Presumably because he, Philip, had not found the Amulet of Eneydos. How and where the hell *could* he have found the damn thing, not even knowing what it looked like? Nowhere in *Dark Entropy* was it actually described. Its powers were hinted at, obliquely, and Morl's savage desire for it was repeatedly emphasized; but Pocket had withheld any information about it that might actually be useful. As a literary device, this was cunning. As something of any help to a desperate author, it was about as much use as tits on a fish.

Within a fortnight of getting back to London, Minerva had secured from Gorgon a million-pound advance for *Murdstone Two*. Philip had come back from a walk and the answerphone had been bleating.

'Hi, genius. Where are you? Writing? Call me back this minute, OK? And make sure you're in a sitting position when you do so.'

So he'd called her back and she'd told him. She mistook his cry of terror for one of elation.

'And the buggers balked at it at first. On the grounds that there wasn't even a synopsis or anything. A *synopsis*! Can you imagine?'

'Yes,' Philip had said. 'I mean no.'

But Minerva had clinched the deal by lunching conspicuously at The Ivy with A. J. 'Razor' Merkin, the UK CEO of Hanser & Hawk, Gorgon's main US competitor.

'And guess what, darling? By the time I got back to the office Gorgon were on the phone, more or less offering to have the cheque couriered over.'

Since then Philip had made five fruitless pilgrimages to the Wringers; two of them at eleven thirty at night and three at four thirty in the afternoon.

On the last occasion he had taken great pains to replicate exactly his behaviour on the day of Pocket Wellfair's first visitation. He'd dug out the old clothes and shoes that he'd worn and was at the bar of the Gelder's Rest shortly before one o'clock. He'd eaten one of Denis's Ploughman's, as before, minus the pickled onion. Inevitably (but perhaps crucially) the guest beer was no longer Dark Entropy; it was something called Rector's Old Chap. Philip managed to down several pints of it anyway, so that by a quarter to four he was able to read his Rolex only by closing one eye.

He'd made heavy weather of the hike to the Stones and was in poor shape when he got there. He'd urinated unsteadily, but copiously, on Long Betty, then taken up position slumped against Growly's Thumb. He had thought that his anxiety might prevent him losing consciousness, but happily it had not. He'd passed out in less than two minutes.

He had been awakened just before six o'clock by a fierce squall of rain that had icy teeth in it. The moor was as bleak as his imagination. In an agony of grief he'd clambered onto the Altar Stone and howled Pocket's name into the gathering dark. He'd desisted only when he noticed a party of elderly ramblers gazing at him monkishly from beneath their rainproof cowls.

Later, his hangover had turned into the heavy cold that restricted his diet to paracetamol and single malt.

Now the phone trilled again.

'Hi, *c'est moi.*'

'Hello, Binerva.'

'Philip? Is that you?'

'Yeth, I thing so.'

'You sound a touch rough. What's the matter?'

'Bid of a cold,' he said bravely.

'Oh, poor you. Listen darling, have you Googled yourself this afternoon, by any chance?'

'Whad? No, I . . . No.'

'Good. This will be news then. I had a call just now from Jane Somethingorother. She's the administrator of the Nutwell Prize. Ring a bell?'

'Um, yeth. Disdandly. You said someding about it on the blane back.'

'Indeed I did. Well remembered. Anyway, the shortlist was announced this morning. And you're on it.'

'Oh. Good. Thath nice.'

'Indeed it is. But what Jane Thingy tells me, OK, is that the shortlist is bollocks. The winner has already been decided. And that winner is, ta-ra, *Dark Entropy* by Philip Murdstone. That's *you*, darling, if you need reminding. Congratulations.'

'Gosh. Well, I doan know whad to say.'

'The money's not huge. Thirty grand. Pays for half your new car, I suppose. Almost. But that's not the point. The point is that the Nutwell is very posh. *Prestigious.* It's for the year's best work of Fantasy Literature. That's *Literature* with the capital L, OK? The judging panel is heavies. Oxbridge profs, *Newsnight* presenters, that kind of thing. Last year, the snooty bastards didn't award the prize at all, because there wasn't anything they deemed worthy of it.'

'Righd,' Philip said. 'Thath good, then.'

'You've not lost your talent for understatement, I see. What it means, darling, OK, is that it gives us a broader base for marketing strategy. It's not just another gold sticker on your covers. It means that the broadsheets will have to take you seriously now. Receptions at Number Ten. Possibly even Number Eleven, seeing as how our overseas sales must've wiped out the trade deficit. I'm seriously considering taking on extra staff.'

He had a brief vision of all being well. That this would be enough. Laurels to rest on. A little place on the Croatian coast. Money in a low-yield but safe investment account. A life without laptops. An older but somehow younger version of himself wearing a pale suit strolling down an Adriatic street for an aperitif. A long way from everyone. Enough money in his pocket.

Pocket.

And no Amulet.

A million quid.

And no book. Not so much as a germ or wind-blown spore of one. Not so much as a single brave blind sperm battling against the dark uterine tides towards the unseen egg of one.

Minerva was still talking into his ear, into his head-ache. 'Not a word to anyone. OK? The Nutwell people are very strict on this. Jane Wotsit has told me to tell you because you'll have to think up a nice little accept-ance speech, which will have to sound kind of improvised because you didn't know you'd won because the winner is only announced on the night because otherwise the losers and their people and so on wouldn't bother to turn up. OK?'

'When is dith?'

'The award ceremony? Um, hang on. The twentieth of next month. It's fancy dress, by the way.'

'Whad?'

'Monkey suit. Bow tie and shit. You know.'

'Binerva . . .'

'Fret not. I've been on the net, and the nearest proper tailor to you is in Exeter. I've made an appointment for you. I'll email the details.'

A short silence.

'Philip?'

'Whad?'

'How's *Two* going? I know I'm not supposed to ask, OK, but . . .'

'Well. You know. Sequels . . . You carnd just forge ahead like the first dime. You have to connect everying backwards. Condinuity and so forth. I've had to make a sord of plan on a big sheed of baber.'

'Darling, Gorgon will assemble a crack phalanx of editors for that sort of thing. Don't worry your pretty head too much about it. Just hurl your inspired prose at the screen, sweetie, and we'll iron out the goblins later.'

'Gremlins,' Philip said. 'Nod goblins.'

'Whatever. You're the expert. Right, must dash. A million things to do.'

He flinched at the word.

When she'd gone he stood for a while holding the

phone. Then he drank more whisky, which made him cough. He subsided into his armchair. The coughing gradually transmuted into sobbing. Later, he wiped his eyes on his sleeve, got to his feet and went to the window. Instantly, he recoiled from it. The Weird Sisters, Francine and Merilee, were out in the lane again. Merilee or Francine took her thumb out of her mouth and waved shyly.

2

The Nutwell Prize ceremony was a bloody rum do, in Minerva's considered opinion. Sort of High Table meets Bottom-Feeders. During pre-dinner drinks, she'd experienced the utmost difficulty escaping from an Indian academic who had strangely assumed that she would be fascinated by his theories apropos the relationship between the *Mahabharata* and *The Lion, The Witch and The Wardrobe*. She'd mistaken him for that Asian chap who did stuff for Channel Four. Next, she'd almost made a fool of herself by mishearing the phrase 'inter-genre discourse'. Then inadvertently she'd found herself in one of those Who's Shagging Whom (carnally or commercially) seminars, this one chaired by Colin 'Cruella' Devine. It was peculiar that the life went out of it when she joined in. She was, after all, the font of all knowledge on that subject. Maybe that was why.

Or maybe it was because she had Philip in tow. 'In tow' was the right phrase, actually; she felt like the doughty little steam tug in that painting by Turner, hauling the hulk of a once-glorious man-of-war to the breaker's yard.

It was absolutely terrifying that he was so useless. He was the bloody *winner*, for Chrissake, and he . . . well, he was hardly bloody *there*. God!

She'd been appalled when he stumbled into the Dorchester. It had almost drained her arteries of *sang-froid* not to scream. He looked like someone on Schindler's list, not a shortlist. As soon as she'd dragged him into the suite she forced him into a hot bath laced with aromatherapy Crisis Oil. Then she sorted him out a haircut and full facial. Helping him into his new clothes, she realized that he'd lost quite a bit of weight since he'd been measured for them. There was a good deal of slack in the trousers. But at least he now looked merely mad, rather than actually homeless. Which was OK, since at least half the people here were clearly nutters.

But where oh where was the Murdstone of yesteryear, the Murdstone of *Late Review*, of Hay-on-Wye, of New York, of Los Angeles? How had he been replaced by this person who looked like he was wearing someone else's dentures?

She glanced sideways at him over her champagne. Watched him nodding vacantly in response to the intense babble issuing from the mouth of Perdita Holmes. She wanted to slap his face, scream at him, 'This tedious bitch is the Head Buyer of MetroBooks, so show her some sodding respect!'

She drained her glass, then signalled for a boy in a black and gold waistcoat to bring her another.

She'd been in denial. Oh, yes. And it wouldn't do. She

took a deep breath (oh for a ciggie!) and let the words form, like a row of bloody tombstones, in her head:

Philip couldn't write what everyone was calling *Murdstone 2*. (Let alone *Murdstone 3*.)

He couldn't do it.

Dark Entropy had been a glorious flash in the pan.

He'd passed across the sky like that Bill Haley Bop comet or whatever it was called and disappeared.

A One-Hit Wonder.

A huge global Number One, and that was it.

All over.

Nothing wrong with that in itself, of course. Loads of people had retired on less. Much less. She knew professionally several people who'd lived for years on a Number Two.

It wasn't his fault. It was hers. She should have *read* him. The person, not the wretched book. Should have said to Gorgon, 'OK, you've got a huge bestseller, thirty-seven foreign language deals, the movie, the spin-off marketing, all of it, but that's it. This writer is now a desiccated bloody locust, OK, and there's nothing else to suck out of him. Go on to the next thing.'

But she hadn't said that. Because, apart from anything else, Minerva Cinch didn't represent flash-in-the-pan clients.

And she didn't *have* the next thing.

The drink came. Another admirer had approached Philip. She clocked his swivel-eyed panic.

There were two alternatives, neither of them ideal.

She could take him away. Take his arm and lead him along Park Lane to the pedestrian subway, then into the darkness of Hyde Park. There, by the Joy of Life Fountain, she would kiss him – tongue in, if she could bear it – thank him for everything, pull a small pearl-handled revolver from her handbag and shoot his brains out of the back of his head. She had nothing, in principle, against mercy-killing and the sound of the traffic would drown the shot. The countervailing arguments were that she didn't have a gun in her handbag, and that, given the weather and what she was wearing, she'd freeze her tits off before they were halfway there.

Or, when Philip was announced as the winner, help him to his feet, aim him at the stage (if this snootfest featured anything as vulgar as a stage), fake a period cramp and hasten unto the nearest exit. Home to Notting Hill for clothes, the EuroStar to Paris before midnight, the French cottage by dawn, rip the phone line out of the wall. A year later, come back and try to reconstruct her credibility.

Anything, really, rather than have to sit there watching Philip fail to make a speech, to watch him stand there in his droopy cummerbund like a wet firework and be displayed as the personification of Failed Second Novelist in a modern morality play. Not even a play. A *mime*. A sodding *tableau*.

There were – had to be – other possibilities; but before she could think of them a person wearing long white hair and a cloak appeared from somewhere and struck a gong.

Almost simultaneously, the doors to the Banqueting Suite were opened inwards and she and her neurasthenic client were swept towards their ghastly destiny.

They found themselves seated at one of the six tables closest to – yes, there was one, with a lectern in front of blue curtains – the stage. Three of the other tables featured a doomed shortlisted writer. They all knew. She could tell at a glance. More than a glance, actually; she met and relished the bitter gaze of her arch-rival, Bronwyn Yronwode of Rawnsley and Yronwode, two of whose clients were here as losers.

The dinner was, considering the occasion, less than fantastic. Minerva drank recklessly, hopelessly. She and Philip shared their table with four others: a terribly anx-ious aristocratic girl called Jonnie from Gorgon PR; Gloria Rowsel from the BBC, who looked, and pos-sibly was, pregnant; someone from Amazon, whom she should have schmoozed but couldn't be arsed; and one of the judges, the Ikea Professor of Utopian Studies at the University of Gateshead, who spent most of the meal staring with pessimistic lust at Minerva's bosom.

Had it not been for Jonnie, who suffered from log-orrhoea, and Gloria, who held the world record for name-dropping (thirty-two in under four minutes), there would have been no conversation at all. The only intel-ligent thing Philip could manage was 'Yes', when the Utopian asked if he wanted the salt. He prodded and dis-membered his Coq au Cidre like a clueless haruspex.

When, at the end of the meal, they were offered port

or brandy Minerva demanded both and poured them into the same glass. She draped one arm over the back of her chair and gazed about her, but mostly at Bronwyn Yronwode, with a devil-may-care expression on her face. Then the stage was lit up, and she prepared herself for the worst.

In accordance with the tradition that governs these events, a great deal of time was taken up by people whose only function was to introduce the next person who would introduce the next. Eventually, the verbal torch was passed to the person who really mattered.

It was astonishing that this was, apparently, a female impersonator. Minerva studied him/her with one eye closed and then the other; either way, she beheld a lantern-jawed individual in a black wig and a voluminous evening gown. A muttered consultation with Jonnie rendered the information that this was, actually, the Chairperson of the Judging Panel. Whose name was Terri Paragus, Head of the Department of Enigmatical Hermeneutics at Cambridge, also the world's leading authority on cabbalistic languages and the editor of *RIM*, a quarterly devoted to Religion, Imagination and Magic.

Doctor Paragus spoke for several minutes in a strangely modulating voice that resembled the upper register of an oboe. Other than the titles of the four shortlisted books and their authors, Minerva understood scarcely a word of what she said. Once or twice the Utopian professor responded to a phrase with a short snort of bitter appreciation. When the speech and its polite applause were over, four black-clad persons – three men and a woman – trooped onto the stage, each carrying a book. Minerva was squiffily baffled; she thought for a moment or two that some sort of hideously sadistic joke had been played, and that these were the real shortlisted writers. But no; they were, it turned out, actors. Who now commenced to read extracts from the competing novels, beginning with Aaron Ashworth's *Blood Bankers*. The extract from *Dark Entropy* was the third reading. The guy's Pocket Wellfair voice was far superior to Philip's (which she had always found a bit embarrassing, to be honest). It was breathy, light, fast; and the occasional coarseness of the vocabulary seemed entirely natural, with none of the nudge-nudge yokelism that the author himself too frequently indulged in.

When the fourth reading (from Melanie Zubranski's *Reflections in a Griffon's Eye*) was over there was protracted applause. The actors (all second-stringers from the RSC, so a bit of budget had been saved there) trooped off, and Doctor Paragus re-approached the rostrum.

Somewhat matter-of-factly she said, 'It is now my great pleasure to announce that the winner of this year's Nutwell Prize for Literary Fantasy is Philip Murdstone, for *Dark Entropy*.'

Cacophony ensued. Manual applause; vocal applause, led by Gorgon's strategically placed whoopers and whistlers; one or two boos (Minerva sought to locate their sources, scowling); and a specially commissioned atonal fanfare that blared from hitherto unsuspected speakers.

A spotlight played over the congregation and came to rest on their table.

'Get up there, you bastard,' smiling Minerva said into his ear.

He stood, to her surprise. She calculated the distance between her and the emergency exit.

Philip walked to the stage like someone in another person's dream, and when he reached it he halted, apparently baffled, gazing at Doctor Paragus's stout knees. After a moment or two she managed to draw his attention to the steps, which he mounted robotically. The applause, which had faltered, now swelled. Philip crossed the stage and, to Minerva's relief, managed to place his hand in Paragus's outstretched and outsized paw. A long scintillation of camera flash, and the applause died away.

Minerva then experienced one of those most unwelcome moments of lucidity that occur when terror changes gear. Between the shadow and the act. Just before the upraised axe descends, or the windscreen implodes. Or just before your star client reveals himself to be a hopeless shitwit.

She had long known, of course, that opposite extremes of passion tend to result in similar facial expressions. Certain of her lovers had appeared, in the climactic seconds of physical ecstasy, to have glimpsed the horrors of premature burial. But what she understood now, glancing about her, was that it was all about context. Expectation.

On stage, Philip stood gaping like someone coshed but yet to fall. His mouth opened and closed silently. The slump of his face and every angle of his posture suggested an instantaneous onset of moronism. And the audience loved it. They resumed applause and combined it with knowing laughter. Because – context and expectation – it was an *act*. A class act. Philip Murdstone, veteran of talk shows and award rituals, had abandoned his worldly persona and, before an audience of his peers, was beautifully enacting the role of the yokel who has inadvertently plucked the sword from the stone. Of the stammering Claudius who finds himself declared Emperor. The applause and the laughter increased when he made a helpless gesture and turned as if to depart.

There were cries of 'No! Speech! Speech!'

Minerva groaned loudly and, when Gloria Rowsel glanced at her, disguised it as a belch and covered her face with her hands. Through the slits between her fingers she saw the Learned Doctor seize Philip's arm with one vast hand and raise the other in an imperious gesture that would have silenced a swineherds' saturnalia.

'As you doubtless know,' Paragus intoned, 'the recipient of the Nutwell Prize benefits from a small, yet I trust, not entirely insignificant, pecuniary enhancement. In addition, he or she traditionally receives a unique and cunningly wrought artefact, not to say *trophy*, which we – my fellow judges and myself – hope will outlast the, er . . .'

'Money,' someone called hoggishly.

'Indeed. And tonight this, ah, *keepsake*, will be presented by an Oscar-winning thespian who has flown in from New Zealand where, as you know, *Dark Entropy* is being translated onto the cinema screen. Colleagues, ladies and gentlemen, please welcome that cynosure of all eyes, Miss Arora Lynton!'

Gasps, murmurs, swoonish cries, and another atonal fanfare, this one with a certain erotic charge. The blue curtains parted upon a slender yet curvaceous shape silhouetted against pinkly backlit mist. A gentle adjustment of the lighting revealed the American actress costumed for the role of Mesmira at the moment of her exile from the Realm. She wore, beneath a night-blue mantle, a skin of silvery diaphanous mail which, perversely but bravely, left much of her fabulous frontage exposed to all manner of harm. Her pale exquisite face was framed by swoops of raven-dark hair; she seemed made of moonlight and midnight clouds.

She approached Philip (who, Minerva shamingly observed, was actually *goggling*) with her eyes lowered, her hands held in front of her, cupped so as to conceal what they held. When the two were face to face she murmured something which, even in the electrical silence that had descended, only he could have heard. He continued to gape at her, so she murmured again.

At last he lowered his head, and the actress parted her hands, revealing some sort of medallion on a chain which she looped over his head. Philip did not move. Minerva thought she knew why. As did other members of the audience, to judge from the wavelet of titters and envious murmurs that swept through it. In his position, he had to be relishing a close view of the famous Lynton breasts and, quite possibly, depending upon the subtle architecture of her costume, whatever wonders lay shadowed below them. That, certainly, was what the Utopian professor from Gateshead imagined; above his narrowed eyes his brow was pearled with moisture like the sweat on warm cheese.

Arora took Philip's head in her hands eventually, and lifted it. As he straightened, the medallion swung and settled against his shirt front. He clapped his left hand over it, pressing it to his breast in a possessive and protective gesture. Then Arora kissed him on both cheeks and took her leave, retreating into the mist from whence she had emerged.

There were renewed calls for a speech. Minerva closed her eyes, hoping to find in private darkness the courage to endure her imminent humiliation. When she opened them again, her mouth quickly followed suit.

Philip had taken up a somewhat Dickensian position at the lectern, grasping its ledge with his right hand while his left remained clasped upon his chest. By some trick of the lighting, he seemed to fit his clothes. The expression on his face might have been that of a benevolent khan or king called upon to bless a peasant wedding. He then delivered a speech, without notes. (There *were* no notes. Minerva knew that. She'd frisked his clothes and found none. She'd said, 'Where's the sodding speech, Philip?' And he'd said, from the bath, 'Same place as the sodding book, Minerva, for all I know.')

He spoke for thirteen and a half minutes in perfect, complex and unfaltering sentences. Minerva didn't understand the half of it. Not then, nor later when the speech was reproduced verbatim in the *London Review of Books*, nor when it appeared – with copious footnotes – in *RIM*.

He began by thanking the judges by name (despite, Minerva knew, not knowing who they were). Next, he praised, with analytic precision, the other books that had made the shortlist (despite, Minerva knew, not having read any of them). Indeed, so incisive and concise was his praise that it left their authors feeling grateful for so little and thankful there was no more. Then he embarked on an erudite yet passionate defence – no, a celebration – of the Fantasy genre. Like a magnificent intellectual animal he ranged across its entire landscape, pausing to browse on Ovid and Pliny, on Frazer's *The Golden Bough* and Bettelheim's nourishing study of fairy tales, on the rich truffly delights of Tolkien, Lewis and Le Guin, on the sharp juiciness of Carter and Lanagan. He sniffed appreciatively at Pratchett – 'absolutely *sui generis*' – Hoban and Garner, but passed them by unsampled. Replete, he spoke with icy disdain of the moral relativism that characterized so much of contemporary 'realistic' teenage fiction, of its obsession with squalid domestic arrangements, of its obsequious trendiness, its feigned concern for the hobbled and the disadvantaged, its fear of transcendence. Only Fantasy, Philip risingly asserted, could lead children into that magical grove where the deep human myths were gathered, and there arm them with the weapons and the means to confront and exorcize those Grendels, those Smaugs, those Megrums that daunt the unfolding soul.

When he finished speaking there was a silence as when the sea waits to surge; and when the tidal wave of applause broke it lifted Philip from the stage and bore him as if on wings of sound back to his seat beside Minerva.

'Where the fuck did all that come from?' she asked, reasonably enough.

Some of the familiar glaze returned to Philip's features. He touched his chest where the trophy hung.

'From here,' he said. 'I think.'

3

In the station car park at Exeter St David's, it took Philip some time to find his car, despite the fact that it stood among the lesser vehicles like some huge and warlike pachyderm. (Even after all this time, he still found himself searching forgetfully for the horrible old Ford.) When he at last he found the beast, he saw that the letters *WANKA* had been inscribed into the coat of reddish dust that filmed its rear end. He stood for a moment or two studying this Japanese-looking word while he rummaged for the keys with their laser fob. At the second attempt the Lexus bleeped, winked its lights, and unlocked itself with a sound that he still found thrilling. *GerSchlunk.*

He climbed aboard and allowed himself to enjoy the gentle arse-clasp of the leather seat, the subtly lit array of magical switches. Leaning back against the sculptured headrest, his gaze rose to a tower block perched on the hill (when terrible lizards roamed Mesozoic Exeter it had been a sandstone sea-cliff) that overlooked the river and the railway. This horribly inappropriate building – it was a college of some sort – was, in this late afternoon, adorned by a pearly light that made it look almost delicate, insubstantial. Then someone inside his head said, 'Time's got its boots on,' and Philip pulled the seat belt across his body.

Instantly, there came again that pulsing grasp on his chest that he had first experienced at the prize ceremony: a sort of crab nebula coming into being on his skin, reaching its electrical tentacles into previously unknown crevices, filling him with words, with cinematic visions. In his ear, deep in it, nibscratch and hoarse distorted whispering.

Beyond the windscreen, some sort of vast suction took place. The car park, the busy road beyond it, the magenta-uplit Premier Inn and the boarding houses that climbed the hill vanished and were replaced by a slope of rugged wilderness in which invisible but awful violence thrived. The college tower now stood jagged and burning against a green sky. Vampyrical shapes poured from its upper windows and formed an immeasurable spiral in the smoky upper air like a murmuration of gigantic starlings.

Something breathtakingly telescopic happened to Philip and he found himself closer to the conflagration. He felt its furnace breath on his face, felt wetness pooling in the V of his collarbone, but could not turn away. He had dreamed the massive portal of the College before, recognized the ancient inscriptions above it. He also knew, somehow, that the great doors were about to open; and now they did, slowly, releasing a spreading red glare that forced him to screw his eyes shut.

When he dared to open them a figure of the direst authority, cloaked in swirling silver and green, had emerged. Even in the violent and uncertain light Philip could make out the predatory handsomeness of the face within its aureole of fire-tipped hair, the depthless glitter of the eyes.

Despite the heat on his skin and the foul smell of burning alchemicals in his nose, Philip had assumed he was a detached and invisible witness to this fiery cataclysm. But now, in a bowel-loosening moment of realization, he knew he was not. He was a part, a vital and unprotected part of it. For Morl had seen him. The necromancer raised his left hand, and with index and little fingers extended, uttered Philip's name followed by incomprehensible words in a voice so sonorous that the roar of burning paused to listen.

Philip found himself unable to turn, to run, to move at all. He could only watch, numb with dread, as behind Morl and within the very matrix of the inferno, hideous forms assembled. Swelts. Hulk-shouldered, tusked, deformed, they lolloped out of the flames and gathered behind their master; then, at some unspoken command, they advanced upon Philip. Simultaneously, the sky above him was riven by howling. Looking up, he saw winged Swelts descending, plaintive with blood-lust, their leathery cockchafer bodies trailing thorny legs. A thin wail of terror came from Philip's throat and he threw himself forward onto the ground in final and abject submission.

His head struck something firm but cushioned and there was a slithering across his chest. It was the seat belt recoiling into its socket.

He sat for perhaps a minute with his forehead on the steering wheel, and eventually his breathing became almost regular. He raised his head when he heard a hesitant tapping. Turning, he saw that he was being studied by a young man with a polystyrene food carton in one hand and a mobile phone in the other. Philip turned the ignition key a notch and lowered his electrical window.

'Yorl rye, mate?'

It took Murdstone a second and some effort to peel his tongue from the roof of his mouth. 'Yeg. Ahgghum. Yes, I'm OK. Thanks. I'm fine.'

'You don' look it, mate. I fort for a minute . . . well, I was finking I might have to call a hambulance.' He held his mobile higher, as if to demonstrate that he could indeed have summoned the emergency services.

'No,' Philip said. 'That won't be necessary. But thank you. I'll be fine.'

'Or rye, mate, if you say so. But you mind how you go.' The man stepped away from the window. 'Nice motor, vough. XL3SE4WDTDSi, innit?'

When the man had gone, Philip eased open the top buttons of his shirt and removed the Amulet and stowed it carefully in the CD storage compartment. Then he lifted his eyes unto the hill where the sunlit tower block stood perfectly crass and intact. After a while he switched the engine on and tapped the number three on the radio console. Wagner, halfway to tumescence.

As he squeezed the Lexus through the barrier, two leering hoodied goblins with low-slung crotches appeared from nowhere and mimed frenzied masturbation in his wake.

The frowsty odour of desperation still lingered in the living room, but instead of throwing open the window Philip drew the curtains across it and lit the table lamp. He laid the Amulet in the pool of light.

Until now, he'd not had an opportunity to study it closely, in private. Secretly. The thirty-six hours since his speech – not a word of which he could recall – had accelerated into a sort of flickering delirium beyond his, or anyone else's, control. His memory of it consisted of random clips and stills. The last was of Minerva, in a bedroom mirror, wearing improbable underwear. Except that her thing, her thong, was not where it should have been; she was wearing it as a blindfold. He lifted his face like a parched man hoping for rain, but could not remember what had happened next. After several useless attempts to urge the movie onward he sat and focused his attention on the Amulet.

It was nothing special to look at. Not quite square, maybe five centimetres by four. It was thick enough to be hollow but he couldn't find a seam in it, any sign that it might be prised open. When he shook it close to his ear he could hear nothing. He couldn't tell what it was made of. It was quite heavy, dark greenish grey and slightly mottled, as a kind of stone might be. Soapstone, was that what he was thinking of? But it felt more like metal. Very smooth, but not as though polished by age. It warmed rapidly when he cupped it in his hand, but was ice-cold within a moment of his releasing it. At the corners of the slightly shorter side there were eyelets to which the chain was attached. The chain itself was clearly nothing to do with it. Nice enough: an expensive bit of silverwork but obviously modern, from Aspreys or somewhere. Originally, he supposed, the thing would have hung from a leather thong.

Thong. Why had she? To not see what? God, he'd give anything to remember . . .

On the Amulet's surface was a design carved, or cast, in shallow relief. Earlier, in stolen moments when he'd glanced at it, he'd thought it represented a holly leaf. Or maybe a stylized pointy-winged figure. A bat, perhaps. Now, the angle of the light falling onto it revealed something quite different: the backs of two hands with their index and little fingers extended, the fingertips of one hand touching the fingertips of the other. In a moment of recognition that was similar to a small electrical shock, he remembered Morl's gesture as he emerged from the burning College of Thaumaturgy above St David's station.

Now he saw something else, something etched into the symmetrical space formed by the folded fingers of the two hands. Peering closer, he made out what looked like a compressed figure eight. There was a dot inside one of its flattened loops. He turned it in the light for a better view and it disappeared. Puzzled, blinking, he rotated it slightly. Nothing. He moved it again, and again. Nothing, and nothing.

He gave up and stood up. He turned away from the table and felt that he was not at home but in a cave.

He groped for light switches and lit the place up.

He fiddled with the controls for the recently installed central heating until he heard the boiler go *whumph*.

He found the remote for the new flat-screen telly and pressed a button at random. Scary girls in bondage wear dancing to terrible pop music. He hit mute and spent a minute marvelling at the eroticism of unattainable girls squirming in silence.

He touched the answering machine and it said: YOU. HAVE. THIR. TEEN. MESSAGES. MESSAGE ONE.

He stopped it there and went into the kitchen and selected a can of soup at random. He opened it and tipped the contents into a pan, then licked the inside of the lid to see if he could tell what flavour it was. He ate the soup without toast because his bread was speckled with tiny blue flowers of mould and he couldn't remember if that was OK or lethal.

Before he'd emptied the bowl he went and ran the bath because he couldn't bear the thought of any gaps of inactivity between things.

He finished the soup and poured himself a large glass of whisky and went into the bathroom and tipped

Cranberry Body Milk into the hot water and took his clothes off and lowered himself into the pink amniotic.

Less than a minute later he climbed out and went downstairs to fetch the Amulet, terribly shocked that he'd left it lying unguarded. As he picked it up the phone rang. He stood undecided with the Amulet dangling from his right hand and vitamin-enriched foam dripping from his penis. The answering machine clicked in and he listened to his own voice and then Minerva's.

'It's just me, *cheri*. Again. Thought you'd be home by now. Are you OK? You looked magnificently *raddled* this morning ... Philip? You're not there. Are you at that dreadful pub? Darling, I can't remember *anything* I said last night, but there is one small matter we *must* talk about, OK? So give me a call the minute you're *compos mentis. Ciao!*'

He plodged upstairs and hung the Amulet on the hook on the bathroom door. Then he slumped back into the water, took a slug of whisky, closed his eyes and tried to think rationally about things that made no sense.

It *was* the Amulet of Eneydos. There could be no doubt of that. 'You'll know it when you've got it,' Pocket had said. And he did know. How it had come into the possession of Doctor Paragus and his/her prize committee he could not imagine, and would not bother trying to.

According to Pocket, in *Dark Entropy*, the Amulet had the power to bring about those things most earnestly desired by those who wore it. Which was good. Depending, of course, who was doing the desiring.

127

Obversely, the results could be unpredictable. For one thing, what the wearer *thought* he desired might not be what lurked furtive in his heart. Thus had the saintly and virginal Prester Nullus died, raving and desiccated, in a knocking-shop staffed by insatiably concupiscent hermaphrodites, after being entrusted with the Amulet for less than a week. It was after a sequence of comparable disasters that, for the duration of the reigns of the Third and Fourth Fractus Lux, the High Scholars had sequestered the Amulet, spellbound, in the scriptorium below Farrin.

Then again, there were those for whom the Amulet would do nothing. Against whose chests it would hang stubborn and inert. He was not one of those, though. Clearly not. It had saved his bacon, had plucked it sizzling from the skillet of hell, at the Nutwell do. Christ, that'd been a close call.

The memory chilled him. He sat up and ran more hot water into the foam.

Then that . . . vision, or whatever it was, fucking nightmare, actually, at St David's. When the seat belt had pressed the Amulet to his chest.

But the thing was, the really interesting thing was, that it was a new . . . bit. At the end of *Dark Entropy*, the College of Thaumaturgy was still standing. Very much so. Therefore . . .

He opened his eyes. His sluggard pulse quickened.

Therefore it was, could only be, a scene from the next . . . volume. Part Two! Pocket was somehow sort of *channelling*, or trying to channel, *Murdstone 2* through the Amulet. My God!

Did that make sense? Yes, more or less.

Good old Pocket. Dear old Pocket! He lifted the steam-clouded glass and drank a toast to the Greme.

Mind you, it had been a bit disturbing that he'd found himself sort of *in* it. Bloody terrifying, in fact. It didn't really make sense that Morl had seen him, spoken to him. That those Sky-Swelts or whatever they were called had come at him.

Probably nothing to worry about. A heightened vividness. Something to do with the magick of the Amulet, no doubt. Dealing with things beyond our ken here, after all.

But anyway, what it came down to was that the Amulet, well, *liked* him. Was on his side. Because what he desired, most earnestly and sincerely desired, was the fucking follow-up to *Dark Entropy*.

Murdstone heard, or thought he heard, a light scratching sound from the direction of the door. He turned his head. The dangling Amulet had the look of something that had just stopped moving.

He smiled at himself. Imagination running away with him. And thank God – or Pocket – for that.

Briefly, he considered the possibility of starting work at this late hour. Taking the Amulet to his chest and settling himself to whatever miraculous events revealed themselves on his monitor. But no. He was elated but knackered. He'd take the weekend off. A nice long walk to clear his head. He finished his whisky and sloshed his genitals. The action conjured up that image of Minerva. He thought about giving himself a quick one. Masturbation was a natural part of the writing process – indispensable, really – but something told him that he would need to husband his resources. He hauled himself out of the bath.

4

Considering the importance of ritual in the book that had made him his fortune, Philip paid scant respect to it in his private life. So he surprised himself by having a somewhat ceremonial Monday morning. He'd again forgotten to turn the heating off, so when he awoke he flung aside the duvet to let himself cool, adopting the position of an effigy on a medieval tomb. When he dressed himself it was entirely in white and black: white Calvin Klein trunks and socks, black Lycra-mix elastic-waisted trousers, black trainers and the white chenille sweater from Harrods. He waited in reverential calm for the kettle to boil and made himself tea with a tea bag. He sniffed the milk like an augurer and rejected it. He added white sugar to the cup, stirred it widdershins twelve times then carried it in both hands across the lane and drank it in regular sips while contemplating the dank landscape that withheld any promise of spring.

Despite appearances, he was not composed. He was cautious. It seemed to him that he was carrying – no, that he *was* – a fragile blown-glass bubble filled with volatile liquids. After some considerable time he shuddered slightly, perhaps in response to a chill gust off the moor. Then he took himself carefully indoors, looped the chain of the Amulet over his head, tucked it inside his sweater and set about earning his million quid.

It was different this time.

First of all there was the seating problem. Pocket Wellfair's text scrolled up the screen only when the Amulet was wholly in contact with Philip's breast. However, he leaned forward when he typed, and so the Amulet swung forward very slightly and then the transmission broke up. He tried to type leaning back in his chair, but after a short spell of working in this unnatural position he became uncomfortable and the tendons in his hands hurt. Eventually he hit upon the idea of tying the belt from his dressing gown around his chest, thus keeping the Amulet pressed to his bosom; and this seemed to work.

Then there was the matter of the text itself. When he had written – perhaps 'received' was a better word – *Dark Entropy*, Pocket's words had flooded the monitor in such a swiftly rising tide that while Philip was transcribing the top lines the lower ones were still forming themselves out of pell-mell wriggling inkage. This time the upscroll contained pauses, deletions, instantaneous rewrites. There were moments when he was terrified that he would catch up. Use it all up before the next bit was ready. Even have to *invent*. Although, mercifully, it never quite came to that.

The visuals were not the same. They were there all right, a sideways glance, a click away, as before. And unimaginable and terrible and astonishing beyond the range of ordinary human description. But slightly dimmer than the first time. As though the film projector was operating at a lower wattage.

Nor was Pocket's voice quite the same. There was something slightly forced in the Greme's humour. Now and again it was like the patter of a comedian whose jokes were fed by pain. Which made a sort of sense because he was writing, transcribing, a darker tale. Five hours in, he could not imagine whence the light might come.

In *Dark Entropy* there had been an almost symmetrical pattern of brightness and shade. In chapter eleven, Morl had hoisted the hideous stillborn prototype Swelt out of the genetic cauldron in the bowels of the College of Thaumaturgy. In chapter twelve, Cadrel had settled kite-sized moths on his arms and carried them into his foster-mother's cottage so that she could see her embroidery by the moonlight stored in their wings. Philip could not yet see the possibility of any such captive moonlight, nor any other kind of illumination, in Part Two.

And it was odd that Pocket urged the story onward into deeper darkness without any hint of misgiving or regret. With a sort of eagerness, actually. Christ, this was a fast book. One damned thing after another. Event. Event. Event. Most of them desperate and murderous. Was it, tactically, a mistake that Pocket depicted the inner workings of the Thule? Was it a defiance of narrative logic that he appeared to know what he could not know?

Even odder was that he, Philip, could think this way. That even while his hands flew over the keys he could consider the unfolding of the story so dispassionately. It had not been this way the first time. Then, he had been dumb, numb, a mere receptor impervious to the demands of his belly, his bladder, his brain. Not so this time. Could it be that he had some kind of *control*? Dear God, let it not be so . . .

Oddest of all was the interruption. The very long interruption.

A hundred and one pages in, he became aware of sounds in his own world. A sequence of noises like someone practising on a muted trombone. He strove to ignore them – he was right in the middle of Strummer Augarde's discovery of the Vibrating Rune – but could not. He untied the knot in the belt of his dressing gown, freeing the Amulet.

It was like tearing a part of himself away from his body. The screen froze and the visuals went dead. In his right ear there was a sound like money getting lost. Then his brain went *What? What? What?* because there was someone in his bathroom. He got up and crossed the landing and yanked open the bathroom door and saw Pocket Wellfair fumbling with his breeches. The room was full of acrid reek.

'Always wanted to use one of these,' Pocket said. 'Arsewipe scroll is a good idea an' all. Soft paper is a sort of miracle.' He peered into the pan. 'How do you make it go away? Is it with this here?' He pressed the flush lever experimentally and jumped back going 'Whoa!' when the water gushed. 'Off they swim,' he said. 'Fancy. Brown fish is a land animal where I come from. How are you, Marlstone?'

Even to Philip's banjaxed ear the casual jollity in the voice sounded forced. And the Greme looked tired. Grubby too. The hem of his coat looked scorched.

'No need to ask, no need to ask. Right as rain and rich as badger's milk, you are. Ho, yes. How are *you*, Pocket, I hear you ask. Glad to see you again, I hear you say. Or do I? No, I don't. Bugger, have I turned deaf?'

'I,' Philip said. 'What. How did you . . . ?'

'Ah, yes. I'd quite forgot you were the man for the questions. Be "Who?" in a minute, I wouldn't wonder. Got me mixed up with one of your other Greme visitors, dare say.'

'No, no. I just didn't expect . . .'

Wellfair turned instantly into a miniature embodiment of pure rage. 'Didn't flukin expect? Didn't flukin *expect*? We made a *deal*, Marlstone. Swore the fluker on our eyes and eggs! Three nights on the bogging trot I've been up at that Devil's Pisspot or whatever it is you call that miserable collection of prickrocks. Waiting. Waiting for you, you slimepaddick. You goathole. Took me another half-night to find the gap into here.' He stepped, staggered, a pace towards Philip and held up a thumb and forefinger, white and blue-nailed, a millimetre apart. 'I was this far, *this* far, from calling the Oath in, leaving you blind and bleddy withercrotched.' Then he groaned and leaned heavily against the bathroom wall.

'Um,' Philip said. 'Are you all right?'

Wellfair was silent for a moment. His eyes were closed, their lids like crumpled kidskin gloves. 'In a pig's arse am I all right. No. I reckon I got blaggered on the way through. I'm dry as Great-granny's tit. Can I drink out of that?' Nodding at the toilet bowl.

'No, wait,' Philip said. 'I'll get you some water from the tap.'

When he came back upstairs with the glass he found Wellfair sitting on the single bed in the study gazing at the screensaver, a photograph of Minerva protruding her tongue, curled in at the edges, nestling a cherry.

'You britch-fumbling sod,' Pocket said. He took the glass and drank eagerly. Wiped his chin on his sleeve. 'Right. Give us the Amulet. Come on, give it here. It's under your poncey jerkin. I can feel it from here. Come on. There's things happening I've got to put a stop to.'

It was a simple reflex action, Philip's protective hand going to his chest. Pressing the Amulet against his flesh. But he had to let go almost immediately. It was too weird. Strummer's raptured face at the vision-edge. Nibscratch. Pocket's voice uttering untranslated speech while Pocket himself sat hostile in the room. Awful complication.

'No,' Philip said, not meaning to say it.

'*What?*'

'No, not no. I mean . . . I don't understand. Why now? We're only, I don't know, halfway through the book. Less.

136

We've, I've got to finish it. Got to. And you're coming through the Amulet. You were talking to me just now. So why do you want to take it away? Christ, Pocket, you can't. We're a million quid in the shit. Come on. What's happened?'

The Greme cocked his head like a chicken. His old eyes closed and reopened. 'Was that language just came out of your facehole, Marlstone? Cos either your brain's fluked or mine is. What are you on about? Book? What book? We've done the bleddy book. Deal's done, my end. Don't you try and frolic with me, you bugger. I'm stronger than I look.'

Philip was fairly sure that this was true, so he began to plead. 'Please. Let's just finish this one. It's all I'll ever ask, I promise. What'll it take? Another ten hours? Twelve? Just let me keep it till it's done. Don't pull the plug on me *now*, for God's sake.'

The Greme's eyes were full of owlish calculation. Eventually he said, 'It's like worms in the head, listening to you. Just you sit gobshut while I try and sort it.'

He seemed to sleep for about six seconds.

When he woke up he said, 'It's maybe I've been warped. Morl might've been screening me. It's not beyond him.' He hummed quietly to himself, then said, 'Marlstone, put your hands on the top of your head. Come on, do it. Right. Now then, stay like that while I go back to your shitter, understand me? Close your eyes, an' all. Right. When I come back in I'll clap my hands and then you open them. Got that?'

Philip nodded.

'Shut them, then.'

He did, and almost as soon as he had done so there was a massive bang. Wellfair was back in the room and sitting on the bed, cross-legged this time.

The Greme shuddered. 'Does me over, doing that,' he said. 'Shouldn't bleddy have to, if all was square. Still, my angles hadn't been boggled, cos here we still bleddy are. So then, what's all this drabble about a book? Have you been getting another one?'

'What do you mean? You know I have. You've been telling it. Dictating it. For God's sake, Pocket, you were doing it, sending it, no more than ten minutes ago.'

'Through the Amulet.'

'Yes. *Yes*. That's why you can't—'

The Greme shot out a hand, the forefinger and the shortest finger extended, aimed at Philip's throat. Philip's larynx contracted. His voice became a squeak then died because he was being garrotted by the muscles of his own neck.

'That's second time you've used the word *can't* to me, and if you're partial to breathing there better not be a third. Elsewise I'll leave you thrapple-clamped and bugger off homewards. Point took? Nod?'

Pop-eyed, Philip nodded. Wellfair withdrew his hand and waited patiently for him to recommence breathing. The Greme got to his feet and stood staring at Minerva.

'Why's she doing that, anyways?'

'Ar-harrgh. Well. She, um. She'd just sucked the stone

out of the cherry without squashing it or anything. She's showing me that it's still . . . intact. It's a sort of trick she does.'

'I wager it is. Must have taken years of practice, wouldn't you say?'

Philip said nothing.

'Righty, then,' Wellfair said. 'This book. Remind me where you'd, we'd, got to.'

'The bit where Strummer discovers, well, accidentally discovers, the Vibrating Rune . . .'

'Strummer?'

'Strummer Augarde, yes. Of course, I don't—'

'Did I happen to mention his age?'

'Yes, er, eighteen, I think. Hang on, I'll check.' Philip reached over and dabbed the space-bar. Minerva vanished to be replaced by half a page of text. 'No, seventeen. It all goes out of my memory quite quickly, actually. You go so fast.'

He turned to see Pocket standing next to him, staring at the screen with something like horror in his ancient eyes.

'Looks like rows of drydead insects raked up on a bedsheet. Is that *your* inkage, or do all of you do the same?'

'Well, there are different fonts, of course. I tend to use Times New Roman, or Microsoft's version of it, anyway. Arial is quite popular, though.'

'Don't it move? There's no shiftage in it, as I see it. Is it dead?'

Philip gaped for a moment and then understood. 'Ah.

Right. No, it's not like what you do. When I write, the words are finished. They don't do that wriggly chasing thing that yours do.'

'Write some.'

'What, carry on with the story, you mean? Can we do that?'

'No,' Wellfair said sharply. 'Just write the first thing that comes into the foulpot you call your head. No, wait. Write this: "Pocket Wellfair is standing next to me."'

Philip pecked at the keys as the Greme watched intently. The words hobbled onto the screen.

'Shrivel my life,' Wellfair muttered. 'It's like tapping on tombstones. I'd never've thought . . .' He hung his head for a moment. Then he inhaled lengthily through his nose and sat down on the bed again. 'What's it say now?'

'What?'

'Does it still bleddy say "Pocket Wellfair is standing next to me"?'

'Well, yes. Of course.'

Wellfair nodded, slowly, several times. Then he rested his forearms on his knees and lowered his head. He muttered something that Philip couldn't catch. After a minute he looked up. His eyes had changed, somehow. Philip had no word for what had happened to them. And when the Greme spoke, the voice was different too. It contained a note of nervous caution.

'Right. Now then. Let's sniff back along our tracks a way. What came just before we got to Strummer Augarde?'

Philip frowned, perplexed. 'Don't you . . . ? Right. OK. Sorry. Well, you led the Greme expedition into the Wandering Crags to find the Fourth Device. Into Morl's False Winter. It was brilliant. Well, terrible. The passage where Rinse Pitcher freezes to death was incredibly strong, I thought.'

Wellfair lifted a pale narrow hand and Philip fell silent. He watched, seriously alarmed, as the Greme wrapped his arms around himself and rocked his huddled body back and forth, moaning.

'Pocket? What's the matter?'

The Greme sniffed lengthily again and shook his head slowly, several times.

Philip waited. He wanted to reach out and lay a consoling hand on Pocket's shoulder, but could not quite bring himself to do so.

Eventually the Greme sighed and sat upright. He clasped his knees with his pale thin hands.

'Right. Listen up. Strummer Augarde is fifteen, in your money. Not seventeen. *Fifteen.*'

'Oh, right. We can change that, then. It's not a problem.'

'Stap me, Marlstone! Listen! Never have I led any sort of bleddy expedition to the Wandering Crags. Never been anywhere near them. Wouldn't want to. No one's ever come back from there without his wits curdled.'

'Well, I'm amazed. You imagine the whole thing so vividly. You're great, Pocket. I mean it.'

If Philip had hoped that this compliment would soothe

his guest, he was immediately disabused of the notion.

'I don't make things bleddy up, you arsecrack!'

'Don't you?'

'No! What d'you take me for, you hobble-brained lummox?'

'But,' Philip said, baffled, gesturing at the computer screen, 'what about all this, then? What about . . . ?'

'There you go again! Fluking *what* and *what* and *what*! I'll tell you fluking *what*, Marlstone. You're writing things that haven't happened yet! *Yet*. That a word you know? *Yet*?'

The lexical part of Philip's brain conceded that it was an oddly complex little word. And repetition seemed to remove its meaning. Made it a noise, like a reaction to pain. Stand on a drawing pin. *Yet!*

But what he said was, 'Is that a problem?'

An innocent question that converted Pocket Wellfair into a small but monstrous hurricane full of blue-tipped hooks like fingers that sought throat.

Philip wailed and fled stumbling down the stairs. He got to the front door but the Greme was already there.

5

Philip retreated to the fireplace and grabbed the poker. Wellfair pointed two fingers and the poker turned to soft liquorice and drooped in a loop. The phone rang. Wellfair turned it into pinkish meringue, then, snarling, aimed his hands at various parts of the room like a demented pistolero. For a few frightful seconds it seemed that he intended to transmute all of Philip's domestic belongings into forms of confectionery. However, the storm in him abated as rapidly as it had brewed, and he slumped back against the door, hands falling to his sides. He looked exhausted.

'Rein up, Pocket,' he said quietly. 'Leave yourself enough to get home with. If the Old Boy knew you'd been wasting like that he'd put an Ache right up your back passage.' He lifted his old eyes. 'Pardon begged, Marlstone. Not your fault. No. The fault sits right here with me. I should've told you. Should've warned you. But I didn't. And now you've got yourself frolicking with Powers beyond your wottage. Beyond mine, come to that. Way beyond.'

He moistened his lips with a pale indigo tongue.

'You're writing *the future*, Marlstone, and it can't be allowed. Not by one of your lot, least of all. Not in dead inkage. Not when it's lies. So just hand over the Amulet, there's a good pony, and I'll leave you in peace.'

Philip didn't move.

'Come on,' Pocket said wearily. 'Come on. Don't you get me naggled up again. You've seen what I'm like.'

'What about the book?'

'What book?'

'The one I'm, we're, writing.' Philip raised a shaky finger in the general direction of his study.

'Marlstone, there *is* no bleddy *book*. That what you've got hidden up there behind that pip-sucking doxy of yours is a winterborn misbegot. I don't know how it got there, and I don't want to. Just get rid of it. Bury it outside the parish and forget it. Top advice, that. You take it. Hear me? Now give me the Amulet. You don't want to keep it, believe me.'

'Please, Pocket. Listen. You don't understand. I *owe* this book. I've got Gorgon on my back. Minerva. My fucking *public*. My credibility is at stake, Pocket. I've taken a million Jesus pounds for it. I've *got* to finish it! Can't you see that?'

'No. Nothing to do with me. Bugger, you do my head over. You need to do another book, make it up.'

'I can't. I can't, I *can't*! Not without you. Or the Amulet. Please . . .'

The Greme tipped his head. 'What d'you mean, you

can't? You do flaky ledgers, don't you? That's why we angled you in the first place. You haven't led me on like a blind goat, have you?'

'I . . .' Philip said. 'I don't know what you mean. Did you say "flaky ledgers"? What are they?'

'Bollix,' Wellfair groaned. 'Whatyoucallums. Hold fast.' He hoisted up his coat and fumbled in the pockets of his breeches. 'No, lost it. Had a list. Not a long one, mind. Something about a horse race. First Past the Post, or summat. Another one about a chicken. That *was* you, wasnit?'

'Do you mean my novels? Is that what you mean?'

'*Nobbles*, that's the badger. Forgot the word for it.' Pocket shook his head sadly. 'Time was, I could catch words easy as shag-season trout. My old brain's going threadbare. Hardly bleddy surprising, all things considered. Yes, nobbles. Give 'em one of those. Now . . .'

Philip bent in a gesture of desperate supplication, his hands in front of him, cupped. 'That's not what they want. That's no good. They want *your next book*. That's the *deal*!' He stopped short, aghast.

'Aha,' Wellfair cried. 'Now there's a word I *do* remember. Along with *Oath*, *Four*, *Vital* and *Orbs*. They clap your bell, Marlstone?'

If Philip had anything left to say he was saved from saying it by a loud whirring noise. Something apparently alive wriggled visibly in Wellfair's coat pocket. The clerk fished in there and produced a blueish egg. He twisted it, separating it into two halves which he peered at intently.

He displayed them to Murdstone. Each had an internal surface of some dark substance inlaid with designs formed of what looked like brass.

'That,' the Greme said, 'tells me I'm down to a fiftieth. That's about ten minutes, in your money.' He screwed the egg together again and returned it to his pocket. 'So no more cackle. Last chance. Hand over the Amulet or I call in the Oath.'

'No, wait. Look, maybe you haven't thought this through. If you're right, if what I'm writing, what I'm . . . receiving, is, like, the future, right, we should finish it. See? Then you'd *know*. You'd know what was going to happen. And you could use that against Morl. Somehow. Couldn't you? See what I mean?'

Philip was startled by the effect these words had upon the Greme. Pocket's eyes closed. His mouth turned down at its corners and his chin trembled. He waved feebly with one hand as though trying to dispel some airborne contagion. For a second or two he resembled a child in an ecstasy of terror. Then, very quickly, he regathered himself and forced his face into an expression of amused impatience.

'Craze my arse, Marlstone, you really have got toad-shite for brains. Real futures can't be had. No one would do anything if they already knew what it was. A sprog at the tit could work that out.' Wellfair rolled up his sleeves. 'Right. I have to do this by the Book. So I have to demand Render three times. Don't let me get to the third. Your eyes and bollix are hanging by a jimp. Have a little frot of them, Marlstone. Imagine them gone. Here we go . . .'

The Greme extended both arms and cleared his throat.

'By the Terms of the Oath,' he intoned, 'square made between me, Pocket Wellfair of the Realm, and one Marlstone, of Another Place, I demand Render of the Amulet of Eneydos.'

He paused, his owl-gaze fixed on Philip's face.

'I herebys make demand of Render the first time.'

He jiggled his fingers, waiting. Philip shrank against the wall, shaking his head. He sobbed, once.

'Come on, come on, you cloutstreak,' Wellfair whispered.

Philip shook his head once more. Wellfair sighed.

'I herebys make demand of Render the second time.'

Philip made a sound like a lamb's first bleat.

'Don't make me do this, Marlstone.'

Wellfair waited.

'Last flukin chance.'

Philip screwed himself up into a defensive position. He bit his bottom lip. He closed his eyes tightly.

'In a pig's arse, then,' Pocket cried. 'I herebys make demand of Render the . . .'

'All right, all right!' Philip screamed, fumbling at the chain around his neck.

Too late.

'. . . third time.'

Something fast and only just discernible occurred in the air. Fleeting and turquoise, like the glimpse of a kingfisher. Philip experienced an icy tingling in his genitals, as though the fluids of his scrotum had turned to champagne. It lasted for no more than a second or two and was not entirely unpleasant, although he cried out just the same. Simultaneously, his eyes smarted as from the effects of smoke. He blinked tears away.

And to his very great surprise discovered that he could still see.

He could see Pocket.

The Greme was rubbing his thin white hands together, warming them. Muttering and humming to himself in a dejected manner. Looking around the room, apparently assessing the difficulties it might present to a sightless eunuch.

'Ho-hum. Well, well. Dumdee-doo. Bogger. Who'd have thought. Knew you was a bit of a dimmock, Marlstone, but never had you down for a complete spatch. But here you are, darkled and gelded by your own stubbornness. Ah well. Ho-dee-doo.' He sighed, pulling himself up into the fullness of his small height, and tried to seem businesslike. 'Spose I'd better sort out your tellingbone, so's you can call the Blind Office. And that strumpet of yours. Tell her she might as well chew that cherry now, if it's juice she's after.'

He gestured wearily at the phone, which reverted to its original substance. Then he turned and gazed sadly at motionless Murdstone for a lengthy moment. He raised his voice a notch.

'Can you hear me, you poor poxdrip? The freeze I put

on you will wear off afore too long. Then you'll be able to bumble your way about. By then I'll be long gone. I'd like to say it's been a pleasure knowing you, but it's been an arse-ache, truth told. But fair do's, you did get the Amulet. So when you're lying abed fingering your empty crotchwallet, you'll have a spot of comfort knowing that you might, just might, have done your measure towards the saving of the Realm. Mind you, you better pray on whatever you've got left that Morl never finds out. Bogger, no. Shouldn't even have said that.' He made a hasty sign in the air, then took a step towards Philip, his hands reaching for the Amulet.

Philip took an involuntary step back.

Wellfair froze. 'Marlstone?'

'What?'

Wellfair went into a crouch. Glanced swiftly around the room. Straightened. Thrust out a hand. 'Marlstone? How many fingers'm I holding up?'

'Three.'

'Was that a guess?'

'No.'

Moments went by in slow motion. Then the Greme went into a demented spasm, like someone trying to dance pain to a standstill. His cries filled the room, writhing and wriggling and chasing each other, their sounds like harpooned whales seeking places deep enough to die in.

When they ceased, when the fit was over, Pocket did not look at all like his former self. He hunched, apparently studying a damp patch on the carpet.

'So you can see, Marlstone?' A tragic whisper.

'Yes,' Philip said apologetically.

'Both nadgers still warm and present?'

'I think so. Yes.' The air in the room was thick and stationary. 'Er, it doesn't seem to have worked,' Philip said. 'The Oath, I mean. I think it might be because—'

He didn't finish the sentence. The Greme was upon him suddenly. Up on his body, like a frenzied child. Biting. Scrabbling. Hard clammy fingers up inside the Harrods sweater, grasping at the Amulet. Seizing it.

What happened then was like an explosion, except that it was cold rather than hot, and radiated violent silence rather than sound. It threw Wellfair clean across the room like a doll. Philip hadn't felt a thing. He watched anxiously as Pocket rolled himself over and staggered to his feet.

'Are you all right?'

Pocket mouthed words that didn't come. He tried again. 'Listen, Marlstone. I reckon we're in deeper shite here than you could fathom. Don't move. It's worse than I thought. I think that bleddy thing is dark-charged.' He braced himself, hands on his knees, and struggled to steady his breathing. 'Right. Making this up as I go along, I am, like a pissed fiddler. But don't panic. I reckon what you do is take the Amulet off, nice and easy, and put it down on the floor. Then I'll have another go at it. Maybe you're earthing it somehow, see what I mean?'

'Well, no, actually.'

'Square do's. Nor do I. Worth a try, though.'

The loud whirring again from Pocket's pocket. He moaned terribly, slapping at it.

'Come on, then. Take it off and put it on the floor. Hurry up, hurry up!'

'No,' Philip said. 'I don't think I will.'

The Greme groaned liked something deeply subterranean. 'Don't give me any more of that. *Please* don't start on that again, you mad flukin bumweevil. We're right on the edge here, man. It could turn on *you*, don't you see that? *Take the bogger off!*'

'Shan't.'

Pocket didn't hesitate. He took just one stride and sprang at Murdstone's chest. He didn't reach it. Before he'd even made contact with the Amulet, its force again flung him away. The Greme struck the back of the sofa, then disappeared arse-upwards over it.

A short silence. A smell something like urine and roasted chestnuts in the room.

'Pocket?'

Christ. He'd better not be dead.

The blue egg rolled into view. It remained stationary for a moment, then moved in wobbly ellipses around the floor, chirruping desperate high-pitched Morse. Pocket emerged from behind the sofa on his hands and knees. He looked dreadfully altered. Reduced and slack, like the victim of a hit-and-run liposuctionist. At a second attempt he grabbed the egg and stumbled to the stairs. Halfway up them, he managed, heroically, to turn his head and gasp last words.

'Flukin *nobblist*!'

Then he was gone.

Philip heard the bathroom door slam and a dying wail. He waited for two whole minutes before setting off upstairs. He tapped on the bathroom door and said, 'Pocket?' just the once. When there was no reply he went cautiously in. One end of the towel rail had been ripped from the wall and had swivelled to the floor. The free end of the toilet roll trailed into the pan. Of Pocket Wellfair there was not the slightest sign. Philip looked fearfully up at the ceiling, but it was intact.

Alone in the room he said, 'I think it didn't work because you got my name wrong. It's Murdstone, not Marlstone. That might've made the difference.'

He peered into the toilet bowl, just in case.

'Murdstone,' he said into it. '*Murdstone*.'

6

For much of the rest of the day, Philip's relief at having evaded blindness and castration kept his other worries at bay.

After Pocket Wellfair's involuntary resyphoning into the Realm, he smoked a couple of cigarettes while waiting for his jumpy nerves to settle. Then he returned to his computer and tightened the belt around the Amulet. Nothing happened. No visuals, voice, or text. He was not dismayed; not even surprised. After what had happened there was bound to be a hiatus.

He went downstairs and drank a large malt while microwaving a frozen Green Thai Chicken Curry. He was thinking that, on reflection, risking one's eyes and testicles for a million pounds hadn't really been sensible. He already had a million – more, in fact – in a Swiss bank and it wasn't really that much money. It was far less than it used to be.

He ate the curry, which was like a bath additive with lumps in it, then watched the early evening television news without taking it in. He took the whisky bottle to his study. After a while he decided to change his screen-saver. Minerva and her cherry no longer seemed ... appropriate.

He clicked through the rest of My Pictures, but of the few that didn't feature her there were none that took his fancy. There was a fairly good one of the neon riot that was Times Square, but you couldn't make out the icons against it. In the end he chose a pre-installed Microsoft sample of the Taj Mahal because the *Murdstone 2* folder looked nice in the blue Indian sky. Then he went to bed.

He awoke to the early sounds of bird-chirp and tractor-snarl because something like a dream had startled him. But no, it was only memory. He blinked at the blank ceiling then turned his head and saw the usual. He checked the contents of his scrotum and found everything still present and more or less correct. He spent the morning doing housework, occasionally diddling himself through the lining of his trouser pockets, sometimes looking out at the world's wintry things in a chuckly appreciative sort of a way.

This smug interlude, this honeymoon with himself, didn't last long, however. By the time the vague sun had leached into the dim of the Dartmoor afternoon the mantra *I got away with it* had lost its power.

Because there was still the book.

The unfinished book.

And all the shit that went with that.

He went to his study and tried to think in sentences.

He had, what, a quarter of it?

Well, nearly a quarter of what *Dark Entropy* had turned out as.

Bloody good too. Dark, yes, but . . .

Pocket would definitely try again to get hold of the Amulet. For sure. Had to. So he would be back.

Get yourself ready for that, Murdstone. Stay away from the Wringers. Keep your eye on the lav.

Or maybe he wouldn't. Because the Amulet had, obviously, turned against him – Pocket – because, obviously, it wanted (could inanimate things *want*?) to be with him. Me.

Yes.

Because it had a story to tell him. Neither here nor there, all that bollocks of Pocket's about it not having happened yet. Gorgon wouldn't give a toss. Imagine saying to them, 'Sorry, I can't give you the new book because the things in it haven't happened yet.' They'd have him dragged off in a straitjacket to the agony dungeon of some corporate lawyer.

Or—

There wouldn't be any more. It was over.

No. Don't Go There.

There is the dark bourne.

There is the windowless room where the spiders live.

In which Minerva would rip him apart.

He couldn't take the Amulet off, of course. It might restart transmission at any time.

Was it safe to go out of doors with it on, though, with livestock roaming about? Come to that, it wasn't entirely unlikely that the Amulet might mistake the inhabitants of Flemworthy for Gremes. Indeed not. There would be very tricky repercussions if he popped into Kwik Mart for a bit of Stilton and inadvertently blasted a brace of locals through the freezer cabinets. Best not to risk it. He was fairly well stocked up. He could do without milk and the *Daily Telegraph*.

Time passed, days that left no traces.

Then one morning or afternoon he lifted his eyes from the Taj Mahal and saw that the small window of his study was also joyously blue. He went downstairs and opened the front door upon a new season. The grey old skull of the world had been aerosolled pale green and the air was full of birds talking about it.

He touched the Amulet through his pyjama top and silently told it *I am not your slave*.

He got dressed. He put on his Barbour and buckled green wellies.

He took the familiar route down the zigzag path of red mud and mottled stones through the sloping pasture. Here and there he caught the coconut whiff of gorse blossom. At his approach, new lambs ran on awkward legs to suckle reassurance from their mothers. At the bottom of the coombe, where Parson's Cleft emptied its trickle into the main stream, he paused on the little wooden bridge and gazed about him. Catkins, soft greenish worms, dangled against the flawless sky. The tea-coloured water burbled. Those yellow flowers that he could never remember the name of (they weren't buttercups, he knew that) blazed in patches of sunlight. A bird with a wagging tail (a wagtail, possibly?) alighted briefly on a watersmoothed stone and then flickered away. From high above, the kittenish mew of a buzzard.

He inhaled deeply, twice, and went on. He followed the old lepers' track that wound its way towards St Pessary. Three hundred metres later, he emerged from dappled shade into pure light. At the small group of tilted rocks known as Three Fingers he stopped. Far enough. Leaning his back against warm and lichen-mottled granite, he lifted his face to the sun like a willing Inca sacrifice. He closed his eyes and something resembling a soft collapse, an intense mellowing, took place within him. For the first time in, oh, who knows how long, he felt as though he was living in his body, that the lively coursing of his blood and juices were for his benefit alone. Yet, simultaneously, he felt on the verge of departure from himself; that at any moment he might be wonderfully, weightlessly, distant.

His face grew warm. His torso absorbed heat; heat like warm fingers reaching into his core. A tingling web of heat, centred on . . .

Oh, shit.

The Amulet.

Was it? Christ!

He fumbled at his clothing, thrust his hand up inside his shirt. The Amulet was trembling.

No, that was his hand.

No, it wasn't.

Shit, oh shit!

Now the hot spider occupied the centre of its hot web; he could feel the pulsing of its legs against his chest.

He ran, awkward in the unfamiliar boots, sobbing for breath. As he lurched across the Cleft, a sudden gust of wind set the trees rustling. Or was that nibscratch?

'Wait,' he cried, stumbling onto the bridge. 'Please wait!'

Beyond the edge of his normal vision there was something shimmering, or vibrating.

By the time he'd reached the top of the track he could no longer draw in air; panic alone powered his legs onto the lane. At the cottage he wasted precious seconds searching for his keys before he tried the door and found that he'd left it unlocked. Up the stairs, bugger the mud. Chest burning inside and out now. Stabbed the space-bar. Couldn't see properly. Sweat stinging his eyes. Forced his fingers to steady on the keys.

And – of course – there was nothing.

It was, had been, just a warning.

Half an hour later, Philip pulled up his sweater and looked at the cold Amulet. The squat little hieroglyph was there again, and this time he understood what it was. Knew its strange familiarity. It appeared every time he turned his computer on. Telling him to wait. It was an hourglass. But now the dot in the upper chamber had sunk closer to the narrow neck that connected it to the lower, the chamber of time already trickled away.

He had fifty-two days left to deadline. He knew that because he had been counting.

7

Evelyn Dent was arranging ten quid's worth of daffodils in the blue spherical vase when she heard and saw her employer arrive. The kitchenette looked down onto the small parking bay at the rear of their Camden office. The BMW came to a halt slantwise, blocking in Evelyn's Clio.

As soon as she saw Minerva unfurl from the car Evelyn knew it was going to be a rough start to the week. Minerva was wearing a severely elegant black suit over a blouse the colour of blackcurrant sorbet. Extra bounce in the hair. Conspicuous jewellery. When Minerva looked like this on a Tuesday, Evelyn knew there had been a rough weekend. The visit to Devon had not gone well. No surprise there, then.

Evelyn abandoned the daffs and hurriedly stoked the coffee machine with extra-strength Monsoon Malibar. She peeled the stubborn cellophane from the pack of Marlboro Lights that she'd bought Just In Case.

'Just don't say anything, darling,' Minerva said, 'unless it's to ask whether I want it black, in which case the answer is yes, or if I want sugar, in which case the answer is two. Please. Got any fags?'

When Evelyn brought in the tray Minerva was reclining on her sofa gazing blankly at the toes of her Jimmy Choo shoes. Evelyn served the coffee, lit two cigarettes and passed one over, along with the ashtray they'd nicked from the Groucho Club.

After the first coffee, and half the first cigarette, Minerva said, 'He's having a nervous breakdown. At least, I hope that's what it is. I prefer to think he's not gone permanently bloody mental. Have Gorgon phoned yet?'

'Once at eight thirty-two and again at five to nine. Plus two emails.'

'What did you tell them?'

'That you were still consulting on the draft and wouldn't be back until mid-afternoon. Was that OK?'

'That bloody *place*,' Minerva said flatly. 'I said to him, Philip, *darling*, we went to all that trouble getting you that gorgeous little pied-a-terre, against tax, in the nice bit of Paddington, just two minutes from the station, OK, you can be back in Devon in two and a bit hours. Big, big windows, lots of lovely light, places to go when the day's labour is ended. Why, I said to him, *why* must you insist on working in this ghastly hobbity little hovel? It's no wonder you get depressed.'

Evelyn said, 'And he told you it's because he has to be there because that's where he gets *inspired*.'

By way of response, Minerva smoked the rest of her Marlboro. 'Guess what he was wearing when I turned up.'

'The skin of a rare beast and a studded leather codpiece.'

'Don't. Wait, I've just remembered something. I parked about a mile or something from his place, which is, OK, the nearest place you *can* bloody park. I'm walking down the road, lane, whatever, and just as I get there I see these two weird creatures standing there watching Philip's cottage.'

'Gremes?'

'Good as. Bent-over little creatures wearing those transparent things, like macs with hoods, you know? They looked like bags of fog. On closer inspection they seemed to be female, except that they had moustaches. So I said hi, or whatever. And they didn't bloody speak. Just looked at me, you know? And you know what? They had their thumbs in their mouths.'

'Never.'

'I swear.'

'Hell's teeth,' Evelyn said. She refilled the cups. 'So what *was* he wearing?'

'Well, just clothes. But, *but*, OK, he had this belt from a dressing gown knotted around his chest.'

'Why?'

'Ah. Well.' Minerva turned to look at Evelyn. 'I'm not in the mood for kiss and tell, OK? Let's just say that the whole weekend I couldn't get him to take it off.'

'Not for anything?'

'No.'

Evelyn's phone rang. She and Minerva waited in silence

until Val Sneed had completed her tetchy message.

'So, why? I mean, why not?'

Minerva drew in a deep breath. 'He's got that Nutwell thing lashed to his bloody chest, that's why. You know, that thing that Arora Lynton gave him. I thought at first that it was about her, you know? Like some pervy fetish-istic thing he had going. But it wasn't that.'

'So what was it, then?'

'I dunno. I really don't know. He said, once, something about coordinates. Didn't make any sense. Another time he went on about it being his lucky charm. Said some-thing about his four orbs, whatever they might be. Mind you, he was pissed. Knocking back the Glen Moronic like there was no tomorrow. And he was *most* peculiar about the loo. Hated me going in there. And when I did, he skulked outside the door. Awful. I mean, you know how hard it is to *go* when you're with a bloke, even at the best of times. But to sit there knowing he's on the other side of the door, going, "Are you all right? Will you be much longer?" Dear *God*. I'm still seized up. If I ever take it into my head to go down there again, handcuff me to my desk and lock me in. I mean it. Make a note of that and date it, OK?'

'Like I did last time? Sure.'

The two women shared silence for a while.

'So,' Evelyn said. 'Dare I ask?'

'He says he's done a hundred pages.'

'And has he?'

'Christ knows. He wouldn't let me read anything. Not

until late Sunday afternoon, after a session in that grisly pub.'

'Ah.'

'Ah, indeed. God, the things I do for literature. I got him to print out the first ten pages, and it was like pulling teeth. Worse, in fact.'

'And?'

'Brilliant, Evie. Extraordinary. Like nothing I've ever read. *Loads* better than *Dark Entropy*.'

'Can I read it?'

'Nope. He grabbed it back as soon as I'd finished it. Like it was MI6's address book or something.'

'And now he's stopped?'

'Yes, he's fucking stopped. Give us another fag. Please.'

8

Twenty-three days to deadline and Philip had grown a beard, although he was scarcely aware of it. He was conscious of the fact that his hand brushed against something hairy when he lowered his hand from his forehead to press the Amulet harder into his chest, but it had been a very long time since he had looked into a mirror.

It was hot in the little room, and it suddenly occurred to him that he ought to have air. With some difficulty he forced the window open. He was surprised that it made little difference. Outside was hot as well. And the physical effort of rising from his chair and opening the window made him dizzy. That was because he had run out of food some time ago. The emergency supplies that Minerva had bought in the village during that terribly awkward weekend had long since gone. The only thing left in the freezer was a thin plastic wallet of something that might once have been smoked salmon. He'd looked at it the night before and seen the date 2001 on it.

Both tea and coffee had become distant memories. He

missed them sometimes – in the morning, usually – but only in that mistily regretful way that old people remembered sex. He did not really miss food; it seemed to him that he burned more brightly, concentrated more fiercely, without it. And not eating eased the toilet paper problem. When he'd run out of old newspapers, he had been forced to use books. He'd gone through *The Rainbow* in short order, but he was working far more slowly through *Sons and Lovers*. In a week he'd reached only the third chapter. And if he ran out of Lawrence, there was always Kingsley Amis. None of that was a problem. But he had run out of alcohol, and that was.

There had been two further warnings since his abortive springtime stroll, one in the Gelder's during the Minerva weekend, and another when he'd tried to reach the village after finishing the bottle of curdled Irish Cream Liqueur. On both occasions, that sensation of hot crab claws moving under the skin of his chest, that electrical vibration, had sent him scuttling home. False alarms, of course, but frightening (or did he mean reassuring?) proof that the Amulet was still . . . active. And wanted, needed, him to be on station. He was pretty certain that if he tried to make another dash to Kwik Mart the same thing would happen again. If he ignored it, defied the Amulet's power, it was entirely possible that it would transmit in his absence in order to punish him. Yes, that was a reasonable assumption. That was just the kind of thing that Amulets might do.

On the other hand, there was the insuperable,

monolithic, non-negotiable fact that he could not go on, *could not* go on, without a bloody drink.

Then he remembered something, something wonderful. He wobbled down the stairs and into the kitchen, yanked open the cupboard under the sink, hauled out and scattered detergenty things; and there it was: most of a gallon of Ratt's Farmhouse Scrumpy in its plastic container. He sat it on the draining board and wiped the greasy cap with a dishcloth, and as he was doing so he noticed that there seemed to be something in the container that should not be there. Holding his dismay in check, he unscrewed the cap and was forced to pull back from the incredibly astringent gas he had released.

When the water had cleared from his eyes he saw that just below the surface of the cider there floated a thick gelatinous mass. He cautiously inserted the handle of a wooden spoon and some of this stuff clung to it. It was like the caul of some grotesque alien birth.

Bitter rage flared within him. It was not much of a flare, no more than a match struck on a windy night, but it was enough. He howled a single obscenity and then moved through the house incanting some sort of checklist.

'Money? Wallet. Where? Jacket pocket. Yes. Notes, several big ones, good. Shoes, yes, shoes. Keys? No, sod it. Wait. Walk or drive? Drive. Can I? Shit, will it start? Stood there ages. Shit. Try it, must be quick. Oh please, *please* let me, you bastard.'

Then he was gone. On the draining board, inside the cider, the slimy bacterial matrix reformed itself with a faint gulp.

At twenty-six minutes past one Merilee let herself into the library and leaned back against the door in a pose that belonged in a silent movie. Francine looked up from her lunch-time task – deciding whether to catalogue Anaïs Nin's *The Delta of Venus* under Geography or Astrology – and gasped.

'Law, Merilee, you looks white as a scalt pig. Whatever is it? Don't say they was out of curry pasties.'

'Oh, Francine, Francine. Never you mind about they pasties. Less us go on through to Children's. I need to subsidize onto a beanbag afore I can talk. I never seen anythun like it.'

'What?'

'Murdsten. Down the supermarket.'

'No.'

'Yes. An bring that Malibu and the Pepsi.'

When the sisters were settled and looking, in their orange corduroy nests, like failed desserts, Merilee twitched her nose and said, 'Have someone pissed in here agen?'

'Not as I noticed. Come on, don' keep me in suspension. Tell us about Murdsten.'

Merilee took a pull on her cocktail as an aid to recollection. 'Well, I didun reckernize him at first. I thought it wuz Raspitoon the Mad Monk, or that homeless plays the widgerydoo outside a Boots. Hair downta here, big ole beard . . .'

'Never a beard!'

'A beard, Francine, and lissun – shoes an no socks.'

'Oh, no. You'm maken that up, Merilee.'

'I swear. My blood run cold when I noticed.'

'So what you'm sane, then? He've gone maze?'

By way of reply Merilee raised and tapped her glass of Malibu and Pepsi while treating her sister to a significant look.

'Ah,' Francine said.

'Which I reduce from what wuz in his trolley. Loads a they pricey whiskies come in cardboard tubes, you know, left over from Chrismuss, an two bottles a Bailey's, wine, all sorts. We come face to face at cakes and biscuits . . .'

'Aisle Three.'

'Aisle Three, and when I works out who it is, I says, "Well, Mister Murdsten! Aren't you a sight for sore eyes" or somesuch. And he just stand there starin at me like he never saw me afore in his life. Well, it wuz proper awkward, Francine.'

'My law, Merilee. I can't hardly pitcher it. Whatever did you do?'

'Well, it wuz either stand there like a rabbit at a stoat's picnic or say somethun, so I looks down at his trolley and says, "Havin a party, Mister Murdsten? Got a new book to cerebrate?"'

Francine squeezed her legs together. 'You wuz doin just a bit a fishin there, Merilee. Naughty.'

'True. I didun get a bite, though. You know what he done? He done that thing Basil Fawlty do, like wakun up from sleepwalkun, and run off.'

'What, out?'

'No, just down the aisle, then back he come with a harmload of bags of coffee and sugar. Dumps em in his trolley and off he go. So of course I sets off after un, and blieve me, Francine, tas none too easy cos he's goin like the clappers. People gettin out a the way of un, more or less climbing up the ready meals case he runs over um.'

'He musta had that bit a rumpy a his from Lunnen waiting outside on the yeller lines.'

'Thas ezackly what I thought. *Ezackly*. Can't fault you there, Francine. But no.'

'No?'

'No, as it did turn out. But you'm getting ahead a me. So he scream down through dairy produce . . .'

'Aisle Six.'

'Five.'

'Six.'

'Bleddy hell, Francine. Five, Six, who give a crusty fuck? Us's losing the bleddy narrative flow here.'

'Sorry, Merilee. I's just tryin to get the pitcher straight. Five is cleanin products an dog food. It might make a diffrunce.'

Merilee steadied her breathing and softened her glare. She took a drink. 'Well, you'm right, as it turn up. Cos Denzil wouldn't have been in Aisle Five.'

'Who?'

'Denzil Gadder. Like to come in of a Tuesday to comb his hair in fronta the cheese?'

'Oh, yeah. That Denzil.'

'Well, Murdsten's goin hell fur leather down to the checkouts, and Denzil don't see him comin and go arse over tip inta the cabinet. Murdsten stop then. Denzil's got his legs up in the air an his comb in his hand, goin *What?* Murdsten just look at him like there's nothun peculiar about findin a sex offender sittin in the yoghurts an grabs up lumps a cheese an a big milk an set off agen. So us gets to the checkouts and whichun do he choose? Seein as how he's in a hurry?'

'Not Sigourney Hookway.'

'Oh yes.'

'Oh no.'

'Ho yes.'

And here the Weird Sisters lean towards each other and press their foreheads together and harshly draw in noisy breaths. (This is their mode of hysterical laughter, a bonding ritual. It is one of the things that persuaded their parents, twenty years earlier, to depart without them in the middle of the night and move to Shetland.)

'Cos,' Merilee continued breathlessly, 'Murdsten dunno no one go to Sigourney's till cos she don know a bar code from a dead zebra. So there she be, fumblin away with his stuff, four or five goes, random like, before the bleddy thing go beep, and there's I, right behind un, seein he's like a man with a stag beetle up his chuff, which Miss Special Needs Hookway don't notice at all. So's to

170

detract him I says . . . Did I mention he had a belt round his chest looked like from a dressun gown?'

Francine looked blank for a moment. 'No, you didn. Why did he?'

'*I* dunno. Bleddy hell, Francine. Anyway, he's grabbin all the bottles offa Sigourney soon as she put them through and stuffin 'em in the bags, an I'm standin there tryun a make conversation about his beard an what all, and he's jiggin about going *Ahhh* an *Hmmm* with his eyes rollin about in his haid like a steer lookin in a butcher's winder, an then's when things got peculiar. You wunt believe what happened next.'

Here, for dramatic purposes, Merilee paused to take a further draught of Malibu and Pepsi. Francine, expecting it, did likewise.

'So,' Merilee said, daintily wiping her moustache with the back of her hand, 'Sigourney's somehow managed to put about halfa Murdsten's stuff through when he clutch both his hands to his chest, right where he've got the belt knotted, an he stagger back and let out this horrible groan. No, that don't do'n justice. More like a *wail*, it was. Made the hair on the backa my legs stand on end, Francine, I swear to God. Then he start sayin things like *No* an *Wait* an *Please, not yet*. Sweat standin out on his forrid like the lumps on a toad. Well, everyone shrunk back, a course. An you know what I thought?'

'Heart attack.'

'Heart attack is *ezackly* what I thought, Francine. Specially when he start goin, *Pocket! Please, pocket*!'

Francine looked puzzled.

'*Pocket*, Francine. *Pills*. Quick as a flash, I thought, He've got a heart contrition, an he've got the pills for it in his pocket. But he's holding onta his chest so hard he dusn't go for em. So I says, "Which pocket, Mister Murdsten?" Cos I was all set to put my hand in there if needs be, an don't you look at me like that, Francine. But I've got my hand only halfway to his trousers when he whirls round and stare at me like . . . well, I can't say as I've ever seen a face like it, not in real life. An he yell, *No, get back! Get away from me! All a you!* He've still got his hands clammed onta his chest, and then somethen horrible flash through my mind.'

'That filum. *Alien* One.'

'*Alien* One, Francine, you'm right on the money there agen. I had a vision of it. A gret long slimy thing like a donkey's todger with teeth at the enda it burstin outa Murdsten's chest an scuttlin along the floor.'

'An did it, Merilee?'

'As it happen, no. Might as well a done, though, cos by now there's pandominion breakin out. That thick mare Lesley on Cigarettes and Lotto start screamin *Tas a sewerside bomber! Us's all gorna die!* An a course that start everyone off.'

'Was you scared, Merilee? I'd a wet maself, I think I honestly would.'

'Acourse I wasn scared, Francine. Well, not *that* way. Cos I knew it was Murdsten not Al Kyder, beard or no beard. Mind you, I did back off on account a how he's carryin on. Lookin up at the ceiling shoutin, *Don't! Don't! They're not creams! They're not creams!*'

'Creams, Merilee? Whatever did he mean?'

'Buggered if I know. He wasn on about biscuits, though, cos he hadn bought any biscuits. Nor choclates. Anyway, then he sort of hunch up and let go a his chest with one hand and fish about in his pocket . . .'

'For them pills, Merilee.'

'Thas what I thought, but no, he brung out his wallet and fumble about with it, going *Fuckfuckfuck*, which is somethun I never thought to hear a novelist of his statue say aloud, and then he just chuck a buncha money down in fronta Sigourney who's sittin there with her mouth open wide enough to get a bucket in, then he grab up the bags with the bottles and that in and take off down the street like a dog with its arse afire. An thas it.'

'The End?'

'The End. Then I jus run back here on legs like jelly a tell you.'

The sisters stared at each other for quite some time. The only sound was of polystyrene granules shifting rhythmically inside the beanbags beneath them.

Then Francine said, 'So, did you get them curry pasties?'

9

Philip shouldered open the door to his cottage and almost died of shock because there was a blackened mannequin sitting in his fireplace. Without taking his eyes off it he sidled into the kitchen and with a thief's cautiousness placed his bags on the counter. He extracted a bottle of Highland Park from its festive tube and took a slug straight from the neck, and then another.

He closed his eyes while he shuddered and kept them closed as he felt his way back to the door into the living room. When he opened them the mannequin was still there. Its legs were splayed, one of them slightly bent. A rustic coronet of dirty twigs sat askew on its head, which was resting against one of the fireplace's granite flanks. It appeared to have no eyes. There was a good deal of soot fanned onto the hearth rug, and granules of it drifted in the light beams from the window like a descending cloud of midges.

Philip realized that the Amulet had become cool and passive against his chest, but was so fascinated by what he was looking at that his anger and grief lasted only a moment. He crept across the room until he was within touching distance of the small and filthy corpse. The only thing moving on it was a reddish trickle coming from a wound on the forehead; it oozed down, gathering black grains like magma seeping from a tiny volcano. He was stooping to examine it more closely when the thing opened its eyes.

Eyes that he knew only too well.

It spoke. 'Murdstone?'

'*Pocket?*'

'Murdstone.'

'Pocket!'

'We could go on like this all bleddy day.' A pale tongue appeared and cleaned soot from lips. 'Me going *Murdstone*, you going *Pocket*. Still got water?'

'Yes,' Philip said. 'Shall I get you some?'

'No. I was only asking out of polite bleddy interest. Fluke me, Murdstone.'

Philip went to the kitchen and filled a glass from the tap, then grabbed up the whisky and brought both back to the fireplace.

The Greme drank, gargled, spat.

'You've hurt your head,' Philip said.

'Not as bad as you've hurt it, you piddick. Never mind it. Comes of getting your shitter mixed up with your chimbley. Whoa. Ought to be a saying, that. I might slip it into the ledger.' Wellfair drained the glass and set it down in a small soot-dune. 'I see you still got the Amulet lashed to yerself.'

Philip took two steps back.

The Greme lifted a limp black hand. 'Ease up, ease up. Don't get your clouts up your crack. I'll not be trying the rough stuff. Bruised as a charity apple I was, after the last time. No, there'll be none of that.'

'Promise?'

'On my Old Dame's bollix. Solemn, that is.'

'Right. OK, then. Do you want a hand up?'

'No, I'm fair set as I am, thankee. I don't expect to be here long. So. How's tricks, Murdstone? The Amulet coughed up the rest of your nobble, then?'

'What?'

'You know,' the Greme said, casually aiming a filthy thumb in the general direction of Philip's study. 'The Great Work. Wondered how it was comin' on.'

Philip stared, speechless for several seconds; then all his weeks of frustration and misery and bitterness formed a ripe boil and burst.

'You, you . . . fucking little . . . You think this is *funny*, do you? It's a bloody laugh, is it, keeping me up there going through ten thousand silent hells a bloody hour for what feels like a fucking year? That's what passes for comedy, is it, in those stinking little bloody burrows of yours? Keeping some poor sod on the hook, torturing him, pulling him up, dragging him down, seeing how much he can take? You *bastard*. And, and, and then you, you just *materialize* in my fireplace and take the piss? How's *tricks*, Murdstone? How's the *nobble*? When you *know* there's no bloody nobble because you haven't, you won't . . . *give* it to me, you – you sadistic little fucking gnome! All right, all *right*! I can't take any more. Is that what you want to hear?'

Pocket Wellfair sat in his soot, immobile and silent, for the whole of this soliloquy and for some little time after. Then, thoughtfully, he murmured, 'So. Hum-de-hum and doodle-dee,' and looked over at Philip, who had slumped onto the sofa, snuffling. 'Right. Done? Now then, sit up straightish, there's a good pony. There's a thing I have to do.'

He raised his left hand and released a charge that for one second converted the contents of Philip's lymphatic system into formic acid. Savaged by internal ants, Philip screamed and sloshed Highland Park onto his lap.

'Pardon begged for that little wibbler, Murdstone. You called me a gnome, see, and so I had to. Ordained Comeback, Cantle Two of the Greme Code. Can't frolic with anything in Cantle Two. Stings a bit, I expect. Drew that snot back up your nosehole, though, didn't it? You have another swig of your damage there, and you'll be right as a trivet.'

Philip drank, then sat glaring sullenly.

Pocket hitched himself more upright, wincing a little.

'So then, down to business. Cos, appearances contrariwise or otherwise, this is not a social call. Now, you listen up, Murdstone, and oblige me by not chipping in with your usual Whats and Whys and Wherefores. Since our last little misunderstanding, which, surprise bleddy surprise, earned me an Ache as would bring your arsecheeks up to your collar, certain things have come about.'

He cleared his throat importantly.

'Which are as follows. After ferking back and forth and mumblin and jumblin for about a bleddy moonpassage, Scholar Volenap finally agrees to call a Clear Table Colligation of all the surviving Readers.'

Here Pocket paused to allow the enormous significance of this to sink in.

'First one for over seven Circuits. Sod of a pig to organize it was, what with the scatter and most of our Lines bollixed by Swelts. Bleddy risky an all, as even you can imagine. Despite of which, most of 'em made it. First matter arising, of course, is the fact we haven't got a Clear Table.'

'I know,' Philip said. 'It was lost during the—'

Wellfair's icy glance silenced him.

'So we had to use a door set atop of my truckle. There's a mighty flapdoodle about that, naturally, and so there has to be a whole flukin day of Abjurations and Revouchments and Solemn this and Solemn the other, before we can even get down to the rabbit. Naggled me to the wick, I can tell you. Anyways up, to trim the fat off the tale – and a bleddy fat tale it was, Murdstone, some of them frowsty old wrinklers think even their farts is High Rhetoric, make Volenap sound sharp as a tree-pecker – we did come to a Clear Resolution.'

Pocket paused again, to let the weighty phrase settle.

'Want to know what it was, Murdstone?'

'Er, yes. Yes, of course.'

'I should think so. So, the Clear Resolution was that I, Pocket Wellfair, do write a flaky ledger. Being the first time such a thing has ever been attempted in the annals of the Realm. What you think of them parsnips, Murdstone?'

'Flaky ledger? You mean a novel?'

'Indeed I do. A nobble.'

'Right. And, er . . .'

'And I have done one? Ho yes. Settled the inkage about, lessee, two hours back, in your money.'

'Christ, Pocket, that's . . . I mean, is it . . . ?'

'Any good?' The Greme blew soot from his fingertips and admired his nails. 'Well, 'tis like judging cats in the dark, for me, of course. But I'd say it'd do.'

Philip was trembling now, and took a shot to steady himself. 'And are you going to, I mean, is it, will you . . . ?'

'Give it to you? Course I will. No bleddy use to me, is it?'

Philip put his bottle down carefully on the sofa beside him and covered his face with his hands. He made small plaintive noises.

'Well, in a pig's arse, Murdstone. I reckoned you'd be pleased.'

When Philip uncovered his face it was wet with tears. 'Oh, God, I am, I *am*! You've no idea . . . Thank you, Pocket, thank you, thank, you, thank you. I can't tell you what this . . . You've no . . . Oh, God.'

'Fluke me, Murdstone. No need to carry on like a tupped granny.'

Philip collected himself. 'When can I have it? Today? Tomorrow?'

Wellfair raised a hand. 'Rein up, rein up. Whoa. There's more.'

'More? There's more?'

'Ho yes. Cos the Clear Resolution comes with a Clear Pendicle.'

'Pendicle?'

'Yes, Pendicle. What you might call a, bogger, what's your word . . . ?'

Philip knew. 'Condition?'

'That's the badger. Condition. Which is, that in exchange for the prescribed nobble, the Oath of the Four Orbs sworn between Pocket Wellfair and one *Murd*stone be renewed.'

'Ah.'

'Well may you bleddy *Ah*, Murdstone, cos this time there'll be no wrigglemalarkey. You go wormy on me again and there'll be no demanding Render, not even the once. I'll have your peepers and seeders out afore you can say Fork. Got me?'

Philip nodded. 'Yes. All right.'

The Greme squinted at him suspiciously. 'You agreed to that a bit sharpish.'

'Well, I don't have much choice, do I? My deadline is three weeks away.'

'Deadline? What you mean, deadline? You look all right to me, Murdstone. Apart from that twat thatch of a beard.'

'No, what I mean is, I have to finish, have, the book, the nobble, in three weeks. No, before three weeks have . . . passed.'

'Three weeks? That's, er, lemme work this out . . . Bogger, that's more than plenty. Took me less'n half that.'

'My God. Is that true?'

'Well, I was in a bleddy hurry, wasn't I? Now then, where was I? Right. We'll do the deal in a minute. Afore that, though, tell me this, and no flammery. That flyshit inkage of yours, up there on that wordtapper thing. What you was writing last time I came through and we had our little disagreement. Did you do what I told you? Did you do Wake and Banish on it?'

'Did I do what?'

'Did you' – Wellfair fluttered his hands impatiently – 'make it go back where it came from?'

'No,' Philip admitted.

'I thought as much, you scrotewart. You don't know what's good for you, do you, Murdstone?'

'I don't know *how* to make it go back where it came from,' Philip said defensively.

The Greme squinted at him. 'What, you sit there without any say in it? No wiping the slate clean?'

'Well, I can delete it. Is that what you mean? Go back to white paper? I can do that, yes.'

'Thank the Knob for that. Thought we were back in the slurry there. Right, then. So here's what you do, and don't you bollix this up, hear me? You go up there – no,

181

not now, not now, you piddick – and you delite all that hagwrit. All of it, mind. Not a bleddy word remaining, and I mean it. Give me your oath on that, Murdstone. Not that your oath's worth the steam off a rat's piss.'

'I promise. Honestly.'

Pocket cocked an eye. 'You naggle my wits, Murdstone. We spent untold amounts of time looking for you. The man for the job, we reckoned. Thought you'd know how dangerous ledgers are, let alone flaky ones. Turns out you've got no flukin idea. None of you do, to be fair. All just mumble and money. But it's come to this. Everything depending on a human nobblist. Buggers belief, don't it?'

'I'm sorry,' Philip said. 'Everything just got a bit out of hand. But I'm sure it'll be all right in the end. It usually is.'

The clerk laughed sootily. 'Well, we'll see. So, let's get on. You know what to do. Fingers on your eyeballs, that's it, and your other hand on your . . . No, no, *inside* your britches. I want to be sure you've got 'em cupped snug. Right. Here we go, then.'

Wellfair recited the Oath of the Four Vital Orbs, enunciating Philip's surname with pedantic exaggeration. The room dimmed while he spoke. Then the Greme reached into his coat, took out the blue egg and rotated its upper part a quarter-turn. He put the egg away again, and fixed his owlish eyes on Philip's face.

'So,' he said. 'We're done, and this time we're square-done. Don't you make a bumscumble of this, *Murd*stone, cos if you do I'll drag you to damnation by the back legs, and that's solemn.'

'OK.'

'So you go up there and delite that shite. Then at, lessee, give me . . . Well, at what you call ten o'clock, I'll start to send you my flaky ledger, pardon begged, *nobble*. Same as before. And when you've got it all, I'll be back for the Amulet. Can't say exactly when, so don't you go rambly. Got that?'

'Yes. Fine. OK. Ten o'clock.'

Pocket sat silently contemplating his amanuensis for a second or two. It seemed that he was about to say something further, but then, to Philip's considerable alarm, the great granite blocks of the fireplace seemed to sag and flex and the Greme was gone. The updraught of his passing hoovered soot from the rug and the hearth so that when the stonework had resolidified the fireplace was as clean as a baby's conscience. Only the empty water glass remained.

Cautiously, Philip went to peer up the chimney's black throat. Seeing nothing more than a patch of lesser darkness, he picked up the glass and poured whisky into it, shakily.

10

Later, he discovered that one of the Kwik Mart bags contained a vacuum-packed chunk of industrial Cheddar and a plastic tub of coleslaw. He chewed his way stolidly through the food, even though the salad had been dressed with a gluey and bubbly substance rather like a chain-smoker's sputum. The same bag also yielded up a jar of instant coffee and a bag of white sugar.

He took his cup across the lane to the gateway and watched the onset of dusk. His heartbeat was a pendulum that swung between unbearable eagerness and intolerable anxiety. To fill in time he returned to the cottage and attacked his beard with kitchen scissors, but when he tried to shave with the blunt razor the pain was too much for him. He washed the soap away and the mirror showed him that the lower part of his face resembled a guinea pig that had narrowly survived a savaging by a Labrador. He took a bath and put on fresh clothes. He drank some more whisky. By eight thirty he was so stressed that he was forced to run on the spot to avoid hyperventilating. This made him dizzy and he had to sit down.

Sitting down was impossible, so he went to the kitchen, filled an empty bottle with water, then carried it and the remains of the Highland Park, plus two glasses, upstairs. He settled these supplies next to his keyboard, drew the curtains closed and lit the lamp. From the malodorous heap of discarded clothes in the bathroom he retrieved the belt and tethered the Amulet tight to his breast. He was not sure if this was any longer necessary – strange that Pocket had said nothing on the subject – but he could leave nothing to chance. He sat down, took a deep breath, opened the file labelled *Murdstone 2* and began reading.

Hagwrit, Pocket had called it. What else? Misbegot something-or-other. But it was so bloody *good*. Rich and bitter as quality chocolate. After twenty pages he put his elbows onto the desk and propped his head in his hands. After thirty seconds in this position he found himself quite literally paralysed by indecision. He could not so much as blink. The grey cubes of his keyboard magnified under his gaze, loomed up towards him. He began to feel a kind of vertigo, a fear that he might topple into the bottomless chasm between Y, U, H and J.

How could he delete all this? It would be an act of literary vandalism, apart from anything else. Maybe he could just sort of round it off somehow, publish it as a novella. Ward off the hunger pains of his impatient and voracious readership, that innumerable host of waiting mouths. Get Gorgon off his back. It would be worth a million. No, more. Much more. It would be criminal to erase it. He couldn't do it.

And if he didn't, what? Would Pocket refuse to send the nobble? Probably. Almost certainly. He'd been serious. Deadly serious.

But would he *know*? Gremes knew nothing about computers, obviously. So if the text were hidden somewhere on the hard drive, innocuously labelled . . . or, no, copied onto a CD or that stick thing. Sealed and buried in the garden. A bank vault. Then delete it from the computer. Dare he risk it? Oh, God.

Philip knew that he didn't know what Pocket knew. *How* he knew things. Was the Greme, in some unimaginable way, *watching*?

And on top of all that, there was the question that he only now allowed himself to contemplate: what if Pocket's story was crap?

The first time in the history of the Realm anyone had written a flaky ledger, the smug little bugger had said. There was, therefore, a huge chance that it would be a load of mimsy old toss. Looked at coolly, the likelihood of Wellfair producing a finely wrought work of imaginative fiction was . . . well, it was like expecting Leon and Edgar to entertain the Gelder's with a duet from *La Traviata*. And to gamble on that possibility half a masterpiece would have to be sacrificed. It was so *unfair*! To impose such a choice on someone who had already suffered so much . . .

It was cruel. Inhuman.

He pulled his eyes out of the alphabetical canyon and

saw that the time was nine forty-five. Christ on a bike, how had that happened? On the verge of panic, he lowered his spiritual bucket into the deep well of himself and it came up slopping fear. A moan, a long bovine sound, came with it.

He tapped Ctrl A and the screen turned nasty, the superb text now sad yellow script on a black graveyard slab. His right index figured hovered, trembling, above the Delete key.

Tap.

Gone.

The Amulet shuddered against his breast.

A howl of pain or rage. It came, Philip assumed, from his own throat.

He closed the file, said Yes to Save Changes, opened a new document.

Nine minutes passed, during which he grieved bitterly. At three minutes to ten he drank a large shot of Scotch, tightened the belt a little and sat straighter in the chair, waiting for the Amulet to awaken.

It didn't, but at a minute past ten he began to hear something similar to wind stirring fallen leaves. It was not coming from outside. It was in the room. Rhythmic and deeply pleasant. He quickly entered a state of profound but clear-headed relaxation. Now someone was walking through the leaves, feet making a dry slushing noise. The monitor screen faded and wavered, then steadied itself, brighter than before. At the same instant the susurration in the leaves resolved itself into nibscratch and Pocket's inkage began its slithery unfurling across the bottom of the screen. Of their own volition, Philip's fingers spread themselves over the keyboard and translated. He flicked his eyes sideways: the visuals were there. Yes!

A huge and sallow moon rising over water. Something moving slowly into shot. A barge with a night-black sail. GarBellon, grim-faced, wrapped in his cloak, at the tiller. By the dim light of the barge's hooded lamp, Philip could see a mantled figure. Mesmira?

Yes: his fingers danced her name.

She sat at the prow, her head lowered over the figure – Cadrel? Yes, by God! – whose head lay in her lap. Blood seeping through the joints in his armour. His eyes bandaged.

Just before the critical faculties of his brain shut down, Philip was filled with the joyous realization that everything was going to be all right. Pocket had come up with the goods. It was brilliant. It was what everybody wanted. *Murdstone 2*.

Yes!

Then he entered trance.

Was lost to himself.

Until – there was no way of knowing how much time had passed – there was a brief but terrifying break in transmission. The unravelling inkage paused, then went into reverse, undoing itself and melting away. Philip's fingers typed a few words backwards before coming to a halt. He stared numbly at the screen, trying to remain enwrapt in his hypnogogic trance.

Then the monitor went dead.

He heard owlhoot. It roused the worm of panic that slumbered in his descending colon. He began to rise out of the depths of his inspired catalepsy like a hooked fish. The hook was in his chest.

The Amulet! It trembled, grew cold as an ice cube against his sternum.

The screen blipped on and off again.

He thought or said, 'Wait, Pocket, for God's sake,' and took his hands off the keys and tightened the belt.

Cold turned hot.

He was filled with black light like a swoon. The screen flashed on again, became a mosaic then a kaleidoscope then cleared. Inkage swarmed up the page again.

His hands flew to the keys.

Part the Second

What?

What?

Who?

Always the man for the questions, Murdstone.

Then he plunged again. Became the dumb conduit. The laid fuse waiting to carry Pocket's flowering fire to its powder keg. More or less unconscious.

Under his dreaming gaze his fingers swarmed like fish over the reef of his keyboard.

When it came to its end he was a husk, an oyster shucked and sucked from its shell.

After a while he came to and remembered who and what he was.

The screen glimmered at him and he realized he hadn't saved the text. He hastily clicked the Save As tag. Only then did he realize that Pocket hadn't thought to give his nobble a title. Not knowing what he had written, and exhausted, Philip simply couldn't face the task of thinking of one. Anything would do for now. His eye fell upon a row of ale bottles ranged along the narrow shelf above the narrow bed. *Tanglefoot*. No. *Abbot's Digit*. No. *Doom Bar*. Hmm . . . *Warlock's Pale*. Yeah. Good enough. He tapped the words into the File Name box, omitting the apostrophe. Saved. With considerable effort he swung the chair until it was facing the bed. It was both a short distance and a hundred miles away. Somehow he got onto it.

He dreamed that he was in an open-plan office of measureless proportions. It was night, and nobody was there. Away in the distance a single desk lamp burned, so he headed towards it. Long before he got there, the lamp went out.

He awoke in the same dream, except that the space was much smaller and the desk lamp was his own. It was still night. Or it was night again. He felt OK, but jittery. He made himself go downstairs in search of food and drink. The light in the kitchen was incredibly harsh. He put the kettle on to boil, and found the remainder of the cheese, grooved by his teeth. He ate it with difficulty, then made instant coffee and carried it back up to the study. He sat in front of the computer and stared for a few moments at the ethereal beauty of the Taj Mahal. He added a slug of whisky to the coffee and wished he'd bought cigarettes. He reopened *Warlocks Pale* and read for six hours, frequently using the mousewheel to back-scroll the text, trying to fix the shape of Pocket's narrative in his head. When the words *Part the Second* – he had a vague memory of being alarmed by them – appeared on the screen he sat back in his chair and inhaled moistly through his nose.

He was deeply moved.

He also needed a break.

He went to the lavatory and emptied his bladder, then went downstairs and dragged open his front door. The cool lambent air hit him like an angel's cocaine; he felt pneumatic with hope, joy, confidence. It was, apparently, dawn. Perfect dawn.

He let out a little cry of delight and scurried out onto the lane. Despite the rigours of the past how many hours, he felt dew-fresh and new-hatched.

He stood at the iron gate and watched the new day ripen the landscape. Night's last lingering indigo yielded to peach. He could almost hear the bracken unfurl, the gorse crackle open its spicy yellow blossom. Off to his left, a pony snickered.

Philip smiled ruefully, recalling his doubts. Pocket's nobble was, so far, excellent. He had not expected the Greme to manage so adroitly the tricky balancing of continuity and suspense. Nor to understand the human need for stories to have meaning. To force shapelessness into shape. Pocket had achieved that, of course, in *Dark Entropy*; but that was non-fiction. Sort of. Presumably. But to have built this extraordinary edifice . . . well, who'd have thought the little bugger was that sophisticated?

As in *Dark Entropy*, Pocket's eccentric first-person narrative alternated with passages of half-timbered prose from the Ledgers. Which he'd had to invent. He was ideally qualified to do so, of course, having been a Full Clerk. All the same, it was bloody clever. And, unlike the aborted misbegotten text, light and dark were delicately balanced. The passage in which Mesmira gently and gradually bathes Cadrel's eyes in the colour-gradated waters of Lemspa; Cadrel seeing, after weeks, his reflection in each of Mesmira's eyes: wonderfully done, without any indulgence in sentimentality.

Then there was all that darkly comical stuff about the whatweretheycalled, Vednodians. Philip was pretty sure that they were Pocket's own creation. There was no mention in *Dark Entropy* of Vedno, a remote region of the Realm characterized by uncharted vales and gloomy moors, loomed over by glowering crags. Nor of its community of stoned and hirsute troglodytes whose chief aim in life was to imbibe the hallucinatory waters of Zydor and lose themselves in day-long dreams of heroism and sensuality. Philip, while no fan of comedy, could appreciate the black humour in these episodes. As yet, though, he was unclear as to what part they played in the overall schema, which concerned itself, of course, with the search, the battles of might and will, for the Amulet of Eneydos.

He was beginning to suspect that Keepskite, the singularly disgusting Guardian of the Font of Zydor, might be in unwitting possession of the Amulet. The hints in the text that this was the case were very subtle. So subtle, in fact, that perhaps the only reader able to spot them would be Philip himself. He smiled at the thought. Cunning old Pocket.

These pleasant ruminations were disturbed by a flurry of bleats. A frisky mob of lambs, already abattoir-plump, capered into view, shepherded by their groaning mothers. Emerging from his reverie, Philip was struck by the thought that Pocket, having fulfilled his part of the bargain, might be turning up any moment to demand Render of the Amulet. He might even now be materializing in the fireplace or lavatory. It suddenly seemed terribly important to finish the reading of *Warlocks Pale* before that happened. So he turned away and hastened back unto his cottage.

11

There was no sign, sound or smell of the Greme. Philip settled himself in front of his screen and plunged eagerly into *Part the Second*.

The switch of narrator, the change of voice which, during transcription, had briefly startled him out of his enchantment, now astonished him utterly.

Who in God's name was this omniscient narrator out of nowhere? Why this totally unheralded side-step into the Third Person? What the hell was Pocket up to? His eyes jittered down a page of text. Then he stopped himself, scrolled back up and began again.

Bemused though he was, he had to concede that this new voice was extremely beguiling. Magisterial, yet without the slightest taint of pomposity. Literary but also intimate, conversational. Mellow with dark undertones. Complex yet unstrained, like Henry James cured of costiveness. Avuncular. Strangely familiar. Very, very good.

Better, Philip acknowledged bitterly, than anything he had ever written. Better than anything he would or could ever write. A first-time novelist – and a bloody gnome, into the bargain – had achieved a feat of literary ventriloquism way beyond the reach of his own striving.

The little shit.

He read on. After a slowish start *Part the Second* of *Warlocks Pale* swelled into a major set piece. The Battle of the Bay of Quarternity, for which the scene had been set elaborately in *Part the First*, was in full ding-dong. Cadrel's untrustworthy allies, the piratical Long Bankers under the command of Mock-Admiral Bocksteen (he of the worm-infested beard), came under mort-fire almost as soon as their triremes came within range of the coast of the Realm. This brimstone barrage was the work of the Quernows. Once a fiercely independent clan, these blood-red alchemical miners were now minions of Morl. Despite the best efforts of these bombardiers, Bocksteen drove his burning ships (which were filled with the howling of smouldering oarsmen) through the cordon of Sea-Swelts onto the shore. The chaotic hand-to-hand fighting amidst surging black smoke, the undisciplined savagery of the Bankers, the blood and innards sloshed onto the pale and thirsty sand were all described with a velvety, ironic restraint.

All excellent, Philip gladly admitted. Minerva will wet herself when she reads this, he reckoned. It hits all the criteria of her purple fucking blueprint and then some.

With the battle in the balance, with Cadrel and Bocksteen back-to-back, their swords dripping gore, Swelts swarming towards them over dunes of their own dead, the action shifted away.

To Mesmira.

He had completely forgotten about her. Where was she, again?

Ah yes, in the moated grange belonging to good old Gyle Tether, into whose safekeeping GarBellon had delivered her. There she was, mooching about in her chamber, looking sexy in white silk, thinking about stuff. Back story. Well enough done. Presumably necessary. Suppose there will be readers who for whatever half-cocked reason read *Warlocks Pale* before *Dark Entropy*.

But then she takes up the Verotropic Mirror and looks into it.

And we're back to the battle again. Nice idea. Seeing it in the Mirror. Mesmira gazing at Cadrel's smoke-blackened and blood-stained face. Her love will power his sword. That's what we think. It's like a Mel Gibson film, but good.

Morl in the mirror! What's *he* doing there? Sort of phasing out of, emerging out of Cadrel, then back again. They look a bit alike. Not noticed that before.

Mesmira recoils from the Mirror, drops it. It shatters on the flagstoned floor, dissolves into a trillion motes of prismatic dust that skirl and disappear through the mullioned window.

Bad luck, that, breaking a mirror. Seven years' worth. A plot device? Hmmm . . .

Mesmira stands wide-eyed and aghast, or thrilled, clutching herself. Hands clasped on her bosom. Erotic. Arora doing it. Lovely titsquash. Can see it all.

New chapter. Morl paces within the Observatory atop his Thule. His bitter monologue, his agonized rant to his uncomprehending Praetorian Swelts. How he has been so terribly misunderstood; how the stupid, nostalgic, magic-sozzled inhabitants of the Realm have failed to see the necessity for modernization, modernization, modernization. How he had been hailed as a hero, a deliverer, then been villainized when he put his reforms into action.

Philip was surprised to find himself feeling almost sorry for the evil bastard. Having to admit that much of what he said made sense, all things considered. Clever stuff, Pocket. Subverting the reader's allegiance. Bloody good.

Ah, now here's the author himself. That's a relief. Change of voice is one thing, completely vanishing another thing entirely. Wouldn't do at all. Enormously popular character. There were websites devoted to him on which Pocket fanatics wittered to each other in Gremespeak. In the nobbles his self-portrait was a somewhat flattering one, of course. If his admirers knew what the real Pocket was like, what he was capable of, they might revise their opinions.

Anyway, here he comes, disguised as a Morven pedlar, the lead-sealed Fourth Device concealed in the false bottom of his cart.

Philip cannot remember the significance of the Fourth Device. Never mind. It'll make sense, sooner or later.

Lyrical account of Pocket's travels across the Plain of Wraith and into the Forest of Mort A'Dor. A sort of pastoral idyll after all that violence: golden light filtered through leaf-canopy, shadow deer startled away, glow-vines at dusk. He arrives at a glade and chuckles the cart-pony to a halt. He's weary and so is the pony. He clambers down and gathers the materials for a fire. While it crackles into life he feeds the pony clump-nuts from his satchel and turns her loose to graze. The moon, in its green phase, rises above the trees. The stars choose their constellations and settle for the night. Pocket roasts coney meat on a skewer and washes it down with two measures of barleybrew from his flask. Yawning, he creeps beneath the cart and wraps himself in his blanket. He hums himself asleep to the sweet refrain of an ancient Greme lullaby.

And never wakes up again because his throat has been slit.

Philip jerked back.

Whatwhatfucking*what*?

Read that again.

Christ, yes. Pocket had killed himself off. His pale little body touched by the first light of morning. Blood pumped onto the leaf-litter. A blue-breasted death-warbler perched on his stiffened left thumb. The cart smashed to kindling. The Fourth Device stolen.

Who killed him? No idea. Just happened like that out of nowhere.

End of chapter.

Jesus wept. Philip stared at the screen as if hoping that his dead inkage might find life and change its mind.

But no.

He sat fumbling anxiously at the remnants of his facial hair. This was just about the last thing he'd expected. Pocket was indispensable, surely. *Dark Entropy* owed much of its enormous success to his voice. That he should hand over the narrative to this other bloke was pretty rum; that he should gratuitously top himself and rule himself out of any further part in the action . . . well, that was plain perverse. Shocking. Mind you, what a bloody stroke to pull! Philip imagined millions of readers doing just what he had done: come to a shocked halt, mewling expletives. It was a wibbler that would make 'em sit up straight, and no mistake.

(Which it did. Several months later, Adelaide Pinker, writing in the *Guardian*, will admit that 'like all admirers of *Dark Entropy*, I mourn the demise of the garrulous Greme. I confess to having felt angry, almost betrayed, by his dispassionately described demise. But what a stroke for Murdstone to have pulled! To have killed off his narrator halfway through what we must now confidently expect to be a trilogy. It's as if Dickens had murdered David Copperfield three hundred pages in. Or as if, halfway through *The Catcher in the Rye*, Holden Caulfield is wiped out by a hit-and-run driver while crossing Park Avenue. There is something almost self-destructive in taking such a risk. But it may be that like all great writers Murdstone needed to slough off one persona to explore another. And the narrative voice he develops in the second part of *Warlocks Pale* is an extraordinary achievement. Whether this voice is that of the author himself or a character in his continuously surprising history of the Realm is one of the brilliantly teasing questions that make us wait thirstily for the final part of the Murdstone Trilogy.'

That same weekend, the *Mail on Sunday* will embark on a series of stories about the drink- and drug-fuelled misadventures of Marcus Dalloway, the pint-sized actor who played Pocket in the movie version of *Dark Entropy*.)

Philip read on. It continued to astonish him that he had transcribed this tale through the long watches of the night without remembering any of it. So he was surprised when, eighty or so pages from the end, the narrative set off in a completely unexpected direction. Well, not completely; Philip had read Pocket's earlier hints correctly. *Warlocks Pale* finds its final focus within the grubby, addled Shire of Vedno.

Keepskite is indeed in possession of the Amulet. Morl has learned this. He has discovered that not only is Trover Mellwax, stealer of the Amulet, alive, but has thirty-two, not thirty-one, manifestations.

His thirty-second is a small pink island in The Middle Sea. Morl's Sea-Swelts sever its anchor chains and tow it back to the Thule where it is tethered on the Dimensionless Table of Morl's hastily reassembled necromantic laboratory. For two days it defies form. On the third day Morl manages to clone cells from a finger posing as a sandbar and phases them through the Morph Scrambler until he gets something he can work on.

It's Mellwax's nineteenth manifestation: a young Morven female with the luminous innocence typical of her species. The calm and graphic description of her torture at the hands of Morl and his Swelts – worthy, Philip thought, faint and dry-mouthed, of Louis de Bernières – goes on for several pages. Eventually her agonies yield an imago: of herself being brutally rear-swived by Keepskite, of his dirty fingers relieving her of the thong-hung Amulet while, eyes clamped shut and senses closed down, she simulates gratitude.

All of which left Philip most uneasy. Despite the cool restraint of the prose, this was hardly suitable material for younger readers. Then he laughed at himself. What was he thinking? He had a new readership now, one that was – anatomically, at least – adult. He no longer had to concern himself with what children felt. It was ridiculous that he hadn't fully understood this before, hadn't allowed himself that glorious sense of release. He did so now. Then returned to the text.

The last section of *Warlocks Pale* took the form of a classic chase. Or race, rather. GarBellon the Sage has also discovered the whereabouts of the Amulet, and he, along with Cadrel and Mesmira and a brave (if quarrelsome) band of Gremes and Porlocs, set out on a hazardous expedition to the wilds of Vedno. At GarBellon's insistence, their route takes them across Turbid Hoag, the frightful lake haunted by mirages and patrolled by poison-finned Slankers, and thence into the unmapped harshness of the Vednodian foothills.

Absorbed as he was in Pocket's action-packed mini-epic, Philip couldn't help noting that Cadrel's character had undergone a subtle change during this second part of the story. He had become harder; even, occasionally, arrogant. Less sympathetic. It was rather puzzling. But perhaps this was understandable, after all he'd been through. Or perhaps, like Shakespeare's Prince Hal, he's had to turn his back on youthful lightness of heart to harden himself for kingship. Regrettable, yes, but maybe necessary.

Hmm. Fits the blueprint in a slightly more interesting way. Let the editors sort that one out.

Meanwhile Morl, at the head of a cohort of Battle-Swelts, approaches Vedno from the opposite direction, across the wasteland of Shand'r Ga and through the mazy vales of lexical rocks known as Wylselph.

And it is Morl who wins the race. His army penetrates the wormy labyrinth of the Vednodians while Cadrel's oarsmen yet labour to propel their boats through the deliquescent off-shore sands of the Hoag.

Then, just as it seems inevitable that the Evil One has the Amulet within his grasp, Pocket pulls off a bravura set piece.

The Swelts, thirsty after their arduous trek in heavy armour, and before Morl can stop them, guzzle their fill from the Font of Zydor. The resulting party is an orgy of maudlin camaraderie punctuated by random acts of violence and primitive song. (Philip is reminded of a long-ago occasion in Worthing, when he'd stumbled upon

– and quickly fled – a host of bikers who'd descended on the Sussex coast to get off their faces on beer and magic mushrooms.)

The sound of the Swelt bacchanal awakens Keepskite, who has been sleeping off the previous day's binge in his squalid grotto overlooking the Font. After a horrified survey of the nightmare below, he takes flight; but not before Morl has spotted him.

Pursued by the magnificent necromancer, Keepskite flees through the narrow convoluted rock tunnels known only to Vednods. As he runs, the Amulet grows heavier against his greasy chest, slowing him, seeming to yearn for his pursuer. Twice, thrice, Morl hurls lethal bolts of Transformational Hex at his shadowy quarry, but misses; they strike rock fragments from the walls which turn into metallic earwigs that clatter and squeal away into the darkness.

Slick with sweat and electrical with panic, Keepskite emerges onto a broad ledge that overhangs a dizzying precipice. The brooding day is full of roaring because, to the left, the ledge disappears in the seething waters of a cataract that hurtles from the plateau above and plunges to the Tarn of Gorn, far, far below.

Moaning fear, Keepskite staggers towards the waterfall. He knows what he hopes Morl does not know: that the ledge continues behind the curtain of water and gives unto a perilous flight of rough-hewn steps which, in turn, lead to a lower complex of caverns and passages.

However, the desperate Vednod takes only a few paces then stops, letting out a whinny of terror.

First Cadrel, then the Sage emerge from the shadows of the cataract. Smiling grimly, Cadrel unsheathes Cwydd Harel. Keepskite turns back, then cringes against the rock face as Morl steps out onto the ledge. With an off-hand gesture, Morl pinions Keepskite to the rock with mind-forged manacles. The prince and the necromancer gaze at each other with blazing eyes.

There then follows an exchange of compulsory Sword and Sorcery banter. Philip hurried through it.

After a final curse, Morl raises his arm and unleashes a massive charge of Hex at Cadrel; but the prince uprights Cwydd Harel in front of him and deflects the bolt. The deadly energy ricochets skywards, striking a cruising garfulture; the unfortunate bird is transmuted into a pig, which plummets, screaming, to its death on the rocks that rim the Tarn. However, so powerful is the strike of the Hex on the magickal sword that its shock renders Cadrel unconscious and he falls.

Morl aims his hand again to deliver the *coup de grâce* but reels back, howling, as every cell of his body is jiggled by a blast from GarBellon's periaptic staff. By a tremendous act of will, the Dark Necromancer reconfigures himself and faces his Ancient Foe.

The Sage, age-old, straggle-bearded, his white robes besmirched and torn, looks no match for the still-athletic Antarch resplendent in his green and silver battle-gear; but Philip knew who he'd put his money on.

Pocket's prose takes on tremendous pace and swing as he describes the final duel between Good and Evil. Murdstone now dimly remembers how furiously the inkage had writhed onto his monitor, how his fingers had jittered frantically over the keyboard transcribing it.

The battle is by turns physickal, metaphysickal, psychologickal and magickal. In one particularly vivid paragraph, the two wizards become a black alligator and a white crocodile locked in a savage embrace full of claws and teeth amid the teeming waters of the cataract.

'Stone me,' murmured Philip, 'it's Sherlock Holmes and Moriarty at the Reichenbach Falls. He's nicked that. Can't have, though . . .'

At last a roar of triumph sounds above the booming of the waterfall. And it is Morl who has prevailed, victorious but hideously changed. A terrible asymmetry has befallen him. He moves in a series of lurches, as though his legs are at odds with themselves. His once handsome face is disfigured; the left side of it is now puckered, silvery, scaly, like scar tissue grown over burned flesh. The eye that glares out of it is orange and lidless. His left shoulder is humped up close to his ear, of which only a vestigial stump remains, and his right hand has congealed into a set of hooked and leathery talons.

The triumphant smile which further distorts the necromancer's face disappears when he realizes that he and Keepskite are alone on the ledge. Cadrel and Cwydd Harel have vanished, and with them the Amulet of Eneydos. Hissing with rage, Morl approaches the shackled and gibbering troglodyte. His eyes blaze blue and orange. He extends his claw toward the Vednodian and utters the words of the Withering Cantrip; instantly, permanent night fills the orbs of Keepskite's eyes and his testicles shrivel to pips.

Philip's mouth was suddenly very dry. He scrolled down to the last half-page of the text.

Morl turns and hobbles across the ledge until he stands at the very edge of the precipice. He raises his unequal arms; for an instant it seems that he might launch himself suicidally into space. Then he lifts his face and howls a curse so dark, so savage, that its echoes form a black cyclone that gathers Morl into itself and roils away across the wilderness of Vedno.

The End.

Well. Philip hadn't known what to expect of Pocket's nobble, but it certainly hadn't been this strangely disturbing hybrid.

It would do, though. Yes, by God. It would certainly do. Defeating expectancy wasn't something that happened every day. Quite the opposite.

He could see the cover quotes now:

'Strangely disturbing' Victor Hireling, the Sunday Times.

'Elegant, horripilant, perverse' Dyana Kornbester, NY Review of Books.

He sat staring at the screen for several minutes.

Then another thought came upon him like sunrise in a major key.

Pocket had ended *Warlocks Pale* with a cliffhanger – almost literally so. Morl deformed and crazed and whirled away. Cadrel in possession of the Amulet, presumably. GarBellon dead. (Or was he? No sight of a smashed and water-bloated corpse.) Nothing finally resolved.

So . . .

Go careful, Murdstone. Be delicate. Nothing so untrustworthy as hope.

But it was obvious. Undeniable.

He stood up and left the room and patrolled his cottage, touching walls and furniture as if for luck or reassurance.

Why, though?

They'd done a square deal, eyes and bollocks in hazard, him and Pocket.

The Greme would give him a nobble, a flaky ledger. He would give the Greme the Amulet.

End of story.

Except that it wasn't.

It was still unresolved.

There was *more*.

A third volume.

Had to be.

Why?

He was in the kitchen, staring at the electric kettle as though such a thing was inconceivable, never previously witnessed.

Because Pocket had got the bug.

He'd have no immunity against it, of course, being

the first of his kind that'd been exposed to it. Hadn't known that once you start flaky ledgers there's no stopping. That the desire for admiration – even from worlds you despise – becomes an addiction, once it's granted. Becomes feverish when it's removed.

Pocket would want, need, to go on.

The little bastard had become, unwittingly, innocently, due to force of circumstance, a nobblist.

Yes!

Philip was, he realized, acutely hungry. At that instant an ugly clamour rent the air: the cack-handed campanologists of Flemworthy's bleak Victorian church summoning the sad and the elderly. So it must be Sunday. Damn! Then he remembered, joyously, that Denis had recently taken to opening the Gelder's for weekend breakfasts. Philip found himself salivating at the thought of Denis's version of the Full English: black pudding with sweet and sour pomegranate sauce, kedgeree with pineapple, and wild boar and mint sausages, all washed down with a pint of Guest Ale.

He returned to the study and copied *Warlocks Pale* onto a new memory stick, then clicked on Outlook Express. He typed MINERVA in the address box, wrote 'Will this do???' and attached the text. He waited for the Outbox to clear, then left.

He was halfway along the lane when a worrisome memory struck him.

Don't you go rambly.

He returned to Downside and wrote 'Starving. Gone to

the pub. Back in an hour. Thanks. Brilliant. PM' on two sheets of paper. He put one on the floor of the lavatory and the other in front of the fireplace. Then he hastened unto his breakfast.

12

On his return, Philip discovered Pocket Wellfair standing motionless in the living room.

'Pocket,' he exclaimed, a touch too heartily. 'My dear chap! I hope you haven't been waiting long.'

'Long enough.'

'Have a seat, have a seat. Can I get you anything? Glass of water?'

'I'm fair set as I am, thankee.'

It seemed to Philip that the Greme was a little out of sorts. The twinkle in the old eyes had dulled, and there was a hint of putty in the colour and texture of his face. On the other hand, he'd added a colourful accessory to his costume; a jaunty red and white kerchief was knotted around his neck. This Bohemian touch was encouraging. It strongly suggested that Pocket had recognized his literary calling and had decided to dress accordingly.

'Listen, Pocket. The nobble is brilliant. Amazing.'

'Twill do, will it?'

Philip nodded ironically, belched richly. 'Yes, it'll do.

You have an enormous talent, you know. Enormous. You're a natural.'

'That'd be a compliment, would it, among your lot?'

'Absolutely. But listen, I have to ask you this – why on earth did you kill yourself off halfway through? It shocked me rigid.'

'I didn't kill meself. Some other bugger did.'

'Well, yes, of course. In terms of the actual story. But I mean . . . well, as the narrator, the storyteller. Why you suddenly decided to become someone else. Use a different voice. Adopt a different point of view.'

The Greme stood with his head cocked slightly, as if listening to something faint and far away.

'I got bored,' he said finally. 'And I'm getting bored again, with all this jibber-jabber. So, business, Murdstone. The Amulet.'

'Sure, sure,' Philip said amiably. He took off his jacket and undid the top two buttons of his shirt. Then he paused, and smiled, and said, 'So, when are you planning to start the next one?'

'What?'

'The next book. The next flaky ledger. Nobble.'

'What in a pig's arse are you flabbering about now?'

'Well, you obviously intend to write another one. I assume that's why you left the last one unresolved. Unfinished. On the edge. To Be Continued. Hmm?'

Pocket Wellfair's eyes narrowed. 'I hope your head hasn't come unlatched, Murdstone. I do hope and trust you're not about to frolic me about again.' He raised his right hand and extended two fingers. 'Cos if you do, I'll send a wibbler up your jacksie that'll turn your teeth upside down. Then I'll do your eyeballs and empty your scrote.'

'No, no. No frolicking, Pocket, I promise. The Amulet is yours, fair and square.' Philip pulled it free of his shirt. The clerk's eyes locked onto it. 'It's just that I thought . . . well, that you'd *want* to. Write the last part, you know. You should, Pocket. Honestly. You have a genius for it, and that is definitely not too strong a word.'

Wellfair said nothing.

Philip lifted the chain over his head and held the Amulet in his cupped hands, gazing at it like a widow about to scatter her husband's ashes on a golf course. Then he lifted his face, which wore, he hoped, an expression that was both teasing and beseeching.

'Come on, Pocket, my old friend. Let's do another one. Finish the sequence. You know you want to. And it's not a lot to ask, is it? It only took you a few days to do the last one.'

The Greme's face twitched. A smile or a sneer or something in between.

'Fluke me, Murdstone. You never give up, do you?'

'The thing is, I really *need* another one. These things come in threes, you see? I don't know why, they just do. Look, I know I've nothing to bargain with. I have to give you the Amulet. I know that. I'd be too frightened not to. But we're friends, aren't we? And, and, I found the Amulet. I looked after it for you.'

Pocket's face hardened.

'Please, *please* write me another one. Look, I understand how important the Amulet is to you. To Cadrel. To the Realm. Of course I do. I'm not frolicking about here, Pocket. But what you need to understand is that another book is just as important to me as the Amulet is to you. Really. It would save my life. All right, it *is* a lot to ask . . .'

Wellfair raised a pale and featureless hand, and Philip fell silent. He thought he could hear a faint humming in the room, like the tiny sound a light bulb makes just before it dies.

'You're a greedy little piddick, Murdstone.'

'Yes. Yes, I am. But also *needy*, Pocket. I can only appeal to your better nature. Help me. Please.'

'All right, all right. Fluke me.'

'You mean you will? You'll write me another nobble? Promise?'

'*Promise? You* ask *me* to promise, you backsliding arsewart?'

'No, sorry, Pocket. Sorry. OK. That's fine. Thank you. Thank you.'

'Keep your thanks, Murdstone. They interest me less than a miretoad's quim. Now get up off your imaginary bleddy knees and give me the Amulet.'

Philip held it out.

'No, no. Dangle it by the chain. That's a good pony. Now reach your arm out towards me, nice and steady.'

Philip did as he was told. At this long-awaited and

ceremonious moment he felt the need to lower his head in a gesture of solemnity.

Pocket approached slowly, murmuring words in the Old Language. When he was an arm's reach away, Philip inhaled a little gasp. Where the chain lay across his fingers he experienced an icy tingling. The Amulet itself appeared to be vibrating, in that its edges became indistinct and then distinct again; yet it did not seem to be in motion. It increased slightly but discernibly in weight. He looked up.

'Pocket . . . ?'

The Greme had halted. His wide eyes were fixed on the Amulet. A spasm passed over his pallid face, as though a hundred tiny muscles had twitched beneath the surface of his skin. He licked his lips. The tip of his tongue was dark blue.

'Pocket? What's happening?'

The Greme seemed not to have heard him. His mouth twisted, struggling to utter words that would not come.

Now the Amulet moved. It rotated slowly through three hundred and sixty degrees and when it was facing Pocket once more the Greme shuddered and closed his eyes. When he opened them again, each had extruded a thick white tear that wriggled, rather than trickled, down his cheeks. Pocket put a hand to his face and wiped them away. They fell to the carpet. They looked like grains of rice until they started to move. Philip watched them with horrified fascination for a moment or two, then was distracted because the Amulet jerked on the end of its chain and became so heavy that he had to use both hands to support it.

'Pocket? What the fuck is happening?'

His voice died. More thick white tears were oozing from Wellfair's eyes, eyes that were now darkening into black apertures. The Greme's blue-tipped fingers wiped at them weakly. Those he managed to brush from his face fell and twitched on the floor. His mouth opened. It was full of maggots.

Philip's scream blended with another sound, a sound something like a huge sigh of ecstasy, and the Amulet opened itself, hingeing apart like a tide-wakened mollusc. It sucked the light from the room and concentrated it into a blueish beam that focused mercilessly on Pocket.

Philip struggled, panicking, to let go of the damned thing, but could not. Nor could he speak. Nor take his eyes from Pocket.

Who was decomposing. The Greme's head went back and his mouth gargled a final imprecation that sprayed pale pupae into the air. The neckerchief fell from his melting throat revealing, momentarily, a seething diagonal slash. The pale flesh of his long fingers dissolved into squirming gobbets that dripped to the floor. Then the clothes collapsed, affording Philip glimpses of bone and slackening sinew before the sticky white swarm consumed them.

Then Pocket was gone.

The Amulet drew its blue force back into itself and closed with a muted hiccup.

Philip was now alone in his living room with a vast colony of larvae. He could hear them. They were murmuring, seeking each other, having hectic miniature discussions, forming themselves into groups. Groups that formed larger groups. Piling themselves into shapes. Building something. The air in the room was now a faecal, gangrenous stench. Whimpering, Philip climbed onto the sofa and crouched at the end furthest from the nightmare. He clutched the Amulet with the fingers of both hands, holding it in front of him, without knowing why, yet completely unable to let go of it.

At tremendous speed, the millions of maggots formed themselves into a mound with three increasingly distinct sections. Their squirming surfaces hardened and darkened into a glistening carapace. Long tendrils emerged then thickened into jointed legs, blackened, grew claws, sprouted bristles. Two legs were deformed. Next, with a sound like Velcro parting, big wet buds burst from the thing's back and grew into hard transparent wings stretched on black metallic spars. The head swelled into being: two huge multifaceted bubbles above hirsute, gluey mouth-parts. One of these eyes glittered. The other resembled a diseased grapefruit.

The maggots that had assumed the necromantic form of Pocket Wellfair had become a giant bluebottle that smelled of shit and ammonia.

Complete, the creature was motionless for a moment or two. Then its legs adjusted position, tilting the grotesque head slightly downwards. From the end of its

216

proboscis, the fly extruded its labella, a flat hairy tongue the size of a cow's. It drooled necrotic saliva onto the carpet. Apparently not finding what it sought, the fly turned itself, using brisk movements of its thorny legs, in Philip's direction.

Philip wanted to scramble behind the sofa, but found himself mesmerized and peculiarly listless. He could not tell if it was his soul or his breakfast that threatened to rise into his mouth. The giant tongue slathered across the floor towards him and climbed onto the sofa. It settled on Philip's shoe, ensliming it, then moved, in sticky paroxysms, up towards the meat of his leg.

The Amulet bucked, sighed, opened. Its intense blue radiance coated the fly in flickering light, just for an instant. The monster recoiled and toppled away sideways, its legs flailing, its gross abdomen convulsing. Its immense and frenzied buzzing set the entire cottage vibrating, rattled the windows in their frames.

This shockwave of sound shook Philip from his trance. 'Die, you fucker!' he screamed. 'Die!'

Heartfelt though it was, his wish had the opposite effect. In a fast sequence of spastic motions, the fly righted itself. It stood twitching slightly, silent now, a thick thread of mucus hanging from its complex jaws. Then, briskly as before, it turned towards the sofa once again. Philip thrust the Amulet out towards the giant insect, but there was no blast of light.

He shook it urgently. 'Come on, come on!'

Nothing.

'Oh, please, bloody please!'

The fly advanced.

Then stopped.

Philip, paralytic with dread, found himself gazing into its bulbous eyes. Myriad disfigured faces of Morl Morlbrand looked back at him.

The fly spoke. 'Lower the Amulet, Murdstone. It will not destroy me here, outside the Realm.'

The voice was a thousand voices gnarled into one. The night-voice of some limitless forest. It was sonorous, and – considering that it emanated from a fly so recently swatted by a million-volt blast of Magick – oddly self-assured.

Philip did not, could not, move.

'I enjoy fear, Murdstone. Especially when it is pure. Distilled. Uncontaminated. Is that what I would savour if I were to lick the sweat from your face? Or would I get the bitter aftertaste that traces of hope leave on the palate?'

'Don't touch me. Please. Leave me alone. You can have the Amulet. Really. I don't want it.'

The Morl-fly lowered itself, as though relaxing. 'No? Then why don't you just reach out and drop it in front of me? Go on. Then all your troubles will be over. Go on.'

He couldn't do it. His fingers were locked onto the Amulet, and when he tried to push it away it resisted with a force far greater than the strength of his arms.

The fly laughed stickily. 'You thought, did you not,

that you were in possession of the Amulet. As in all things, you were wrong. *It* possesses *you*. Believe me, it would have been better for you had I relieved you of it. Unfortunately for both of us, I miscalculated. I thought I had plumbed and reconfigured its ancient enchantment. Now I find I yet have work to do. Further depths to mine. Lakes of deeper darkness to angle in.'

Despite the terror that had disabled his normal bodily processes, Philip thought he recognized something familiar in the necromancer's diction, the somewhat scholarly syntax.

'Doubt not that I will succeed, Murdstone. Nothing remains that can stop me; not even Death, with whom, as you have seen, I have reached a certain accommodation. So to speak.' Another oleaginous chortle.

'All I wanted was a fucking *story*,' Philip cried.

'No, Murdstone. You wanted *my* story. And that is a somewhat different matter, as you will discover.'

The phone rang.

Abruptly, the fly contracted its tongue into its chitinous channel and turned away like a guilty thing upon a fearful summons. The legs made another series of angular movements, their claws audibly finding new purchase on the carpet. Philip shrank back, but the fly swung away from him towards the fireplace.

'I regret I must curtail this conversation. Time does not keep well, frozen, even in the Thule. *Adieu*, Murdstone. I shall be back. I have your coordinates now. That's a little crumb of certainty for you. You may find it of some comfort, I dare say, now that the limits of your world have melted. But I, at least, can be depended upon.'

The fly crawled into the fireplace and angled its body upwards. Its front legs found claw-holds in the blackened chimney-throat. Then, with a good deal of thorny scrabbling, it climbed up and out of sight.

13

It took almost a month for the Great Fly of Flemworthy to pass into folklore. The delay resulted from a certain degree of suspicion attached to the key witnesses. Merilee and Francine were, outwardly, perfectly normal. On the other hand, they were twins. There was talk about them of a sexual nature. More significantly still, they were librarians and therefore fanciful. As Leon said, on a night when the Fly was being warmly debated in the Gelder's Rest, "'Tain't by chance they calls them places *lie berries.*'

Francine and Merilee themselves maintained a quiet certitude. There was an increase in traffic through the library of people feigning an interest in aerobics videos, but in response to questioning, Merilee, or possibly Francine, would say, 'I seen what I seen, an thas all I'm sane.'

When the monthly livestock market took over the abandoned industrial estate on the outskirts of the town, things swung in the sisters' favour. Posh Widow Flaxman, the broad and reputedly lesbian owner of the Toggenheim Goat Stud the other side of Grimspound, was the improbable backer of their story. Between the Ready Porkers and the Overwintered Sterks she held forth in the refreshment tent.

'Sunday, it was. Hello, Bernard. You what? Forty fucking quid a beast? Hell's teeth. What can you do? Bloody Europe. See you later. Anyway. Yes, the same again. Cheers. What was I saying? What? Oh yes. Lunchtime, it was. Just got to the paddock when this shadow passed over it. Thought nothing of it, of course. Cloud. Then, bugger me if six of the nannies and both billies didn't fall down in a faint. Just like that. Like they'd been shot. Couldn't believe it. No, Gerry, I had *not* been on the sherberts, as you so quaintly put it. But while we're on the subject . . . Thanks. Splash of water with it. Cheers. The goats? Came round after a minute or two. They're still not right, though. Poor old Ajax is still off his rumpy. Might have to shoot the bugger if he doesn't pull his socks up. Say what you like, it was a bloody rum business.'

Further confirmation – of a sort – came later the same day when the insanitary mystic Krishna Mersey came down off the moor for his weekly Vedic encounter with the fish and chip van from Okehampton. It wasn't easy to understand Krishna at the best of times, and on this occasion he was so full of a jittery sort of gloom that he made sense only intermittently. But those queuing for their haddock and scratchings were left in no doubt that an Avatar of really Bad Karma, man, had passed over his encampment on Sunday. It was, like, a really intense shadow. And, like you would, Krishna had looked up to see what was casting it. Nothing, man. Like, *nothing*. Clear blue beautiful spiritual empty sky. All the same, there was this shadow. And it was so intense, man. And full of *negativity*. As soon as it touched his tomatoes (in reality these were marijuana plants disguised with red Christmas baubles) they'd like just wilted and *died*, man. Half the crop gone. It was like a sign, man. Had to be.

But because Krishna was a Liverpudlian who lived in something called a yurt his evidence could not be trusted entirely.

Then it transpired that Lieutenant-Colonel Sir Arthur Rogers-Jelly MC JP of Sullencott Manor had suffered a similar experience. On Sunday afternoon he'd been whiling away the time between volumes of his memoirs by breathing on the glass of his library window and playing noughts and crosses against himself. He'd just completed a drawn game when a shadow passed across his vision and the room went utterly dark. He'd assumed, naturally, that he'd had a stroke. He'd pressed the panic button on his desk to summon his housekeeper, who'd bustled in to confirm that he was both conscious and more or less upright. After a large and restorative pink gin, Sir Arthur had made a patrol of his grounds. He'd been dismayed to discover the south lawn disfigured by a broad brown swathe of withered grass. It ran diagonally from the ha-ha to the wall of the kitchen garden. Further reconnaissance revealed that in the garden itself four rows of brassicas and three of strawberries had been devastated by a sticky black mould.

The colonel delivered a briefing on these matters to his fellow Rotarians at their monthly meeting. It was followed by a half minute of silence, during which uncomfortable glances were exchanged and throats were cleared.

'Well,' ventured Pharmacist Allcock, 'we, I at any rate, have heard these, er, reports of a, ah, unnaturally large, er, emerging from Philip Murdstone's chimney.'

'Claptrap,' the colonel said. 'Superstitious nonsense. Stammering eleven-toed halfwits around here will believe anything. I should know. Have 'em up in front of the Bench on a weekly basis.'

Another silence was broken by Surveyor Gammon. 'So you think there is a rational explanation for this phenomenon, do you, Colonel?'

'Course I do. Rational explanation for everything.' The old soldier looked sternly at his colleagues, then leaned forward over his clasped hands. 'Gentlemen,' he said, in a quieter voice, 'I want your absolute assurance that what I am about to say will go no further than these four walls. Understood? Yes?'

All nodded.

'Very well. It is my considered opinion that what we're dealing with here is a drone.'

'Ah,' Gordon Chouse exclaimed. 'A bee.'

'Not a bloody bee, man! A *drone*. Unmanned aircraft. Spy in the sky.'

The Rotarians gazed at him.

'Now then,' Sir Arthur continued, 'if you plot the course of this thing on the map – meant to bring it with me, forgot, sorry – from Flemworthy to the Manor, you get a line running south by south-west. Project that line forty miles or so, and where do you end up?' He was forced to provide his own answer. '*Plymouth*. And there is, in the vicinity of Plymouth, a certain establishment involved in what we might call, ahem, Military Futurology.'

'The Technical Support Unit,' exclaimed Malcolm Sweet, proprietor of Farm and Leisure Footwear. 'The wife's brother does the catering. They don't half—' The colonel's glare withered him and he fell silent.

'I am certain in my own mind that what overflew the Manor last Sunday was something dreamed up by the boffins of the TSU. Test flight. Heading back to base. Nothing whatever to do with your writer chappie.' Sir Arthur leaned back in his chair and folded his arms.

Gammon said, 'What puzzles me is this fly business . . .'

'Ah, well. It's possible, very possible in fact, that the drone was indeed disguised as a fly. The big eye thingies packed with cameras and whathaveyou. Spot a tick on a stag's arse from a mile up, that sort of thing.'

Heads were nodded.

'Why a fly, though, Sir Arthur? Why not, I don't know, a bird or . . . ?'

'Obvious, isn't it? Where are the theatres?'

The Rotarians blanked. Well, there was the Plough Arts Centre at Torrington. The Northcott in Exeter. Bristol Old Vic . . .

'Afghanistan. Iraq. Somalia. Iran, if we're lucky. What

do they all have in common? Flies. Bloody flies everywhere. See what I'm getting at? Johnny Raghead looks up, sees a fly. One of thousands above his sweaty little turban. Doesn't notice that it's much higher up than the others. Doesn't realize that it's taking photographs of the rust on his Kalashnikov, the attack map he's drawn in the sand with a stick, the Semtex he's stuffing into his cummerbund. Get the picture? Bloody clever. I take my hat off to those chaps. Quality intelligence is what tips the balance every time.'

Irritating Gordon Chouse persisted. 'And how, if you don't mind me asking, Sir Arthur, do you explain the business with Mrs Flaxman's goats? Or the damage done to your garden? Or, for that matter, to Krishna's secret dope plantation?'

'Ray,' the colonel said.

'Pardon? Who?'

'Ray. A *ray*. Laser sort of thing. State-of-the-art weaponry. Fired by mistake, I imagine. Some chappie down in Plymouth pressing the wrong button. Or simply a gremlin. Takes time to iron these things out, y' know.' He waited. 'Any further questions?'

Gammon drew in a breath and looked around the table. 'No? Thank you, Colonel. I'm sure we'll all sleep easier in our beds. Now then, item one on the agenda. Apologies for absence.'

14

Had Rogers-Jelly not sworn the Rotarians to secrecy, the fearful thrill that possessed Flemworthy might have been quickly suppressed. Instead, reports of, or imaginings of, the Great Fly became almost the sole topic of conversation. Visits to the library increased tenfold; sometimes there were more than five people at once in there, pulling books at random off the shelves and spending an hour or more at the checkout desk. Now that persons of quality had come out in support of their story, the Weird Sisters began to wax loquacious.

'It pulled itself outer Murdsten's chimberly like a fat rat outer a pipe,' Merilee said. 'Us didn' notice it at first. We wasn' really lookin, was we, Francine, being as we was just on our walk.'

'No.'

'Then there was this rustlin, like someone undoin a parcel. Come from up above. So we looked, and there twas. Our heart stopped in our chest, didn' it, Francine?'

'Oh, worse'n that. I felt like I had a paira hands acrost

my throat. I tried to speak but I couldn. There it was, head goin this way and that, wings whackin together with a sound like cardboard. Then it takes off backards an go back'n'forth for a bit like he's pissed, then set off in the general drection a Nodden Slough.'

Their audience shuddered satisfactorily.

Pale-faced Pauline from the post office said, 'Wasn't you tempted to hev a peek through the winder?'

'Us did try,' Merilee admitted, 'but we cudden see nothun cos the glass were covered in condescension. And us was buggered if we was gorna knock on the door.'

A great deal of lively conversation centred on Philip Murdstone.

That he was a queer fish had never been in doubt.

The way he'd just shown up out of nowhere and bought that damp hole Downside Cottage after it had lain empty for six years since its previous inhabitant, old Ma Birtles – who was definitely a witch – had been found dead in her armchair with the Bible upside-down – *upside-down*, mark you – in her stone-cold claws and half her left ear eaten by her cat.

The way he'd lived poor as a church mouse, and then suddenly made millions with a book all about Black Magic and Neck Romancers and what have you.

The way he'd lurk up at The Devil's Clock at all hours.

And lately, he'd been acting very strange indeed. Who could forget how he'd turned up, bearded and sockless, at Kwik Mart and caused mayhem?

'I thought at the time,' Merilee or Francine said, 'he was pissed as a two-legged stool. Now I hevta ask maself if I wasn wrong. Whether what we witlessed wasn a boner feeday case of demonic possession.'

Even those unconvinced by the Weird Sisters' analysis had to concede that it was very significant that Murdstone had disappeared at the same time – perhaps at *exactly* the same time – that the Great Fly had launched itself from his chimney. Simple logic seemed to insist that the fly *was* Murdstone. And that, therefore, Murdstone's return was a thing to be feared.

On the fifth Sunday after the Fly, the Reverend Colin Minns was somewhat surprised to discover that the congregation at Evensong was thrice its normal size. No fewer than twenty-four worshippers, some of whom he barely recognized, huddled together in the tall gloom of Saint Jude's. He knew that this burgeoning of the faithful was not the result of his going amongst his flock inspiring them with the love of the Lord because it had been some time since he could be arsed to do much of that sort of thing.

His first inkling of the explanation came towards the end of the Lord's Prayer.

'*And lead us not into temptation; But deliver us from evil,*' he intoned; and in the following short pause his congregation loudly murmured, 'And from the Great Fly.'

He glared down at them, but none would meet his glittering eye.

Later, emerging from the vestry with gin on his breath

and microwaved Chicken Tikka on his mind, the vicar found a deputation awaiting him. It was headed by his sexton, William Sexton.

'Bill,' Minns exclaimed, more or less heartily, and popped a Polo mint into his mouth.

'Vicar,' Sexton said.

All stood silent for a long moment in the dimness that smelled of mould and wax and unanswered prayer and moth-eaten military banners.

Minns rubbed his hands together. 'So, er, how can I help you good folk? You do look most dreadfully solemn, I must say. Is there a problem?'

Someone almost discernibly female poked Sexton from behind and whispered something urgent. The sexton braced himself and spoke.

'Us wants you ter perform a extersism, Vicar.'

'Beg pardon?'

Sexton shifted his feet. 'I dunno if perform be the right word. Do one, anyhow. On Downside. Philip Murdsten's place.'

Minns put his hands into his trouser pockets and lowered his head.

All waited.

'William. My friends. I really do think that this fly business has got out of hand.' He now looked at them squarely. 'There are those of this parish who have, shall we say, rich imaginations. And, to be frank, there is a, shall we call it tradition? Of superstition? In this part of the world? Mister Murdstone is a successful writer. That

230

is, of itself, no reason for suspicion, let alone fear. I've met him once or twice and he seems, well, a perfectly normal sort of a fellow, really. I don't know if you are familiar with the phrase "mass hysteria", but—'

Sexton the sexton cut him off. 'The place is evil, Vicar. Allers has been. Ask anyone. Any dog'll whine goin pass, and if a dog dunno the Devil no one do.'

Minns opened his mouth and shut it again. The faces that glimmered at him were stonily, anciently, determined.

Hell's bells, he thought.

When he got home he poured himself another stiff one and called the Bishop.

15

There had not been a midnight event in Flemworthy since the public burning of a Spanish ventriloquist in 1828, so the procession that wended its way towards Downside was joined enthusiastically by almost the entire population of the town and its nearer environs.

Even so, it was strangely quiet. Children – normally thrilled or querulous past their bedtimes – were silent in their all-terrain buggies. The usually and randomly garrulous inmates of Sunset House stumbled or trundled along quietly. Also there, or represented, were the Friends of Abused Donkeys, the members of the White Knights of St George (who also represented UKIP), the Young Farmers, the codpiece enthusiasts of the Francis Drake Society, the Saint Jude Optimists, the grizzled Young Conservatives, both members of the Watch Committee, Eric who pretended to work for the Council, the addled punters who hung around the Gelder's for an hour after closing time and, in the vanguard, the Weird Sisters. Only the Methodists, the Women's Institute and Leon and

Edgar, for reasons of ideology or indifference, boycotted the occasion.

All were led by the Reverend Minns, who wore a rucksack and as solemn an expression as he could muster, and William Sexton, who bore a large wooden cross. A great many in the train were holding candles; others burned cigarette lighters which flickered off when thumbs were scorched and flickered on again when thumbs had cooled. However, there fell a light but persistent rain, so these various flames and their bearers were sheltered by an almost continuous carapace of umbrellas. These lent the parade a spectral, almost sinister aspect. Viewed from some height and distance – from, say, Krishna Mersey's smoky yurt halfway up Beige Willie – it might have been mistaken for an improbably large millipede, bearing glowing eggs within its innumerable crotches, creeping towards some unspeakable hatchery.

At the cottage, Minns and Sexton halted, facing the gate. Their followers fanned out behind them along the lane.

Sexton shuddered bulkily. 'I can feel the evil coming offut in waves, Vicar.'

Nonsense, Minns didn't say. For all his ecumenical scepticism, he was forced to admit that there was something unwholesome about the place. The way it beetled into the flank of the hill like a trapped and watchful animal, candlelight reflected snakishly in its glass eyes. The thatch lowered like a scowl. A whiff – probably imaginary – of staleness and corruption.

He shrugged the rucksack off his back, turned and raised his voice. 'Friends. *Friends*. Thank you. Mr Sexton and I will now enter this house and conduct the exorcism. I cannot say for certain what will happen during this procedure. But whatever happens, I must insist that none of you try to enter the house or take any other unconsidered action. I mean that most sincerely. Mr Sexton and I would appreciate it if you stayed where you are and supported us with prayer. Thank you. Bill?'

The two men opened the gate and approached Murdstone's front door and hammered loudly upon it.

'Admit us in the name of God Most High,' Minns demanded, twice. When nothing happened Sexton put his shoulder to the door, which yielded on the instant. The sexton slipped on a slithery dune of junk mail and tumbled into the living room. Struggling to save himself, he collided with a low table and sent the telephone clattering into the darkness. His dropped torch struck the floor and went out.

'Bill? Are you all right, Bill?'

'Vicar?'

'Wait. I'll light a candle. By all that's holy, it smells like a dead badger in here, doesn't it?'

'Ar. Tis the stink of the Devil's chuff.'

Minns groped in his bag and pulled out a beefy beeswax and lit it with his lighter.

(It never occurred to either man to try the light switches. Had they done so, they would not have had to proceed umbrageously. South West Power, having not received Philip's quarterly payment, had assumed he had switched allegiance to EuroLec and, in an attempt to woo him back, had granted him a reprieve. A letter to this effect was one of the things that had sent Sexton's foot on its skid. On the other hand, turning the lights on would have seriously disappointed those waiting outside, for whom flickering flame and uncertain light were essential elements of the long-anticipated ritual.)

The clergyman held his flame aloft until it illuminated a table. He set the candle down and lit another. Sexton had located and relit his torch and was now reciting, loudly, the Lord's Prayer. Minns thought it unwise to silence him and used the opportunity to scan the text he had downloaded from an American website. He was frankly embarrassed by the prospect of addressing Satan directly and in stentorian tones, but it was some consolation that the only person who would hear him do so was an idiot.

Sexton got to the end of the prayer and said 'Amen'. He waited expectantly.

'Ah. Yes, *Amen*.'

'What do us do now, Vicar?'

'Well, we arrange ten candles in the shape of the cross. In the middle of the floor. Six down and the other four across. Two either side. See what I mean?'

Sexton drew in a sorrowful breath. 'I knew twud be complercated, Vicar. I'd best leave it ter thee, I reckon.'

'Yes. OK, Bill. Shine your torch on my bag, there's a good chap.' Minns rummaged again.

Sexton said, 'I did wonder if he mightn't be here.'

Minns looked up into the dazzle. 'What?'

'Well, like we haven seenum for some time don' mean he mightn't be here. Holed up, like.'

'What?' Minns' eyes skittered around the gloom. 'Are you telling me you think Murdstone might be here?' He lowered his voice to a whisper. 'Bill. That would be . . . terrible. It would be so embarrassing. If he—'

A noise came from above them. A crash followed by a small howl of pain.

'Oh, fuck,' the clergyman said.

An upstairs door opened. A hoarse voice was heard. 'Fluke me, I can't be doing with that much longer. Like being puked up by a goat been eating thorn. Murdstone? Murdstone!'

Minns and Sexton drew closer together. Sexton held forth the cross. He aimed the trembling beam of his torch at the head of the stairs.

'Aha! So you are here, you frolicking arsewipe. We were beginning to think—'

A demon walked into the light. A demon in the guise of a child wearing a hoodie and sandals. But its eyes were dark and ancient; they flinched from the glare.

'Stap me, Murdstone. Turn that flukin lamp off!'

'Don't, Bill,' Minns warned.

'I won't, Vicar. Tis a thing of darknuss!'

The demon crouched, peering. 'Who the bollix . . . ?'

When the torch found its face again, the fiend hissed and thrust out two white talons. Sexton cried out in horror when the torch turned to hot biscuit and crumbled in his hand. Men and monster, motionless shadows, stared at each other for an eternal moment. The two candle flames burned in the creature's eyes.

Sexton said, 'Vicar?'

All saliva had departed Minns' mouth. He croaked, 'In the name of the One and Only God . . .'

It was as far as he got.

The demon snarled, 'In the name of the crack of my arse!' Then it turned and scuttled into darkness. A door banged against a wall. A shudder thrilled the house. Then silence.

Time not measurable by the normal means passed. When it had gone, Sexton walked backwards and cautiously to one of the candles and picked it up.

'Us'd better check, Vicar,' he whispered.

Minns rallied himself and picked up the other candle. 'Yes. You're right. After you, Bill.'

With the cross leading the way they ascended the stairs. The only door open was that of the bathroom which, when they dared enter, was significantly colder than the rest of the cottage despite the smell of scorch that hung in the air. The exorcists examined the room by the light of their candles.

'I'd say tis gone,' Sexton said.

'Yes. Shall we get the hell out of here?'

At the foot of the stairs Sexton said, 'Well, all in all, that were a bleddy sight easier than I thought twud be.'

Book Three

Untitled

1

Slut, although barely an hour's drive from Dubrovnik, has been less ruthlessly improved by Russian Mafia money or British private equity slush funds than other places on the Dalmatian seaboard.

This is because Slut is not quite on the coast. The town is an irritating thirty-minute taxi drive from its beach, and the road is not good. You can, of course, get there by boat. A slow boat will leave from Slut's riverside quay at unpredictable times (and at unpredictable cost) and deposit you, dizzied by diesel fumes, behind the shingle bar that separates the Slut lagoon from the Adriatic. For these and other reasons, Slut has been spared. No cranes loom over its motley buildings, and the occasional Mercedes-Benz with darkened windows pauses but passes by.

Nonetheless, tourists come, attracted by the magnificent Greek amphitheatre and the remains of the Temple of Priapus just the other side of the service station on the main road. They stay for a day, sometimes even two, eating at the restaurant where Vanda works, poring over their copies of *Lonely Planet* or *The Rough Guide*, congratulating themselves on finding The Unspoilt Croatia, and struggling with the menu that Vanda has tried vainly to get Mirko to rephrase. Has tried to explain that 'Lamb Sin Cocked in its Own Hair' is unlikely to sound attractive to non-Croats. Nor yet is 'Tongue of Goat Choked in Sauce'.

Vanda knew these things because she had spent two and a half of her teenage years as an asylum seeker in Cromer, a town on the coast of Norfolk, England. The experience left her with two things: a working knowledge of English and a repertoire of bad dreams in which she flees through the squalid corridors of a crumbling and labyrinthine hotel built in 1906.

She spoke in English to the Englishman who had been, inexplicably, in Slut for more than a week. He was staying at the Vrt, the resort's only two-star hotel. (She could not for the life of her understand why the town's other hotel did not also paint stars on its sign board.) Every day he ate lunch and dinner at The Feral because he had discovered, like other tourists, that the alternatives were worse. He would arrive soon; it was almost twelve twenty-five. She prepared the table he always used, the small one on the terrace in the deep shadow of the awning. She positioned his chair with its back to the wall. And sure enough, here he came now, strolling along the riverside in his light suit and Panama hat as if Slut were Nice. If he wore pince-nez instead of sunglasses, he would look like *Death In Venice*. Vanda was fairly sure he was an artist of some sort, a composer, perhaps, or a poet. Not a painter. Never a spot of paint on his hands or clothes. Or perhaps he was something more interesting. A criminal evading Interpol. A man recovering from a disastrous love affair or scandal.

She had considered having sex with him; he was not that old, actually, and almost certainly more inventive than the local options. He was always drunk when he left at three o'clock, but not that drunk. She could overtake him on her bicycle, dismount provocatively, and discuss her discontent. She pictured his soft and neatly trimmed beard sliding down her belly to intertangle with her own more luxuriant one.

'Good afternoon, Mister Cockling.'

'Good afternoon.'

Philip would have used her name if he could remember it. He was almost inclined to call her Francine or Merilee; these hirsute Croatian women sometimes provoked an unwelcome nostalgia for Flemworthy.

Unbidden, Vanda fetched and uncorked a bottle of the infamous local red. Philip, as usual, scanned the menu and chuckled sadly.

Vanda said, 'We have two good fish, brought in last night, but Mirko will fuck up them. I recommend lamb and kidney kebab. I know you had two days ago, but is a different lamb, and not goat. I make the salad personal.'

'Fine,' Philip said, pouring the wine. 'Thank you.'

'No worries.'

He shuddered as the first gulp of wine went down.

Subsequent mouthfuls would be less bad. Later, there'd be the so-called cognac, which he liked. He also liked being addressed, approximately, as 'Mister McCoughlin'.

The Feral had as yet no other customers, which pleased him. At this time of vertical sun the view from the terrace had a pleasing incorporeality which he preferred to relish undistracted. The river, which was actually sluggish and brownish, danced with light and the harsh cliff on its far side seemed insubstantial as tissue paper. The blue and white boats moored at the quay were shapeless in the glitter except where their awnings cast dense shadows onto their decks. It all had the tipsy imprecision of an Impressionist painting, of dreamy nowhereness.

The waitress came back with bread, a saucer of olives and some of that oily pulp that resembled hummus but wasn't. She set these things down and, since there was seemingly nothing else she had to do, lingered at his table. Cautiously, Philip looked up at her. To his relief, she was not looking at him. She appeared to be sharing his pleasure in the view. Taking it in. Inhaling it, actually, so that her not inconsiderable breasts rose and fell. Her hands rested on the flesh extruded by her low-cut jeans. Philip applied himself to the not-hummus.

'Slut,' she said, startling him. 'What a shit-hole. Remind me of Cromer. Know Cromer, Mister Cockling? In Nuffuck, England?'

'Um, no. Never been there.'

'I was in Cromer.'

'Really? Were you? Is that where you learned English?'

Vanda sighed. 'Where I learn English, where I learn sex abuse also.'

'Ah. Well. I'm sorry that . . .'

'No worries. All in the past. I like English men, in spite.' She pulled up a spare chair and sat down on it; a single, surprisingly fluid movement. She helped herself to one of his olives and licked it before popping it into her mouth. 'I guess, but I think you are a writer, for example. Maybe you do research. A book of love and sex and the wars that break the soul of my people.' She protruded her tongue with the olive stone nestled in its folds.

A memory uncoiled inside him, low down.

'No,' he said.

Vanda furled and flipped her tongue, shooting the stone over the low wall of the terrace. She turned her melting gaze upon him.

'All right, no. You want to be mystery. I like. But you want a story, I tell you one. A fantastic one. Maybe later I will tell you. Somewhere private. OK?'

'Um. Yes. That would be nice.'

'Thank you. Now I go make sure Mirko don't fuck up your kebab.'

Dessert not being an option at The Feral, Philip enjoyed slooshing the treaclish cognac around his mouth then picking the softened meat fibres from between his teeth with the nail of his little finger. His pleasure was diminished by the arrival of four young tourists. They spoke Australian English. Vanda went over to them and bent to their table to translate the menu. The red T of her thong peeked over the waistband of her jeans. After a while he looked away. Memories crowding in. Memories that Ian McCoughlin should not possess.

Then her hand was on his shoulder. 'Another one?'

'Yes, please.'

Her hand stayed where it was. He turned and looked up at her.

'OK,' she said. 'One more. Then finish, OK? You know why. Don't want Roger Red Hat to fall sleeping in the middle of my story.'

'Right,' he said, suddenly dry-mouthed.

Her fingers tracked lightly across his nape, then she was gone.

Two of the Australians had taken books from their backpacks. One was a travel guide. The other was *Dark Entropy*.

Conscious of Vanda's eyes on him, Philip held himself steady as he left the restaurant and walked to the quay. He would sit on the last bench, the one in the shade of the trees, and wait for her. Why not. Bit of a stiffy on, actually. Been a long time. Definitely on offer. Moustache no problem, really. Staff at the hotel on siesta, get in there no trouble, no questions asked. Push the crusty socks under the bed. Then . . .

Then a fierce heat in the middle of his chest.

Christ! Heartburn? That let's-be-honest terrible wine?

No. The Amulet.

Not again. Please.

Not now.

But yes. The fucking thing had woken up again. A meteorite searing his breastbone. His brain hissed. His sight turned bright as burning magnesium around a central darkness. Scary things at the periphery. He stumbled to the bench and tried to blink them away.

The Amulet trembled, then settled and cooled. His sight clarified. His upper body felt concave and wet, like a flushed urinal.

He looked back and Vanda – he remembered now – was wheeling a bicycle from behind The Feral. She waved to him, then threw a leg over the crossbar. Philip, with an effort, raised his arm.

Something fell through the air and landed with a faint slap on the flagstones by his feet. A severed finger with a blueish nail. Maggots in its pulpy stump.

Vanda wobbled to a halt. She watched the Englishman jump up and run away, losing his hat, bleating like the goat he ate for lunch. She was disappointed but unsurprised. She considered setting off in pursuit, but she had her dignity to consider.

2

Anxiety was not something that Minerva Cinch went in for, as a rule. It was bad for her business, her digestion and, most significantly, her complexion. She therefore declined anxiety, much as other women declined saturated fats. So it was extremely vexing that Philip Murdstone was causing her stress. *Again.*

He'd really cranked her handle, going right to the wire with the delivery of *Warlocks Pale*. And now that the damned bloody brilliant thing was in, he was cranking it again by going all incommunicado on her. Since the terse – well, sarky, really – note that accompanied the emailed text there'd not been a peep out of him. She must've left a hundred messages on his home phone, the Paddington phone, and on his mobile. Ditto emails. And nothing.

At first she'd assumed that he was slumped in his farty den exhausted by the rigours of creativity. Or just pissed all the time. Fair enough. But now that several weeks had passed it was getting beyond a joke. And she had *nice* things to tell him. That Gorgon had phoned and waxed *rhapsodic* about *Warlocks Pale*. That the senior editor had said that it was the cleanest text she'd ever received; that apart from typos and such, it needed almost nothing doing to it. That the cheque for half a mill, payable on receipt of manuscript, was in. That Ahmed Timbrel had phoned from LA offering to double the film option fee in order to secure the rights.

I mean, it's all *joyous*, darling, she would have said, if only the sod would pick up the phone.

Despite herself, she began to entertain the extremely vexatious notion that Philip had died. At diminishing intervals a grotesque image flashed upon her mind. His body decomposing in his armchair, the flesh turning purplish, his viscera churned by maggots. She told herself this was ridiculous. He'd have been found by now, surely. But then quite possibly not; he had no neighbours and she doubted that he had much in the way of visitors.

On the morning she discovered a zit budding alongside her nose she climbed into the BMW and fed his postcode into the satnav.

During this stressful interlude Evelyn padded through the days like a horse with muffled hooves. She fielded calls, surreptitiously switched the coffee to decaff, made sure there was always a hundred cigarettes in her desk drawer. She called Murdstone's number on the hour every hour and hung up as soon as the answer machine kicked in.

Until today when, shortly before her employer's return, all she'd got was a strange warbling whine in her ear.

'Good morning, darling. What's new? How's Cuthbert?'

Evelyn looked up, smiling bravely. 'Well, the vet's lanced the boil. Says I can pick him up later today. Would that be OK? Sort of fourish?'

'Don't see why not.' Minerva leaned against the door frame, seemingly reluctant to enter the room.

Evelyn said, 'Well? Was he . . . there?'

'No.'

'Ah.'

Minerva drew in a breath that lifted her shoulders. 'I want you to call Perry Whipple, darling. Lunch, ASAP. He can name the place.'

Evelyn raised her eyebrows.

'I know, darling. But things have got weird. I need to talk to someone who does weird.'

3

Sumtip Hucan Tsay shifted down a gear as the terrible minibus approached the last bend in the pass. Despite everything, the timing was perfect. They'd begin the final ascent to Phunt Kumbum just as the late afternoon light hit it. He turned to his cousin, the tour guide Notip Yucan Bett, and smiled.

'In a minute the Americans will all say "Ossum".'

Notip shrunk deeper into his parka and grunted. The Americans said 'Ossum' all the time. And they would say it again when they saw the monastery's white, red and gold tiers clinging to the slopes below Shand'r Ga. At the last tea shop, Sumtip had asked Sherri, the American with the nice long tits like a goat's, what the strange word meant.

'Well,' she'd said, 'it's like *Wow*, you know?'

It was interesting that Americans sometimes sounded like the Chinese.

He coaxed the bus around the bend, and for a couple of seconds lifted his gaze from the untrustworthy road. The snow on the peaks of Tangulaj was a lurid pink, like blood mixed with milk. Its shadows were the colour of wet Levis. Then Phunt Kumbum itself hoved into view, glowing.

'Wow,' someone gasped from the back. 'Ossum.'

Another said, 'OMG, isn't that truly ossum?'

The guest master watched the bus approach, slaloming between the lines of wind-tattered prayer flags. He gazed down as the visitors hauled their rucksacks from the vehicle and stood contemplating the flight of sixty-six steps that led up to the gatehouse.

The two couples were young, and climbed towards him like sturdy automata. The fifth visitor made heavier weather of it, halting frequently, bent, his shoulders heaving with the effort of breathing. He was older than the others, bearded and somewhat dishevelled. The guest master silently and smilingly greeted the Americans, but did not speak until this wheezing person had tottered onto the terrace.

'Welcome, my friends, to Phunt Kumbum. My name is Sandup Gnose. Guest masters of this monastery are always called Sandup Gnose. I am the one hundred and first. You can call me Sandy.' The monk spoke in lilting but perfect English. Only one of his guests might have identified a slight Glaswegian accent. 'I will show you to your accommodation shortly,' he continued. 'But first things first. You've had a long journey, and I bet you could murder a cup of tea.'

He delighted in the spasm of horror that passed over all five faces.

'No, no. Don't be afraid. Not yak-butter tea. Proper tea. We get it smuggled in from Assam. You can't get better in Fortnum and Mason. This way, please.'

In the dimly lit tea room, Sandy sat down next to the bearded *Injie*.

The man held his bowl in both hands, his head bent over it. 'Christ on a bike,' he said. 'This is wonderful. I haven't had a decent cup of tea since . . .' He lifted his face and stared blankly into the gloom. 'Some time ago.'

The monk clapped his hands delightedly. 'You are English!'

'Yes. Well, Scottish, originally. My name's Ian McCoughlin.'

Sandy's smile achieved an even greater radiance. 'Scotland! Where, exactly?'

'Um, Dumfries.'

'I know it! I know it! Dumfries and Galloway!'

Bugger, Philip groaned inwardly.

'I did a degree in Business Management at the University of Glasgow. Upper Second. Then two years at Millar and Millar, stockbrokers.'

'Really?'

'Yes. Yes . . .' The monk's smile faded away. 'But it played hell with my karma. I found myself contemplating the very real possibility that my next reincarnation would be as a tapeworm. So I came home.' He was silent for a moment or two. His bifocals glittered in the lamplight. 'Anyway,' he said, regaining his alarming cheerfulness, 'how is dear old Dumfries?'

'I couldn't say. I only lived there until I was four. I've never been back.'

Sandy nodded. 'A famously migratory race, the Scots.' Then he closed his eyes, cleared his throat and declaimed, in a throaty Highland brogue:

'*I've seen sae mony changefu' years,*
On earth I am a stranger grown;
I wander in the ways of men,
Alike unknowing and unknown.
'The great Rabbie Burns, of course. More tea?'

Later, standing in the doorway of the cell, Sandy said, 'It's a wee bit less austere than a monk's, but not much.'

A thin mattress and a quilt. An oil lamp, a bowl and a thermos flask on a low chest. A four-legged stool. A small murky painting (of Dipamkara Buddha, but Philip wasn't to know that, of course). The window was unglazed but barred and shuttered. The door looked to be a good ten centimetres thick and hung on four huge hinges with elongated hasps.

'It's fine.'

'Our modest meal will be served in twenty minutes,' Sandy said. 'Then you and the other guests are invited to join us in the *dukhang* for our evening debate. It'll be all Greek to you, of course, but it can get pretty lively. Jolly good fun.'

'Erm . . . I'm feeling very tired, actually. The altitude, I expect. I might get an early night. I'll probably feel up to it tomorrow evening.' The Spartan bed had become deeply attractive.

The monk tilted his head. His smile took on a tinge of puzzlement. 'Tomorrow, Ian? But doesn't your tour depart in the afternoon?'

'Well, actually, ah, Sandy, I'm not really with the tour. I just persuaded the guide to give me a lift up here. Bribed him, actually. I thought I . . . I was hoping to stay for a little while.'

'A retreat?'

'Yes.'

'Hmm. Well, there are the proper channels for arranging these things, actually.'

'I'm sorry. It was a sort of spontaneous decision.'

'Yes, well. Spontaneity isn't something we actively encourage, you know,' Sandy said a little primly. Then he lightened. 'I'll have a word with the Abbot. Ask a favour for a fellow Scot, eh?'

The following morning Philip set out along the *kora*, the pilgrims' path that meandered, rising and falling, around Phunt Kumbum. So slow was his progress that it might have appeared contemplative. In fact, he was still spavined and nauseated by mountain sickness. After only ten minutes he was forced to support himself on a polished basalt *lingam* that had flown there from India during the First Age of Light. As he leaned on its glossy glans the four Americans, clad in bright Lycra, jogged briskly by in a cloud of their own steam. He was too breathless to respond to their jocular greetings. He slumped to the ground and rested his back against Shiva's sturdy organ.

Beyond the great valley a range of mountains loomed, their wrinkled brown flanks topped by a zone of white, blue-shadowed peaks. This ethereal beauty put Philip in mind of the meringue-topped chocolate torte he'd eaten in Zurich soon after leaving his bank. The gnome who administered his numbered bank accounts had turned out to be a brisk young woman wearing pink-tinted spectacles. He had not understood much of what she'd said, but had left with the wherewithal to obtain funds for 'a protracted period of research travel', a wad of cash and the address of a place where false (the gnome had preferred the word 'supplementary') passports could be obtained.

In a barbershop kitschily tricked out in 1930s Cunard décor he'd got his hair cut and chestnut-rinsed to hide the grey and his beard trimmed into a shape that looked deliberate. Four days later and a few thousand Swiss francs lighter, he – or rather Ian McCoughlin, according to his new but well-used passport – flew south. Then further south. Then east and further east. His peregrination to Phunt Kumbum had been wildly erratic. He had not been using conventional travel guides. He'd been flicking through an atlas of fear.

In various places in three continents he had felt calm for short periods of time. Then the dread would surge. In Slut, he'd been almost happy for ten whole days until the finger. And seen a dark raptor, or its shadow, cross the face of the cliff. He shuddered again at the memory.

In Istanbul, crossing the Galata Bridge under a hot and paper-white sky, he'd felt a stirring at his breastbone and entered a patch of chill darkness. The men fishing from the bridge's parapet had turned to look at him, rolling up their collars.

In the human turbulence of Delhi, a crowd had parted when a fakir wearing a green and silver robe and a living necklace of snakes had fixed his single eye on him.

A small gaggle of monks now emerged onto the path below. Fussily, they arranged themselves on a level outcrop of stone and sat, cross-legged. After a minute or so of silent contemplation one of the monks produced a large bag of popcorn and passed it round.

Philip knew, at some numb, dumb level of knowing, that flight was futile. It was possible, just, that he could evade the radar of Minerva and Gorgon and all those other fuckers who had a stake in him, a piece of him. But not Morl. Not Morl. Because, he, Philip, also known as Ian, still possessed the Amulet.

Common sense dictated that he should have left the damned thing behind. In a place easily found by a nightmare that came down the chimney or lurched out of the lav. Good advice, that. You take it. But common sense had been not been a feature of his flight from Downside.

At Heathrow, he had been tempted to drop it into a waste bin. But he couldn't.

It had made him, after all. And he'd earned it. It was, without question, the most important thing that he had ever possessed. To have left it behind would have been like King Arthur tossing Excalibur aside with a casual, 'Ah, sod it, I'll get another one.'

It was also the only thing he had left to trade.

Wearing it, he'd passed through the security arch without a bleep.

Philip grieved for Pocket Wellfair, his saviour, his nemesis, whose small brave life had been cut short in Mort A'Dor. Sometimes Philip entertained a redemptive vision of himself digging the Greme's grave in a sun-splashed dell and lowering the poor little sod into it while murmuring a valediction in the Old Language.

At other times he worried about developments in the Realm. There was, obviously, an asynchronicity, an interdimensional dateline, between the Realm and here, wherever and whenever 'here' was. But things were going on, equally obviously. And they weren't looking good. A blind goat could see that. Morl was on the up, and that was bad. It was the wrong story. Uneasily, Philip recognized that he was partly responsible for this. The responsibility hung from his neck.

4

The *dukhang* was almost full by the time Philip followed Sandup in. He had been dreading an atmosphere of profound meditativeness, and was surprised – and greatly relieved – to find the hall echoing with chatter and giggling. The space was lit with a great many candles and oil lamps and was, to his occidental eye, disorderly. Some two hundred or so monks had gathered. Some sat in clumps or in smiling rows along low benches. Others milled about the room forming loud, voluble groups, which then dispersed and formed others. With their shaven heads protruding from ochre felt cloaks they looked identical; the swirl of their movement, and their chirruping, suggested the nesting rituals of a colony of flightless birds. Here and there – randomly, it seemed to Philip – were tables laden with the kind of stuff you might find in the New Age boutiques of Totnes.

Sandy guided him through the throng to where a knot of older monks was seated and made introductions. The monks greeted Philip with speeches of varying length, each of which Sandy translated as 'He wishes you peace'.

Philip made vaguely spiritual gestures and said, 'The same to you.' This seemed to go down perfectly well, judging by the broad smiles with which it was received.

Something like a quarter of an hour passed, during which Philip was greatly troubled by wind. Asia had not been good for his bowels. He wondered whether the all-accepting philosophy, the deep resignation, of Phunt Kumbum extended to farting. Possibly; there was a good deal of incense being burned. To be on the safe side, he gradually deflated the painful gutbubble in a series of tiny whiffles.

A long blast on a horn (which Philip gratefully exploited) was followed by a burst of enthusiastic chanting. An elderly monk led a small procession to the head of the room. When silence had established itself he sat and held his arms out in front of him. One of his retinue laid a white silk scarf over his hands. Then a second acolyte placed a book upon the scarf. There was another, more subdued, outbreak of chanting.

Sandy leaned his head closer and whispered, 'The Abbot does not always read for the debate. You are rather lucky.'

Philip merely nodded. It was the best he could do. His flatulence had made him taut and attentive; now that it had eased, he felt exhausted. The dim otherness of everything. Peace – or sleep, at least – beckoned him, urged an escape from this strange rookery of orange birds. He forced himself to sit more upright.

The Abbot began to read. At first, his words were

heard in reverential silence. The shadowed bronze faces that filled the room were blank, attentive. Four minutes in, someone interrupted. The Abbot looked up sternly, then smiled. From the back of the hall, someone called out what must have been a joke; there was laughter. A cluster of monks got to their feet simultaneously, chorused a phrase and applauded themselves. Others joined in. From the dim outskirts of the room, a single voice called out a single word, which precipitated an amazingly resonant chant that thrilled Philip's backbone.

The monk who'd handed the book to the Abbot raised a hand. The *dukhang* was instantly silent. The reading resumed.

Eventually, Philip realized that the Abbot was doing voices. He was telling a story.

Soon there was yet another interruption. A young monk gave a short impassioned speech. A few of his neighbours stood and raised their hands in a clenched fist salute. One of them shook a clump of bells. Closer by, an older man got to his feet and achieved a respectful silence. He spoke for a whole minute, then sat down. He had clearly refuted everything the younger monks had said. Surprisingly, they applauded him.

The Abbot returned to the book.

'I dare say you'd like to know what's going on,' Sandy murmured.

'What? Ah, yes. I'm rather baffled, actually.'

'Of course. Well, we are studying a Western text, which is highly unusual. That is one reason why the *geyung*, the younger monks, are especially excited. Wisdom has it that the West has nothing to offer us. Having lived in Glasgow, I am inclined to share that view. However, when one of our community came back from a seminar in Dartington, Devon, he brought back . . . Do you know Dartington, Ian?'

'Yeah.'

'I believe it is very nice. Anyway, he came back with a copy of a book called *Dark Entropy* by Philip Murdstone. Have you read it, Ian?'

Philip managed only a shake of the head.

'That's a pity. It's rather good. I'll lend you my own copy, if you like. It's a fairly easy read. But the thing is, the reason why some of us are so excited, is that allegory is essential to our way of thinking, as you know. In *Dark Entropy* there is this beautiful kingdom called Realm, whose ruler, Cadrel, is exiled. Its people, who live in harmony with their world, are oppressed. They are being colonized by an evil being called Morl, who wants to make Realm part of his Thule. He has a vast army of mindless warriors called Swelts. Hope for the Realm resides with Wise Men, especially one called the Sage, who have Great Wisdom, which the book calls Magick and is recorded in ledgers.'

'Right,' Philip said.

'But, of course, we understand that Realm is Tibet. It is clearly signalled in the text. Place names and so on. It is equally obvious that Morl's Thule is China. That the Swelts are the Chinese, that the grid they are building is the roads and railways that the Chinese are building to swamp us with Han immigrants. That Cadrel is the Dalai Lama, sword or no sword. That the Sage is the immortal reincarnation of the fifth Dalai Lama. And so on.'

Sandy paused while a low groan circumnavigated the *dukhang*.

'That is why what we call the Murdstone Debates are so popular. The *geyung* enjoy saying terrible things about Morl, because they are really talking about China. Which they cannot do openly because there are Chinese spies everywhere. Even here, I am sorry to say. My older colleagues enjoy this aspect of it, of course, but are rather more interested in deciphering the book's deeper, spiritual meanings.'

Philip's mouth filled with saliva that tasted of old batteries. He swallowed it down. 'I didn't know . . . I mean, so this *Dark Entropy* is available in Tibetan, is it?'

'No,' Sandy said, his smile suggesting regret and possibly sad resentment. 'The Abbot makes his own translation. He was at Oxford. First-class degree in Classics, St John's College, nineteen sixty.'

The reading was again interrupted. A short speech from the floor was rewarded with chirrupy laughter.

When the Abbot continued, Sandy whispered, 'We're all rather excited because we expect to receive the second volume of Murdstone soon. Two weeks ago a band of brothers set off for Kathmandu to scrounge a copy from one of the backpacker hostels. They should be back any day now.'

'I hope,' Philip said faintly, 'it won't be a disappointment.'

'That is most unlikely. Murdstone is in touch with the Truth. And Truth, by its very nature, cannot disappoint.'

Sandy put his mouth a little closer to Philip's ear. 'But I am troubled, Ian. This morning I learned from the Americans that Philip Murdstone has disappeared. Vanished without trace, apparently. His friends are appealing for information. I fear he may have been abducted by Chinese agents. London is full of them, as you know, posing as restaurant staff and acrobats. I am in three minds about sharing this information with my brothers. I would not wish to spread dismay. What do you think?'

Philip had a huge desire to sag, fold, crumple. The incense smoke had become oppressive. His eyes were losing focus. The candles were bright smears in the gloom. He turned to the earnest monk, who suddenly resembled Pocket Wellfair in specs.

'I dunno. It's probably, you know, a publicity stunt, or something. He'll turn up. Or maybe he's in hiding somewhere. Gone off to write another book. Doing research. Somewhere quiet.' He knew that his speech was slurred. Attitude sickness. Too high, you're too high . . . Used to be a song.

'Do you think so?'

'Sure of it.'

Philip got somehow to his feet. 'Say nothing, Sandy,

if I were you. No point in spreading dependency. I mean despondency. Lovely evening, really interesting, must go. Unused to everything. Very tired.'

'Hoots the noo and awa tae bed,' Sandy said, smiling Scottishly up at him.

'Burns?'

'Mrs Cohen, my dear old landlady.'

5

Philip tottered down the side of the *dukhang* past a bank of blissfully attentive faces and into a dimly-lit corridor. Partway along it his knees turned gelatinous and he came to rest against a huge ochre and black-painted column. He sucked in thin air.

After a while he noticed that the pillar supporting him was one of a pair forming the entrance to a Protector Chapel. He turned groggily, and looked into its candlelit interior. Its back wall was a large mural. At its centre, a deity of some sort. Red. Lots of arms with swords whirling about. A necklace of severed heads. Peaceful look on its face. Surrounded by blue demons. Ugly as sin. Tusked, slobbering, malevolent. Armoured, implacable.

Swelts, in fact.

They turned as one to look at him.

The solitary monk writing at a low table raised his head. Within the shadow of his cowl a single orange eye glittered.

The Swelts bulged and pulsed, struggling to free themselves from the mural's two dimensions.

The monk smiled then spoke. '*Et in Arcadia ego*, Murdstone.'

The Amulet bucked and yearned against Philip's chest. He fled, stumbling, a silent scream on legs, into the stone-cold labyrinth of Phunt Kumbum.

After what felt like an hour of panicky questing he found his cell. Slammed the door behind him. Slid the bolt. Pressed his forehead against the thick wood. Tried to get his heart and lungs to cooperate, stop his brain cells brightly worming. He'd made some slight progress when he heard sounds behind him: a rasp, a clink, an outpuff of breath. He opened his eyes. Lamplight seeped into their corners.

'By the scrote, Murdstone. When you go proper rambly you don't fluke about, do you?'

Oh no. Not again.

'Wossup, Murdstone? Forget to pack your tongue, did you? Or've you got it stuck in that bleddy door?'

'Go away. I'm not listening to you. You're not Pocket. Pocket's dead.'

'Well, stap me sidewards, Murdstone. I never knew that. Dead, am I?'

'Yes.'

'Bogger. That'd tangle matters. Hang you on there while I stick a finger up my jacksie see if I can feel a beat. Yep. There it goes. Tiddy-boom, tiddy-boom. You nearly had me worried there, Murdstone. But I appear to be in the land of the living still. Mind if I wipe my finger on your bedsheet? Thankee. Norwest corner, lest you wonder. Now, you going to stand there like a pol-lacksed sterk all night or face me man to Greme? I could converse to your saggy arse all night but a bit of respect wouldn't go amiss.'

Philip turned. Pocket was sitting on the bed with his hands on his knees, his face a small yellow moon in the lamplight.

'By the Royal Knob of Lux, Murdstone. You look rougher every time I clap eyes on you. What's all this flabber about me being dead?'

'In the book. You . . . died.'

'Fluke me, Murdstone. That was made up. Flaky. It's a bleddy *nobble*.'

'Then you came to the cottage.'

'Did I now?'

'But you weren't you. It was horrible. You – you turned into maggots. And then the maggots turned into . . .'

'A sod of a huge great fly.'

'Yes.'

Pocket gestured dismissively. 'One of Morl's favourite tricks, that. Nasty if yer not used to it, I grant you. Scares Porlocs witless. They fill their breeks every time, superstitious twassocks that they are. Come over here, Murdstone. Come on.'

Philip approached the bed and knelt because his legs were no longer any good. Pocket held out a hand.

'Take hold of that finger.'

'Is it the one you . . . ?'

'No. That was the next one along. Go on. Take hold. There's a good pony. How does that feel?'

'Cold.'

'Well acourse it bleddy is. It's colder'n the nipple on a witch's tit in here. But squeeze. Do I feel wibbly? Maggoty? Or do you feel bone, hmm? Sinew?'

'Yes.'

'If you cut me, I'd bleed. Got a blade about you?'

Philip shook his head. He tightened his grip on the Greme's finger. 'Oh, Pocket! Pocket, I thought, I really thought . . .' Words became sobs.

'Rein up, Murdstone, rein up. Fluke me, there's no call to get leaky. And I'll have that finger back if you're done with it. Thankee. Now then, to the quick of the matter. Go home.'

'What?'

'Go home. All this ferking hither and yon is bleddy useless, an you know it. Morl—'

Philip's mind rebooted. 'Morl! He's here, Pocket!'

'Whatsay?'

'He's here. I saw him. Just now.'

The Greme regarded Philip gravely. 'Your wits've lallopped, Murdstone. No surprise in that, I dare say. They weren't well tethered in the first place. Comes of spending a life writing flaky ledgers, I'd hazard. Makes you see things what aren't there.'

'No, Pocket. Listen . . .'

'No. You hark to me. Morl's not the problem. Well, he flukin is, acourse. But he's not *your* problem, Murdstone.

Your problem is that you can't get rid of the Amulet.'

This was, Philip admitted by bowing his head, true.

'Not marked against you, to be square. We bollixed it up. Thought it would be easier than it turned out. But that's all trod road now.'

Pocket paused. Philip looked up into his genial smile.

'Why do you want me to go home?'

'I've got a new nobble for you.'

'What?'

'Ah, I thought that'd prickle your lugs up.'

'You've written another one?'

'Seems I recall you saying these things come in tribbles. So I've done you a number three.' The Greme looked at him asquint. 'Gratefulness don't come easy to you, does it, Murdstone?'

'I'm sorry. Thank you, Pocket. That's wonderful.'

'Didn't you like the last one? What was wrong with it?'

'No. It's not that. It was brilliant. Especially the second part.'

'Hm! What, then?'

Philip lowered himself onto the other end of the pallet and wrapped his arms around himself. It was indeed bloody cold in the cell. 'It's just that I, I don't know, I've had enough. I'm tired. I want to stop. Stop writing. Just be . . . quiet.'

Pocket nodded. He sniffed. He huffed. He said, 'Here's a thing or two in no particular shuffle. One. You don't do the writing. I do. Two. You think you're flukin tired, try being me. You've no bleddy idea. Three. You live high as a flea on a hog's back, thanks to me. Fame the length and breadth. Money coming at you like flies to a fresh-dropped turd. Ho yes, we know these things, Murdstone. Four or five, I've lost the count, you do the tribble and you can spend your days quiet as a thriftmouse sitting on your arse like'n addled tosspot if that's your fancy. And last but not leastwise, when the nobble's done, I'll have that flukin Amulet off you. Then your troubles are gone. Life a dish of cherries, pips or no pips, depending on the run of your luck. Oh, and one other item I near forgot. You've got no flukin choice in the matter.'

Philip didn't speak.

Pocket said testily, 'Any of that get past you, Murdstone?'

'No.'

'Good. So go home. Set yourself down at that pewter thing and I'll come through when we – I'm – readied. Square?'

'Yes.'

The Greme stood. He said, 'By the crack, Murdstone, what a piece of work you turned out. I'll be glad to be shot of you, truth to tell.'

Then the cell sucked in a breath and he was gone.

6

Merilee's little scream came out distorted; she had a forefinger questing a good way up her nose. She turned away from the window and called, or rather wailed, her sister's name.

Francine's head appeared from behind the desk. 'Merilee? What?'

Merilee leaned her back against the wall, a hand to her bosom. Several intensifying seconds passed before she could speak.

'He's back.'

'Who is? What you'm on about, Merilee?'

'Murdsten. I jus seen his car go by.'

Francine coughed shock. A morsel of pork pie flew from her mouth and landed on the latest issue of *Men's Fitness*. Eventually she managed to say, 'You'm sure twas his, Merilee?'

'Who else drive a bleddy great thing that colour? Besides, it went dreckly past that ole pokesnout Tom Bladdermore an he fell backards inter the horse trough like he'd been shot.'

The twins stared at each other, thumbs in mouths, sharing a thrill of horror.

Then Francine said, 'Oh, Merilee. What if he come here an find out aller his books've been burned in fronter the public?'

'Shit an biscuits,' Merilee said. 'Thas a thought.'

They considered it.

Francine said, 'Us'll have ter keep watch. Take turns at the winder. If he come, lock the door. Put up a sign sayin Closed Fer . . .'

'Lunch?'

'No. Cause of it might be afternoon.'

'You'm right there, Francine. Sharp thinkin. Stocktakin, then. Or Death in the Fambly.'

Despite being *de facto* orphans, the sisters were comforted by this plan.

Until Francine said tremulously, 'But what if he come as the Fly, Merilee? What if he can shrink inter like a normal one an come in through a winder or the keyhole? Then swell up huge agen?'

Merilee seemed about to faint but gathered herself. 'Nip down the supermarket, Francine. Buy a swatter an aller the inseck spray they're got on the shelf.'

'Aisle Four,' Francine said.

'Five,' Merilee said.

Stoned on jetlag, Philip had driven most of the A30 with the window down and the hi-fi at full whack. Despite these precautions, he'd almost missed his exit and had veered across the inside lane, cutting up a blaring truck carrying two thousand almost featherless chickens to their destiny.

This incident shattered the frosted glass behind which his mind had lurked for the past five – or was it six? – days. Now, as the familiar bends of the country road unfurled, he realized that he felt rather sick. It was a nausea that could not be entirely attributed to thirteen in-flight meals. No. His gastric unease was anxiety. No, again. *Fear.* The return to his tainted cottage, his tainted life, frightened him. As did the prospect of a third and final return to the Realm, despite the promise of liberation that accompanied it. Completeness and Closure were words on the same spider-chart as Death.

He passed the turning to Slewchurch. Ten miles to go. The time, according to the dashboard clock, was 11.21. He slowed and stabbed the music off. He tried to let the autumnal curvaceousness of Devon soothe him. So much more pleasant, really, than the soul-freezing splendour of the Himalayas.

The sign loomed: WELCOME TO FLEMWORTHY, to which a local wit had added TWINED WITH MORLS THOOL.

He passed through the almost deserted square and turned onto Dag Lane. A black-suited bicyclist was heading in the opposite direction. Philip recognized him as the local vicar, but could not remember the man's name. As they passed he called 'Good Morning' from his window.

The vicar opened his mouth as if to reply, but Philip did not catch what he said. He glanced at his wing mirror and was surprised to see the vicar and his bike toppling sideways into the hedge. A bit early for a clergyman to be pissed, Philip thought, even for a High Anglican.

He parked and got out of the Lexus. His legs were unsteady. Quite some time since he'd walked more than four hundred metres of departure lounge carpet. He lit a duty-free cigarette and sought comfort from the view. A sense of belonging.

None came.

He walked to his home. In front of it he halted, astonished. Someone had turned his fence into an artwork of some kind. It had been adorned with swags of garlic, crosses of wood or other plant material, small mirrors, scraps of paper covered in scrawls of writing, CDs, rosary beads, strips of flypaper and little dolls crudely fashioned out of stuffed fabric. On closer inspection, these dolls had been pierced through various parts of their anatomies by pins, nails, sewing needles and cocktail sticks.

Philip was so absorbed in examining these tributes that it took him some time to notice that a white cross had been painted on his door. When he pushed it open he was almost overwhelmed by stench. He stepped over the slew of mail, returned the phone to its cradle and shoved the window open. He located the source of stink as the kitchen waste bin and carried it outside. He dallied with the idea of adding the fence fetishes to it, but decided that it might offend the well-meaning person or persons who'd placed them there.

He was surprised that he still had electricity, that the central heating whuffed into action, that the fridge illuminated its emptiness when he opened it. The rug in front of the hearth was webbed by glittery trails of congealed slime. Only slugs, of course.

He returned to the car for the bags of stuff he'd bought at the branch of Sainsbury's just off the Exeter bypass. A movement tickled the corner of his eye. He looked down the lane and saw, or thought he saw, two figures nip smartly behind a beech tree. On his second trip to the car he paused at the buckled gate and glanced across the coombe. On its far side a gaggle of birdwatchers had their binoculars trained in his direction.

Back indoors, he extricated a pair of sandwiches from their triangular blister and ate them. He gouged mould from the cafetiere and washed it out and made coffee. It tasted of mould. He added a slosh of whiskey to the cup. Better.

He continued to restore things to order, because although he was tired to the edge of hallucination he didn't dare sleep and didn't know what to expect. He'd tethered the Amulet against his chest with his trusty dressing-gown belt, of course, but Pocket had said he'd 'come through', which might mean he'd put in a personal appearance.

The thought jerked him. He went upstairs. The window-ledge in his study was thickly strewn with fly husks. He dabbed the laptop on and endured ten seconds of acute worry before the screen came up. He opened a New Document and gave it the bold title **3**.

Then he clicked on his email and was appalled by the infinite downscroll of little unopened envelopes. He clicked back to the blank page and went downstairs. He repositioned the armchair to where he could monitor both the lavatory and the chimney, poured himself a glass of Jameson and sat down to wait.

He was unconscious within five minutes.

7

Two things awakened him: a warm stirring, a tactile chuckle, against his chest; and a squeal of door hinges. The room was filled with soft amber light. The silhouette of a hooded figure occupied the doorway.

'Murdstone?'

'Pocket?'

'Oh, don't start that bleddy wrigglemeroll again. You sound, Murdstone? Your wits lined up? I see you've been at the damage again.'

'Yes. No. I've only had a sip or two. Come in, come in.'

The Greme came to the middle of the room, sniffing the air like a beagle, then settled himself comfortably on the sofa.

Philip went to the door and scanned the shadow-barred lane. There seemed to be no one about. He closed and bolted the door, drew the curtains, switched on lamps. Only then did something occur to him.

'You came in through the front door,' he said.

'Bugger me, you're sharp, Murdstone. There's not a lot gets past you.'

'No, I meant, usually you—'

'Clap into your shitter or down the chimbly with my arse asmoulder and knocked as a conker.'

'Yes.'

'Ah, well. We smuggled a pair of spellwrights in from Hazy Vale, see. Couldn't understand a bleddy word they said, but they abjurated some of the seals on the Dimensional Projector, diddled the equipollence on some of the others, gave it a quick wipe with a damp cloth, and stap me if twern't good as new. Bugger, do they charge, though. Ole Volenap nigh on fell dead when I read him the price. Mind you, well worth the coin. That's how come I angled you in that Phunky Bum place. And this time I come through to your crib slick as a sea weasel through a sluice. Not a lump nor flecker. Found myself outsider your door not a mollicle out of place.'

'I see,' Philip said, a little surprised by this uncharacteristically prolix explanation. 'That's good, then.'

And Pocket did indeed seem in much better shape than on previous visitations. To Philip's inexpert eye, he seemed to have put on a little weight. His hooded tunic thing was not only unstained and unscorched, it appeared to be new. His lower legs, bare and skinny on earlier occasions, were plumply sheathed in white woven stockings. The Greme sat at ease, his right elbow on the arm of the sofa, his chin resting on a loose fist, looking,

Philip thought, like someone posing for a photograph. And in no particular hurry.

Philip returned to his chair and took a dainty sip of whiskey.

'So, another nobble, eh, Pocket?'

'Yup.'

'Why?'

'*Why?* On account of you were desperate for it. Urging at it like a stalled bridegroom, wasn't you?'

'I suppose I was, yes.'

'And anyways up,' the Greme said, making an airy gesture, 'we left things adangle, end of the last one. Walking round the whole matter, I saw it wouldn't do. It was a two-legged trivet. And that started to naggle me. Flaky ledger or no, it can't just stop, I told meself.' He paused and aimed an authorial finger. 'Tales need shaping off, Murdstone. Top advice, that. You take it.'

'God help you, Pocket. You've become a nobblist. I thought this might happen.'

'Did you indeed? Never had you marked as a man could see round the next corner.'

Philip took another, less dainty, sip of Jameson. He noticed that his hand shook. Cautiously, he said, 'So, did you, er, shape it off? Does it . . . end? Satisfactorily?'

'Ho yes. Time you come to the end of the inkage you wouldn't be hungering after more.'

The Greme's gaze wavered, drifted off to the fireplace. For a few pleasant moments, Philip entertained the possibility of the two of them passing the evening in companionable, writerly conversation. Or even silence. Then Pocket stood and briskly rubbed his narrow hands together.

'Come on then, my pony. A comfy arse gathers no turnips, as my Old Dame was wont to say. You got that device of yours sparked up? Bring your grog, if you can't do without. Won't make a difference.'

Philip seated himself at the keyboard and fastened the Amulet more tightly to his chest. He dabbed the space-bar and the empty page appeared.

'Fair set, then, Murdstone?'

'Yes. No.'

'No?'

'I'm not sure I want to do this, Pocket.' The shake in his hand had reached his heart and brain.

'Say what?'

'I don't know if I can do it.'

'Murdstone, if this's more of your flukin bumgullery to hang onto the Amulet . . .'

'No. It's not that. Honestly. I'm frightened. My head is full of dark patches.'

'In a pig's arse, man,' the clerk said gently. 'We know that. We knew that from start-off. Couldn't figure how you managed with so little candle. Part of the reason we angled you, truth to tell.' Pocket's birdy hand nested on Philip's left shoulder. 'But we're nearly done, Murdstone. So don't you go getting frembly now. Third and last part of the tribble. Then you can rest the plough and graze the hosses. Square?' The hand gripped.

'Square?'

Philip nodded, gasped out a breath. 'All right.'

'Good. I'll leave you to it, then.'

'Pocket?'

'What now?'

'What if the Amulet, you know, doesn't want to, won't let you take it? Last time, it—'

'Don't you bandy your wits about that. It'll come peaceful.'

'Will it? How do you know?'

'Just write the flukin nobble, Murdstone. Then you'll have your answers.'

The door closed. Philip listened to Pocket's footsteps on the stairs. He took a quick slug from his glass and braced himself.

It began as before: a stirring of dry leaves, an unseen walker's whispery approach modulating into nibscratch. The Amulet trembled, awoke. Philip's hands spread themselves, hovering over the keys. In the darkened auditorium of his head images gathered and flickered into smooth unreeling. Inkage writhed onto his monitor.

Into and through the deepening night he saw and transcribed the third and final part of the Murdstone Trilogy.

He saw and wrote the blade of Cwydd Harel shatter a doorway through the outer wall of the Vednodian labyrinth. He saw and wrote Cadrel step onto the ledge and vanish into the cataract. Then emerge, bearing the sorely magicked but yet living body of the Sage, GarBellon.

His flying fingers recorded the rage of the Antarch, Morl, when he discovers that the thirty-second manifestation of Trover Mellwax has disappeared from the Dimensionless Table.

He watched this raging through the purple eyes of a warp-rat concealing itself in the deepest shadows of the laboratory.

He wrote and witnessed the Sage-burdened and perilous descent of Cadrel from the heights of Vedno to be reunited with his fearful troops. He saw them take ship, only to discover that Turbid Hoag has been whipped by the dark storm of Morl's flight into towering hills of water.

He saw and wrote the loss of every ship save Cadrel's. Porlocs and Gremes swept into the furious Hoag. Heard their screams as the Slankers closed in.

Some still-functioning particle of Philip's mind worried that things weren't going too well, Realm-wise. And there was a touch too much . . . *relish* in the account of disaster when it happened to the Good Guys. Bloody good, though. Thrilling.

What next?

What

next?

My triumph, Murdstone.

What? Who said that?

He wrote and saw Cadrel's reunion with Mesmira. Deeply emotional. Good old Tyle Gether, carrying the lantern from the bedroom then tending to GarBellon's damage. Mesmira hungry for Cadrel's touch. His hand limply fondling her before he falls exhausted onto the pillow. Her sigh. They sleep.

A rustle ascends the ivy that coats the wall of the Grange. A slithering through the half-opened sash, a tiny patter of clawed feet across the room. Mellwax the warp-rat hauling himself up the coverlet. Settling himself on Cadrel's pillow. Chewing patiently, silently, through the leather thong that attaches the Amulet to Cadrel's neck. Carrying the Amulet, careful not to make contact with it, to the window and thence into the night.

He witnessed and wrote treachery.

In the eerie half-light of a sullen dawn, a hooded figure leads a cohort of Swelts through the mazy tracks of Farrin. Guides them to the secret entrance to the subterranean library.

He wrote with viscious enthusiasm the butchering of Orberry Volenap, hearing groans which he dimly recognized as his own.

He saw the burning of the Ledgers, heard the squealing of the inkage as it turns into black insects that live for only moments before they disperse as windblown motes of ash.

While the harvest moon made its slow traverse of his window he witnessed and recorded, tirelessly and with deep repugnance in his soul, Morl's conquest of the Realm.

The body of GarBellon on its rude catafalque being hauled along the Third Way towards the Thule. The

Swelt escort standing by as it is pelted with filth and ordure when it passes through the encampments of the dispossessed.

Cadrel's rotting corpse, impaled on the blade of Cwydd Harel, suspended

No!

Yes, Murdstone

in an iron cage for all to see.

He wrote of

Remember this, Murdstone

the leaching of amnesia into the Realm.

Of Gremes, Morvens, Porlocs, Bubblers, moth farmers, wenders, bobbers, framers, barquemakers, wheelwrights, all smiling, forgetful, numb, queuing in the last colours of the day for their Thule tablets and grog.

He saw and wrote long lines of redundant Swelts, marshalled by the Praetorian Guard, waiting patiently in line for the Elimination Chambers. He watches them exit through the vents as rings of green vapour, and dissipate.

He groaned in libidinous agony writing Mesmira. Naked. Reclining languid on a white silk divan. One hand between her thighs. A sound summons her from trance and she looks up. Her blank eyes click on Lust and Brighten. Her lips part.

She reaches out

Something stirring, Murdstone?

and guides a withered hand, a claw, to the rosy aureole of her perfect left breast.

Oh, no. No!

Yes. Oh, yes

Morl mounts the divan. Mesmira, moaning desire, disappears beneath the billows of the green and silver necromantic cloak.

The image fades to black. There is no more.

Philip's hands stopped typing.

From the direction of the village a cockerel challenged the day.

8

It seemed to Philip that his brain had turned septic. That vileness had infected his senses. A greenish darkness edged his vision. The banister rail felt blood-sticky to his hand, the stair carpet marshy beneath his feet. The smell in his nostrils was yellow.

Pocket Wellfair was sitting on the sofa, breakfasting on a hand of bananas. He greeted Philip with manifestly false cheeriness.

'By the Knob, Murdstone, these things are bleddy tasty. What d'you call em?'

'Bananas. You're supposed to peel them.'

'Hum! Each to his own, says I. Want one?'

'You're still here.'

The Greme shook his head admiringly. 'Up all night and still sharp as a bodkin.' He crunched the last of his banana, regarding Philip sombrely. 'You look like a man as has leaked his bone marrow into his boots, Murdstone. Wassup? The nobble not to your taste?'

'Have you read it?'

'What kind of a patecracked question is that? I wrote the bleddy thing.'

'Did you?'

'Yes I did.'

'I don't think I believe you.'

'Fluke me,' Pocket said impatiently. 'Who gives a tinker's toss who wrote what? Not you. Ho, no. You've been more'n happy to put your name to my flaky ledgers, so don't you stand there like a virgin's tombstone and come on all primsy with me.'

Philip nodded meekly and regretted it; it caused slippage in his eyesight. He steadied himself and said, 'But this one's not flaky.'

'Some of it is. The brighter bits, to my manner of thinking.'

Philip made his way to the sofa and knelt before the Greme, lowering his head. 'Take this fucking thing off me, Pocket.'

'Ah. Readied, are we? No need to demand Render this time, my pony?'

'Just take it off.'

'Magick word?'

'Please.'

Pocket leaned forward and looped the chain over Philip's head. He took the Amulet in his pale hand, studied it for a moment, then secreted it inside his jerkin.

'Easy in the end, eh, Murdstone? Just like that. Who'd have thought? Now, are you meaning to spend all day with your snout in my crotch?'

Philip crawled across the room and into his armchair. The glass of whiskey he'd abandoned many hours earlier contained a drowned bluebottle and smelled of burning plastic. He drank from it nonetheless.

Pocket watched him. He said, 'Not the ending you'd hankered, I fancy.'

'No.' It came out as a malted croak. 'It's horrible. Ugly. Perverse. *Wrong!*'

'True.'

'They'd hate it. Gorgon, Hollywood, everyone. I'd get slaughtered. Minerva would have my balls.'

'I wish her stronger luck in that work than I had.'

'It's . . . *hopeless.*'

'That's a tad on the harsh side, Murdstone.'

Philip riled his hair with his hands. 'I can do dark, Pocket. I *do* do dark. But that' – he gestured towards the stairs – '*that* is . . .'

'True,' the Greme said once more. A muted trilling from Pocket's pocket. He took out the egg, twisted it. Hummed a quick calculation.

Philip had sagged in the chair; now he lifted his head. His gaze was wet and reddish.

'And *you*, Pocket. Why?'

'That's a riddle with only one arsecheek, Murdstone. Me why what?'

'It *was* you, wasn't it, that led the Swelts to the Library. Betrayed poor old Orberry. Why, for God's sake?'

Wellfair put his hands on his knees and studied them for a long moment. 'It don't sit well with me, Murdstone.

Don't think that. I'm glad the Ledgers burned, truth told. I wouldn't want my doings inked and fixed.' He looked up. 'But I'd no flukin choice, see?'

'What happened, Pocket?'

The Greme sighed. 'I was square snaffled, Murdstone. Turns out Morl's occulators had angled the Fourth Device. And there was I in bleddy Mort A'Dor asleep beneath the buggerin thing. When I wake up there's Morl smirkin down at me with a dozen Swelts behind him. I near on beshat myself. To cut to the quick of it, there's two ways it can go. One is I get chopped to gobbets, slow. And wakeful while it's done. Or I enter his service. Mince or minion. Not exactly arsy-varsy, is it? Can't say I argued the toss with myself for very long. Would you?'

Philip said nothing.

'But d'you know what really naggled my wick, Murdstone? What proper slived and boned me? I swear thrall, on my knees, and when I'm done Morl says to me, *I should kill you anyway, Greme, for crimes against language.* How so, master, says I, all aback. And he says – hark to this, Murdstone – *my manner of writing was rustic slopshite.* And deribative.'

Pocket was temporarily overcome by bitterness. Philip could taste its sharpness on the stale air.

'Rustic, Murdstone! *Rustic!* And me a Full Clerk with two Ledgers and half a flaky one under my belt!' He thumped his albino fist on the arm of the sofa. He was lost in sullen introspection for several slow seconds. Then he looked at Philip and said, '*Deribative*'s a word not known to me. But I'd wager my bollix it's not by way of a compliment.'

'No,' Philip said, 'it's not.' He eased the dead fly out of his glass with two fingers and flipped it at the fireplace. It fell short.

The Greme sat silently, perhaps in expectation of sympathy or even absolution. When neither was forthcoming he got to his feet and chafed his hands together in a businesslike way, as might a milkmaid settling to the first teats on a cold morning.

'Well, anyways up. You've got the third portion of your tribble and, like I say—'

'I've deleted it.'

'Whatsay?'

'Waked and Banished it. Buried it outside the parish.'

'You're frolickin with me.'

'No.'

Pocket stared at him. 'Stap me, Murdstone, if you aren't the . . . Words bleddy fail me.' He fingered an earlobe anxiously. 'T'won't go down well in certain quarters, I can vouch you that. He wants it known abroad.'

'Sod him,' Philip said sincerely.

'Clamp your gob, Murdstone,' Pocket hissed. 'Fluke me.' After worrying at his ear a little longer the Greme said, 'We keep this close, hear me? Not a bleddy word to a living soul or any other kind. No more talk of Waking and Banishing. And *I* never heard tell of it. I reckon I must've fell deaf as a coffin-nail this last while.' He waited. 'Murdstone?'

'OK,' Philip said listlessly.

'Whatsay?'

'Square, Pocket. Square. Who gives a monkey's, anyway?' Philip was aware that his speech had slurred and thickened. But it wasn't the whisky. He was separating out. Parts of him weren't taking messages. He refocused on Pocket, watched him stretch his back and flare his nostrils ostentatiously.

'Fresh air, Murdstone. That's what we need. I've had as much reek of your manky burrow as my noseholes can handle. Come on, my dabchick. Out of doors. On your feet.'

'I'm all right where I am.'

Wellfair gave an impatient little grunt and made a lifting gesture with his hand. Philip's legs straightened of their own accord and he found himself upright. At the same instant, as if he'd hoisted his head into a nasty stratum, he became aware of the unpleasant odour in the room. It was brownish and hairy.

He tottered to the open door and let Pocket take his arm.

9

The light was too much for him. A sudden white-out, prismatic at its edges. He was obliged to support himself on his voodoo fence until he could see.

Pocket waited, inhaling hungrily like the survivor of a long-haul flight, then escorted Philip to the gateway in the ancient drystone wall.

In autumns past, the view had been a particular delight to him. The soft magenta iridescence of the heather on Goat's Elbow Hill, larch and birch taking on shades of spice and tobacco, slow-roiling mists lending the scene a sad but pleasurable transience. Not so now. It seemed to Philip bleak, smoky, harshly lit: the sinister establishing shot of a violent movie. There was definitely something wrong with his eyes. And now his ears were playing tricks, too; sheep-groan and birdsong phasing into human cries, a dog's furious barking into laughter. Something soft landed on his hand. A flake of ash.

'Murdstone?'

Philip turned. Pocket was gazing up at him. The Greme's eyes were pools of blackness. Philip tried to speak but could only gasp as he was seized, enwrapped, by a force that hosed him into the sky. It was a shorter trip this time. In a mere second he found himself – presumably incorporeal but still in possession of his faculties, such as they were – stationary.

Below him, Flemworthy was burning.

Thick smoke – bringing with it olfactory nuances of monkfish and pomegranate molasses – poured from the windows of the Gelder's Rest. It cast a pall, red-brindled by firelight, over the Square. Flameproof Swelts pushed red-hot trolleys of loot from the inferno that had once been Kwik Mart.

The thatched roofs of the public conveniences and the library were harmoniously ablaze. Francine and Merilee, squealing pleasurably, their plump calves pumping, were being borne on the shoulders of two eager Swelts towards the shrubbery of the Memorial Gardens.

From the roof of the warehouse behind Farm and Leisure Footwear a fireball erupted, a huge red and black chrysanthemum on a tall black stalk.

At the junction of Okehampton Road and Pester Street an articulated lorry had jackknifed, shedding its cargo of blazing bales of straw onto the Chapel of Rest belonging to Lumb & Son, funeral directors, thus saving two grieving families the not inconsiderable expense of formal cremation.

Slowly the holocaust rolled out of Philip Murdstone's appalled gaze. Fresh horrors came into view.

Around the trashed remains of Krishna Mersey's yurt a

platoon of Swelts, smoking spliffs the size of trombones, performed a stumbling victory dance.

Swelts were everywhere, in fact. The landscape was wormy with them. Some, chanting, marched towards some violent purpose. Others roamed in bands, looting and pillaging at random.

The Wringers had been uprooted, the stones laid on the ground to form the letters

M O Я L

At Sullencott Manor, his back to the ha-ha, his service pistol in one hand and a cavalry sabre in the other, Sir Arthur readied himself for his last stand. The walls of his venerable home wore a coat of fire or perhaps, Philip hoped, Virginia creeper.

At the Toggenheim Stud, a festive band of Swelts roasted goats on spits improvised from lances supported on halberds.

Pocket's grip on Philip's arm tightened and they gained height and speed. Beyond Sheep Nose Tor, the high moor stretched into the hazy distance. It became unfamiliar, then took on a new familiarity. They were above Farrin. As soon as Philip recognized it, it gave way to the restless sands of Galling Waste.

Time gulped, swallowing itself; above Homely Plain Philip found himself rewitnessing the disasters he had described a few hours earlier. Groaning, he looked ahead, expecting to see the louring cloud of Morl's Thule. It was not there. In its place an immense and glittering monolith reared into the sky. A vast tower of black reflective glass towards which, *at* which, Pocket was steering him at suicidal speed.

Inside his head he heard Pocket say *Morl's Panopticon*.

The building loomed towards them until all else was blotted out. Philip felt a scream spool out of him like a knotted rope. They hurtled into the dark mirror. The last thing he saw before his death was his own distorted face; then he smashed into it.

Death, it turned out, was merely an icy spasm. When it was over, Philip found himself on all fours closely studying a floor formed of large hexagons of polished white marble. It looked expensive. Cautiously, he turned his head right then left. The floor seemed infinite in both directions.

'Greetings, Murdstone. Our reunion, while inevitable, has been deferred longer than I had anticipated. Please stand.'

Philip did not want to stand. He wanted to continue to admire the ingenious floor and not see anything else at all, ever. He had died, and if Heaven were nothing more than perfect tiling he'd settle for that. He stood.

Morl, in person, was considerably more handsome than his appearances in *Dark Entropy* and *Warlocks Pale* suggested. The Antarch sat in a high-backed black chair, his right leg slung over one of its arms. He wore a simple white tunic and blue trousers beneath the necromantic robe. Between the drapes of his silver hair, his long face was perfectly symmetrical. Eyes – both of them! – blue as an iceberg's shadow.

Peter O'Toole, Philip thought. Before his face went under the harrow.

Nothing wrong with the hands, either. Morl clicked the fingers of the left one. Pocket, who had been kneeling, got to his feet and, with a modest flourish, produced the Amulet. He lowered it by its chain onto Morl's palm.

The necromancer caressed it with his thumb. 'It has taken me no little effort, Murdstone, to disconjure and reconjure this small item. It was deeply spellbound. Its encryption was unique, the key lost. Its allegiance as unpredictable as it is powerful. And my labours were no whit eased by the misguided activities of this meddlesome Greme.'

Pocket lowered his head.

'Yet I succeeded, as I assured you I would.' He smiled. It was a smile that would have domesticated a grizzly bear.

'Now, clerk, let us try its powers.'

'Yes, master.'

Pocket approached the chair and, with due reverence, took the Amulet and looped its chain over his head. It hung peaceably against his belly. He walked briskly to a low table upon which sat a ream of paper and a fat inkpot. He settled himself on a stool and took up a pen. He examined its nib, appeared to find it satisfactory and dipped it in the ink. He flexed his fingers.

'Square-set, master.'

Morl sat straighter and lightly gripped the arms of his chair. He raised his face slightly and closed his eyes. Instantly, Pocket began writing. Writing at tremendous speed, the tip of his blue tongue protruded, his hand a pale blur when it flew back and forth between paper and inkpot. He flicked completed pages away; they formed themselves into a neat pile.

Released from Morl's hypnotic gaze, Philip felt himself sag. It would have been nice to sit down. His head was fizzing like sherbet. He turned it cautiously.

The dimensions of the space he was in seemed measureless, their perspective perverse.

Dark, but not dark. He was standing in one of several oases of light.

In another, some incalculable distance away, a great hemisphere of something like glass rose out of the floor; images, continuously changing and reforming, revolved on its surface.

In another, less distant, a cluster of furniture: a floating rail of hooks from which feminine apparel and soft implements were suspended; a white divan; a coiled black cabinet containing flasks and alembics of multi-coloured fluids.

In yet another, a leafless and muscular plant grew from a shallow bowl. Its branches clasped a huge fruit which might have been an apple were it not blue.

There was no sound other than Pocket's hectic nib-scratch. Philip felt it on his skin. Nibitch.

It stopped. Morl opened his eyes. Pocket let his pen

fall. Unused ink crept from its nib back into the pot.

'Word count, Greme?'

'Three hunnerd and one score, a dozen and two odd, master.'

'Quality?'

'Top, master. Banewood and honey.'

Something was puzzling Philip and it wasn't computation.

'You are at liberty to speak, Murdstone. You have a question?'

'Yes. Well. I mean, you've won, haven't you? You've conquered the Realm . . .'

'I reject the term *conquest*. I have merely brought about a much-needed and long-delayed modernization.'

'Right. Sorry. But I was under the impression that you couldn't do it without the Amulet. But you did. So I don't understand why you went to so much trouble to get it.'

The smile again. 'Your obtuseness continues to delight me,' Morl said pleasantly. 'It has unexpected depths.'

'Thank you.'

'The answer to your question is really rather simple. Nothing is real, Murdstone. Or, to be more exact, reality is fluid. Slippery. There are two ways of stabilizing it. The first is by the use of Magick, of course. However, Magick is difficult, its practice arduous. And even in the hands and mind of an adept as experienced as myself, not entirely reliable. The second is with words. Words and stories. The world *is* the stories we tell of it, Murdstone.

That is why the Ledgers were held in such idolatrous esteem and so jealously guarded. They were also superstitious, confused and helplessly backward-looking, which made their destruction an urgent necessity.'

Philip risked a glance at Pocket, whose face was a whitewashed stone.

'And now I have mastery of the Amulet, Murdstone. When I release my subjects from forgetfulness they will find themselves, through its powers, in a different story. The only story. *My* story.'

Morl seemed to be expecting an appreciative response, so Philip said, 'Yes, I see. That's very . . . brilliant.'

'No, Murdstone. Simple. Merely troublesome to execute. Of course, the story will differ in some respects from the one I vouchsafed you, which was, of necessity, fanciful in parts. But it takes fancy needlework to make a silk purse from a pig's ear. Eh, clerk?'

'It does, master,' Pocket said humbly.

'Nonetheless, I presume your legions of benighted admirers will consume its final volume with their usual avidity? Might I even entertain the possibility of them finding it instructive?'

Pocket grimaced a warning.

'Yes,' Philip said. 'I'm sure they will.' His vision had gone rambly again. The islands of light wandered. He said, 'Can I sit down? I've got the most terrible headache.'

'Have you, indeed? I shall relieve you of that forthwith.'

Morl raised a hand. The darkness behind him was

illuminated to reveal a phalanx of Swelts. The foremost two wore red aprons over their armour. One bore a heavy axe with a long, crescent-edged blade. They advanced, their tusks wetted by anticipated pleasure, and took up position on either side of Philip, whose knees gave way.

'Our business is concluded, Murdstone. I have much to attend to. You will understand, of course, that there can be no question of you returning, knowing what you know, to your own pitiful dimension. However, since you have been, to coin a phrase, a helpful nuisance, I have given orders that you are to be dispatched swiftly.'

'No. Wait. Please. Listen, I'm a writer. I could work for you. I know how stories work. That's what I'm good at.'

Pocket coughed behind his hand.

'In an advisory capacity, even. Editorial. I could be useful. Please don't kill me. It would be a waste.'

Morl chuckled. 'What need have I of writers, Murdstone? Of drunkards and dreamers? Scribblers like you are a thing of the past. I have the Amulet.'

Words ran around in Philip's brain like burning rats. He grabbed at a few of them. 'Ah yes, but but it might . . . run out, lose its charge sort of thing or reverse it or something, then you'd need . . .'

Morl gestured with his head. Philip's executioners stooped and effortlessly lifted him. His feet dangled half a metre from the floor.

'No! Pleasepleaseplease! It's not fair! It wasn't my fault! Tell him, Pocket!'

He was turned. He was in darkness. Being carried deeper into it.

He looked back at the diminishing light and cried, 'I could get you an *agent*!'

'Where were we, Greme?'

'The Lady Mesmira has fled the drunken, boorish attentions of the outlaw Cadrel, master, and thrown herself upon your mercy. Her nightshift, saturated by rain, clings to her. Her pink rosebud nipples are clearly discernible through the flimsy fabric and . . .'

'Ah, yes,' Morl said. He leaned back and closed his eyes. 'New chapter.'

'Bollix,' Pocket said, under his breath. He took up his pen.

10

In the Reform Club, Perry Whipple touched Minerva's glass with his own.

'Happy Christmas, darling.'

'Cheers,' she said cheerlessly.

'I love what you're wearing. You look immensely pluckable.'

Her black feather gilet, worn above black silk trousers by Philip Lim, had troubled the severe doorman of the Reform. However, and understandably, the club's dress code made no mention of black feather gilets.

'Thank you, Master Whipple.'

'The tinsel tiara is especially nice.'

'Yes. Evelyn made it for me.'

'So why the long face, as the barman said to the horse?'

Minerva sighed. 'You know.'

'Hmm.'

Peregrine Whipple, founder, guiding spirit and CEO of the Shaman Agency, was rumoured to be at least seventy years old. His nude and considerable pate fronted a nimbus of white hair that resembled a manifestation of ancient wisdom. The tip of his white goatee rested on the knot of his blue and silver tie. He was currently dating a celebrity chef twice his size and half his age and looked well on it. He sipped his Manhattan, then set it down on the little table and studied it critically for a few seconds.

'I'll tell you what I know, my child. Which is that in two short months *Warlocks Pale* has made, according to my estimates, at least twenty million pounds. That's just print sales. I do not know, and do not wish to know, what your film and other media deals are worth, but I cannot imagine that you'll be dining courtesy of the Salvation Army for some considerable time. BlogsCan, which I check daily while saluting the dawn, tells me that twenty-one per cent of postings concern Philip Murdstone. That's nine per cent more than God, even taking Islamic sites into account. Rumours of his disappearance, madness, death . . .'

'Which, I have to say, you've stage-managed brilliantly.'

Perry dismissed the congratulation with a gesture. 'Nothing at all, my dear. A pleasure. Marketing opportunities like that are as rare as a footballer's adverb. How's your Mojito, by the way? No, please don't shrug. Never shrug when you're wearing feathers. It makes you look as though you're striving to lay an egg. And I strongly suspect that laying eggs in the Reform is considered seriously *de trop*.'

'Sorry. I shall try to be more demure.'

After a delicate pause Perry said, 'Were you fond of him at all, my dear? I don't recall you actually saying, one way or the other.'

'No, there was nothing . . . well. No, nothing like that. And truth to tell, I don't give a toss, at a deep level of toss, that the great Murdstone Trilogy will never be completed. In fact, if all fantasy trilogies consisted of only two books the world would be no worse a place.'

'Amen,' Perry agreed solemnly. 'So, at the risk of seeming repetitive, and considering that you have made a fortune, why the long face?'

'I have failed to deliver.'

'Ah.'

'And I do not fail to deliver. Failing to deliver is something I do not do. I am not happy because right now it looks as though Minerva Cinch will achieve everlasting fame as the agent who came up with *two-thirds* of a work of genius. Two-thirds of the biggest thing since the Bible, the Koran and Harry Potter. And it pisses me off. Professionally and in every other way, it pisses me off.'

'As it must and should. I have given the matter some thought, as it happens. Discreetly lower your sad and lovely head, my dear. I have a Christmas prezzie for you.' From an inside pocket Perry produced a small black object that might have been a coffin for a doll's house. It was attached to a woven chain of white gold links. Perry looped it around her neck. 'I am deeply ashamed that it's not gift-wrapped. The fact is that I took receipt of it only an hour ago. I had to do ghastly things to get it.'

Minerva peeked down at it. 'It looks like a memory stick.'

'It does. It is.'

Perry sipped from his glass while surveying the room. He and Minerva were snugged into a softly-lit corner screened by a trio of columns. The only man within earshot was an eroded, handsome man who had spent so many years impersonating Tom Stoppard that even Tom Stoppard called him Tom Stoppard. He was alone and immersed in the *Telegraph*. In another nearby nook a former ambassador to the Vatican was deep in conversation with an Israeli arms dealer.

Minerva waited. She enjoyed taking cocktails in the absurd grandiosity of the Reform Club. It made her feel naughty. It was like drinking in church.

Quietly, Perry said, 'Sally Quinn. Vernon Betts. Kit Mellors. Those names mean anything to you?'

'Umm. Mellors. He writes for the telly, doesn't he? Or she?'

'They all do. Between them, they've written forty per cent of all episodes of all British soap operas during the past three years. Their fecundity and narrative grasp are extraordinary.'

'So are they looking for a new agent?'

'No. They couldn't. They don't exist.' Perry lowered his voice another notch. 'On that little gizmo you'll find a programme called *Xtrapol8*. It reads previous episodes and generates plot lines and dialogue for future ones. It checks continuity and speech patterns and so forth. I've had a young supergeek of my acquaintance tweek it for your purposes.'

'My God.'

'You exaggerate. I merely have networks.'

'Are you saying that this . . . ?'

'Yes. You slip that little doo-dah into your laptop while you're listening to the King's College Choir. Feed it Murdstone. At the very least it will come up with something we can work on.'

'Perry, I don't know what to say.'

'Say nothing, darling. I shall think of ways you can thank me.'

'I'm sure you will.'

Perry polished off his Manhattan. 'And now, lovely as this has been, I must hasten unto Pimlico, where Merlin awaits. We're going to Bungay tonight.'

'Is that a euphemism?'

'No, it's a perfectly charming little place in Suffolk. Have you been to see him lately, by the way?'

'Who?'

'Philip Murdstone.'

'Oh. Yes, a couple of weeks back.'

Arcadia occupied a little under fifty landscaped acres of Sussex on the northern fringe of the South Downs. The house had been built in the 1780s as a gentleman's estate for the bastard son of a belted earl. His descendants, several of them also bastards of one sort or another, had finally run out of money in the 1990s and had sold the place to Havencare Inc.

It was a hellish schlep from Notting Hill but, Minerva had reflected, turning off the hailswept A26, it was rather handy for Glyndebourne; in the summer she could sweeten the pill with Strauss and strawberries. Mind you, a hundred and fifty grand a year was a lot to pay for discretion, even of the absolute variety. She might have to find somewhere cheaper. Who knew how long he might last?

She declared herself to the speakerphone set into the brick column on the right-hand side of the gates and they slid silently open. At the front door, she was greeted by Gwendolyn, the black and stately assistant matron, who escorted her to the smaller of the two day rooms.

'How is he?'

'Oh, much the same, Miss Cinch. No worse, which is something we can be positive about. Although we did have a slight crisis a few days ago when we offered him risotto for lunch. He became very agitated.'

'Oh dear,' Minerva said. 'Still on about maggots, is he?'

'Yes. When he talks at all, which is not often. Here we are. You'll have the room to yourselves. Tea? And chef has made a rather nice Victoria sponge.'

'Thank you. Lovely.'

Minerva braced herself and walked to his chair. He was wearing maroon pyjamas under a thick night-blue dressing gown. By now, she thought, his hair must have grown back, but he still wore the white woollen cap. There were grey and white strands in his beard.

'Darling,' she said. 'You do look splendid. Like a sage or something from one of your books.'

He did not look up. He continued to stare fixedly at the hands clasped on his knees. He had not known that the dead would still have hands. That would sometimes move. He was watching them in case they did. With his other eyes, his sideways eyes, he was watching, as always, always, the pictures of his death.

They made no sense because, obviously, he was senseless. He knew this in the way that a worm in the ground knows that it is a worm in the ground. The Swelts carry him through darkness and light and darkness again. He can feel the hardness of their paws in his armpits and hear their snuffling and their tread. He feels his bowels loosen. Then there is a gap, hiatus, in the film. He must have fainted during projection because his place of execution is the town square.

Crowded. Two female Gremes with their thumbs in their mouths. A man in black making signs in the air. A Porloc serving food asking questions. Noise and raised fists. An atmosphere of brutal festivity. Death to the Fly. The scaffold lit by revolving light.

He is strapped into a wheeled conveyance. He turns his head to beg. The Swelt has put on a human mask and a luminescent green tunic with silver stripes. And says, 'Hello, mate. With us, are you? That's good. Very good. Stay with us. My name's Gary and the Swelt to your left is Mike. You've had a nasty turn, Philip. We're going to take you to the Hospy Thule in Exeter, OK?'

Then he is on his back, tethered. Instruments of torture are attached to him. 'Just make it quick. Please.'

'Don't you worry, Philip. Mike's a demon. We'll be there in no time.' Examines an instrument. 'So, you are *the* Philip Murdstone, yeah? Seriously sorry to see you in this state, man. You are the absolute dog's bollocks. *Warlocks Pale* blew me away.' Needle in the arm. 'You're gonna get sleepy now, Phil.' Produces a book with a lurid cover. 'Would you mind signing it for me, Phil? Before you get woozy?'

His dying wail rotates above his head. Is still rotating above his head while he is looking at his hands.

The Swelts carry him through darkness and light and darkness again. He feels the hardness of their paws, feels a hand on his head.

'Phil, darling?'

He looks up and beholds a maiden of unnatural beauty standing before him. Shapely golden legs. Thighs and belly like a musical instrument known only to angels. Proud breasts. The soft oval of her face framed by sweeps of auburn flame. Her eyes the colours of the waters of the Middle Sea.

He licks his rough lips and speaks her name.

Perry said, 'Any change?'

'No. He didn't even know who I was. He called me Helen.'

Out on Pall Mall Perry conjured a cab out of nowhere. 'I'll call you as soon as I get back.'

'Do that. And Merry Christmas, Master Whipple.'

His smile was a miracle of dentistry. 'And you, my child.'

She waved him off. A muzak version of 'Silent Night' threaded the rumble and squeal of traffic. A mob of young men wearing business suits and Santa hats or flashing antlers advanced along the pavement. One of them, admiring her plumage, wagged his elbows and crowed like a cock. Minerva recognized him as Wayne Dimbleby, late of Pegasus, now of Click4Books. He invited her to a party. She went on the off-chance that he might still have a brain worth picking.

Night falls upon Sussex. Above the downs the stars take their seats. In the wings, the moon arranges its face. Frost brittles grass and leaf. Standing water quietly pings and crackles its skin of ice. A barn owl, a white shadow, begins its haunt. Crossing a golf course, a fox pauses to assess the darkness. All is calm.

The moon makes its entrance. All is bright.

In Arcadia, it is time for meds.

Acknowledgements

I'm exceedingly grateful to Peter Cox for taking this unruly mongrel on walks. I'm equally grateful to David Fickling and Simon Mason for offering it a loving home and house-training it during my absences. And it's thanks to Elspeth Graham, of course, that I acquired the dog in the first place.

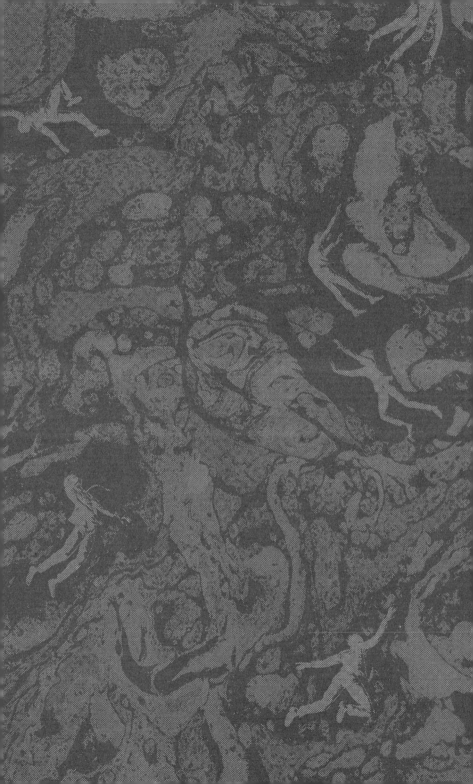